Praise for the Country Club Murders

THE DEEP END (#1)

"Part mystery, part women's fiction, part poetry, Mulhern's debut, *The Deep End*, will draw you in with the first sentence and entrance you until the last. An engaging whodunit that kept me guessing until the end!"

– Tracy Weber,
Author of the Downward Dog Mysteries

"What truly stands out is the development of Ellison as a very realistic and very likable character...Not to be overlooked is the humor and wit that entertains throughout the novel as readers enjoy following an intelligent heroine completely coming into her own as a compelling, funny, and very intelligent woman."

– *Kings River Life Magazine*

"What a fun read! Murder in the days before cell phones, the internet, DNA and AFIS."

– *Books for Avid Readers*

"Intriguing plots, fascinating characters. From the first page to the last, Julie's mysteries grab the reader and don't let up. When all is resolved and I read the last page, I wanted to read more."

– Sally Berneathy,
USA Today Bestselling Author

"Ms. Mulhern weaves a tidy tale of murder, blackmail, and life behind the scenes in the Country Club set of the 70s...an excellent mystery, highly recommended, and I eagerly await the next in the series."

– *Any Good Book*

THE
DEEP
END

The Country Club Murders
by Julie Mulhern

THE DEEP END (#1)
GUARANTEED TO BLEED (#2)
(October 2015)

THE DEEP END

THE COUNTRY CLUB MURDERS

JULIE MULHERN

HENERY PRESS

THE DEEP END
The Country Club Murders
Part of the Henery Press Mystery Collection

First Edition
Trade paperback edition | February 2015

Henery Press
www.henerypress.com

Copyright © 2015 by Julie Mulhern
Cover art by Stephanie Chontos

ISBN-13: 978-1-941962-23-7

Printed in the United States of America

This book is dedicated with love to my parents,
Charlotte and Steve Kirk

ACKNOWLEDGMENTS

To Sally, Madonna and Sara, you made writing *The Deep End* fun–thank you for your advice and support.

To Margaret Bail–your faith and persistence meant the world–thank you!

The Deep End is a better book thanks to Kendel Lynn and the staff at Henery. I am truly grateful.

And, most of all, thank you to Matt, Meredith and Katie. I'd promise that dinners will get better now, but we all know that's not true. Thanks for embracing spaghetti, tacos and eating out. And, thanks for being you!

ONE

June 1974
Kansas City, Missouri

My morning swim doesn't usually involve corpses. If it did, I'd give up swimming for something less stressful, like coaxing cobras out of baskets or my mother out of bed before ten.

Watching the sun rise over the seventh green is often the best part of my day. I dive into the pool while the water is still inky. When the light has changed from deepest indigo to lavender, I break my stroke, tread water and admire the sky as it bleeds from gold to yellow to pink. It's a ritual, a metaphorical cleansing, a moment of stolen peace.

After all, I have a teenage daughter, a mother with strong opinions, a Weimaraner named Max who plots to take over our house on his path toward world domination, and a husband. Much as I'd like to, I can't leave him out.

I kicked off my Dr. Scholl's, tossed my husband's button-down onto a deck chair, dove into the dark water and gasped at the sudden, encompassing cold. That shock of chilly water against my skin is better than coffee when it comes to waking up. Maybe not better. Faster.

My legs kicked, my arms sliced, and I settled into the comforting rhythm of the Australian crawl. My fingers knifed through the water, anticipating the smooth parting of liquid. They found fabric and the horrific touch of cold flesh.

* * *

I watched the sunrise from a deck chair. It was not cathartic or peaceful. It was awful. The police swarmed around the pool like industrious ants, pausing only when someone jumped into the water and floated the body to the side. They fished it out and laid it at the edge of the pool.

I turned my head away. I didn't want to see.

A man wearing a truly unfortunate pair of plaid pants broke away from the ants and sat on the deck chair next to mine. "Are you all right? Do you want a glass of water?" He had nice eyes. Brown. Like coffee.

"Coffee," I croaked.

He waved at the ants and a moment later one of them appeared with a thermos. He poured some caffeinated ambrosia into the red plastic top and handed it to me.

"Thank you."

"I'm afraid we don't have cream or sugar."

"Black is fine." I took a sip to prove it.

"I'm Detective Jones. Can you tell me what happened this morning?"

"I was swimming."

"Without a lifeguard?" I could hear the disapproval in his voice. Detective Jones, purveyor of thermos coffee, wearer of plaid pants, was a follower of rules. I used to like that in a man. There's something comforting about someone who colors within the lines. Problems arise when a strict follower of rules decides to forsake them. He doesn't just jaywalk. Nope. A lifetime of good behavior gives him the right to sleep with other women. Or, if he's slightly more powerful, order a break-in at Watergate. Goes to show, you can't trust anyone these days. Not husbands. Not presidents. Not cops.

I sipped my coffee while the warmth of the cup thawed my fingers. "The club knows I swim in the mornings. I do it at my own risk."

His lips pinched together. Clearly, he took a dim view of swimming alone. "What time did you get here this morning?"

"Around five-thirty."

"Why so early?"

"I like to be in the water at least twenty minutes before sunrise."

"Did you notice anything out of the ordinary?"

Just a dead body. "No."

"What about other people? Cars in the parking lot?"

I shook my head. "No. No people. There's usually a car or two in the parking lot. If someone has had one too many, they leave their car here overnight."

"So you parked your car then came straight to the pool?"

What else would I do? "Yes."

"And?"

"I dove into the water and started swimming. I'd gone maybe half a lap when I..." I shuddered, "when I touched the body."

Detective Jones offered a smile that managed to be both sympathetic and encouraging. "And then?"

"I screamed. One of the groundskeepers from the golf course heard me. He called you."

I took another sip of coffee and glanced around the pool. The morning light still looked delicate enough to break. The weeping cherry tree had lost a few leaves and they skittered across the pool deck in the soft breeze. The police conferred around the body. Then they stepped away and I saw it. Saw her. In that second, my morning went from plain dreadful to the worst ever.

I stared at the ruined dress. Halston. Couture, not off the rack. Everyone who was anyone in Kansas City had heard about how she bought it from Halston himself.

My expression must have reflected my shock because Detective Jones sat up straight in a chair designed for lounging and his nose twitched like a bloodhound's with a fresh scent. His eyes didn't look quite so nice anymore. "Who is she?"

I could have told him she was my husband's mistress. But that word—mistress—it connotes more than an exchange of fluids. Money. Or emotion. Or something.

On the other hand, *the woman screwing my husband* sounded far too harsh. Like I was angry. I got over being angry months ago. *The woman my husband ties to a bedpost and flogs with a cat-o-nine tails* offered more information than I was willing to share. "Her name is Madeline Harper."

"How do you know her?"

He would find out about Madeline and Henry, eventually. No doubt about it. I ought to tell him, but to talk about it, to say the words aloud, would be like ripping off a well-affixed Band-Aid. "I've known Madeline forever. We went to the same preschool, the same grade school, and the same high school."

"Not the same college?"

"Madeline went back east. I went to art school."

"You didn't like her." It wasn't a question.

"How can you tell?"

"You don't seem upset."

"I didn't like her."

"Why not?"

The Band-Aid had to come off. It was going to hurt like hell. That little bit of mental plaster had been hiding all the things I didn't want to see—the things that constituted marriage to Henry. I certainly didn't want to explain any of them to a policeman. I stared at my feet, long, bony, and resting on damp concrete. I had to tell him. I opened my mouth and chickened out. "We have...had...different values."

"When was the last time you saw her?"

"A week ago Tuesday. My husband and I had drinks with her and her husband, Roger." Polite drinks. Ignore the elephant drinks. We're-boinking-like-bunnies-and-you-don't-have-the-courage-to-do-anything-about-it drinks.

"I thought you didn't like her."

"Sometimes sharing a history is more important than liking someone."

He nodded as if he understood. "You told Officer Roberts that you're an artist."

"I did. I am."

"What kind?" Detective Jones sounded disapproving again. Like I'd broken another unwritten rule. You shall not swim alone. You shall not be an artist unless you struggle with poverty and personal hygiene.

"I paint."

"So you notice details."

"I suppose." My gaze traced the celadon threads in his pants. Where they intersected with navy, the threads looked almost green. When they met cream, they looked gray.

"What did you see in the parking lot this morning?"

I closed my eyes and pictured my car's headlights cutting through the lot. Ansil Merriwether's navy Cadillac with the dented fender was parked across two spots. He'd probably been clutching a scotch when he arrived for drinks with his cronies. A jaunty red Mercedes braved the morning dew with its top down. "Madeline's car is in the lot. It's the convertible."

"Any idea why she'd be here in the middle of the night?"

"Middle of the night?" I'd leapt to the assumption that she'd closed the bar, wandered down to the pool after drinks and dinner and more drinks and fallen in.

He nodded. "The club security guard thought he heard something around one. He turned on the lights in the pool. It was empty."

After nearly forty years, you come to know a person. Their likes, their dislikes, their foibles. So I knew. Madeline hadn't stopped by the club for a swim in her favorite Halston dress in the middle of the night.

In the unlikely event that the most self-centered woman on the planet decided to kill herself, it wouldn't be by drowning. Madeline wouldn't want the water to bloat her features. Not an accident. Not a suicide. She'd been murdered.

The shake of my shoulders had nothing to do with the cool

morning breeze. The wronged wife who found her was going to be the prime suspect.

A murder suspect. Me. Ellison Walford Russell. Mother was going to kill me.

I toyed with the idea of asking Detective Jones to put me in protective custody.

Of course, I wasn't a suspect. Yet. I would be as soon as the detective with the nice brown eyes learned that the woman who found Madeline had a good reason to kill her. He'd find out. No doubt about it. Madeline and Henry hadn't been discreet. Not remotely.

Getting caught in the coatroom at the club Christmas party was the rough equivalent of renting a billboard. Apparently rubbing Roger's and my noses in their affair was part of the fun.

I gave it an hour before some helpful, civic-minded woman who spent her days playing tennis or golf or sunning called Detective Jones and told him all about it. I took a deep breath of air scented with damp grass and chlorine. "Madeline was sleeping with my husband."

His gaze sharpened. It shifted between me and the body on the concrete. "Why are you telling me?"

"Because Madeline would never kill herself. Not like this."

Detective Jones drummed his fingers on his knee. Long, almost elegant fingers. He waited for me to say something else, using his silence against me. My father used to do the same thing when I came home late for curfew and he wanted to know where I'd been. It was a good technique. I used it with my daughter. It wouldn't work on me.

The silence stretched. I put down my empty coffee cup and crossed my arms over my chest.

Detective Jones smiled. It was the indulgent smile mothers give to toddlers. A smile that said *I'll let you win this battle, but I'll win the war.* It chilled my blood. "How long have you known?" he asked.

"Eight months."

He nodded as if I'd answered more than just his question.

His fingers stilled. "Did you kill her?"

The birds warbling, the voices of the men by the pool, and the sound of the water as it lapped into the gutter all faded into silence. "No." My voice was too loud. "I'm not a killer." Nope, I was a woman who sounded about as convincing as Dick Nixon when he said *I'm not a crook.*

Those nice eyes didn't look nice anymore. They narrowed.

"Any idea who else might want her dead?"

Who else? Besides Roger and me? I might as well hand him the club directory. I shivered in the sunshine. Someone had killed Madeline. Probably someone I knew. "She wasn't well liked."

He raised a brow. Detective Jones was going to try silence again.

I shifted and focused on a robin perched on the edge of a deck chair farther down the row. It watched the activity near the pool with unabashed interest. Someone in a uniform was zipping Madeline into a black bag.

"What did she do?" Detective Jones sounded annoyed.

"When she wasn't playing tennis or golf or bridge, she worked part-time for an art gallery."

"That's not what I meant."

I forced myself to look into Detective Jones' narrowed eyes. "She slept with other women's husbands, she spread malicious gossip, and she wasn't above a spot of blackmail."

"Blackmail?"

"To get invitations to the right parties. That sort of thing."

He tilted his head slightly to the side. "I'm going to need a list."

He wasn't asking for a list, he was asking me to commit social suicide. I had about as much chance of surviving as a kamikaze pilot. If the ladies who lunch didn't kill me, Mother would. "I can't help you."

Again with the narrowed eyes. I liked Detective Jones much better when he was being solicitous and pouring me coffee.

I lifted my shoulders and let them fall. My path was clear. I couldn't help him. A glowering police detective was nowhere near as intimidating as Mother when she was on the warpath. If I sold out any of her friends or their daughters...Well, Custer's Last Stand would look like a day in the park. She'd massacre me.

Detective Jones nodded. Slowly. "I'll have to ask you to come down to the station to make a statement."

Which is how the worst morning ever got worse.

TWO

I got home and glanced at the clock on the wall—a quarter 'til ten, a full fifteen minutes before Frances Walford ever got up.

Par for the course of my morning—not only was Mother up, she'd driven to my house and taken up a strategic position in my kitchen, ready for battle with a helmet of teased white hair and her everyday armor—diamonds on her knuckles and a serviceable navy dress. Someone must have called and told her that her odd, artistic daughter had found a body.

I'd wanted nothing more than a quiet moment to reflect, a shower, and a decent cup of coffee. Instead, I got my mother demanding to hear about my morning. At least she'd made coffee.

"Are you all right?" she asked.

I stared at her in disbelief. Was I all right? "I found Madeline Harper floating in the pool, spent two hours at the police station dressed in a damp swimsuit and a shirt with frayed cuffs, and I'm a murder suspect."

Mother drew in a sharp breath then her eyes narrowed. "No need to get testy. I'm just trying to help."

Of course she was. Just like the Romans were trying to help the Christians when they introduced them to the lions.

"You look like hell," she added. So much for being solicitous. Mother reached into the refrigerator and pushed things around until she found the cream, then opened the container and sniffed.

"I bought it yesterday."

She sniffed it again. "Why did they take you to the station?"

"I told them about Henry and Madeline."

My mother froze. The cream spilling from the carton into her coffee cup froze. Max, who'd padded into the kitchen in hopes someone would leave food unattended, froze. I'd broken the cardinal rule of the Walfords. *Thou shall not air dirty laundry in public.*

"Why would you tell them that?" Her voice was arctic.

"It was hardly a secret. They were going to find out anyway."

She arched a brow.

"Madeline was murdered."

She wanted to tell me I was being fanciful. Her mouth opened, her lips even formed the words—but she couldn't do it. The morning's events supported me. Madeline was dead, and I'd been hauled to the police station in my swimsuit.

In a classic Frances Walford maneuver, she changed tactics. "I simply can't believe you wore that to talk to the police."

I took a very deep breath and reached for the coffee pot. "I didn't have much choice." All things being equal I would have preferred to wear actual clothes to a testosterone-filled squad room.

"I blame that woman."

Yes. It was all Madeline's fault. How inconsiderate of her to get murdered.

"Although, now that she's dead, you and Henry can work things out."

I took a bracing sip of coffee. "I don't want to work things out."

"Don't be ridiculous. Of course you do."

Henry and I had agreed to stay married until Grace went to college. I'd thought that meant we would comport ourselves with discretion until we dropped her at her dorm room. Henry had different ideas. Ideas that included other women and whips and handcuffs and things I didn't want to know.

"You can't just give up on your marriage."

I gave up eighteen months ago, but I didn't have the energy to argue with her. "I need a shower." She hadn't followed me into a bathroom. Yet.

"Where's Grace?" she asked.

"Working." Babysitting for toddlers. Cheap birth control.

"Where's Henry?"

"I imagine he's at the bank. I haven't seen him today." Not only had I not seen him, I didn't know if he'd been home last night. My coffee cup stalled halfway to my lips. If I was a suspect, Henry might be as well. Although there was no reason for him to murder Madeline—that I knew of.

"Ending a marriage is no small thing. You're sure you want to divorce him?"

"Positive."

Mother patted her hair and donned her contemplative expression, the one that always boded ill.

I tried to ignore it. I wiped down a clean counter top then I got the broom and swept up a few dog hairs. I finished my coffee, rinsed the mug, and put it in the dishwasher. Mother sat at my kitchen island, lost in thought, coming to terms with her daughter's crumbling marriage to a philandering husband.

She could sit there until the cows came home. I needed a shower. I opened the door to the back stairs and took a step.

"Hunter Tafft!"

I blinked. "What about him?"

She patted her lips with a napkin. "He's single again."

Only Mother could travel from a failed marriage to a divorce to a new marriage in the time it took to wipe the coffee out of the corners of her mouth. "No." I tried to sound strong and decisive.

Mother gave me her best don't-be-dense look and waited for me to change my mind. She could wait for a month of Sundays. The answer would still be no.

"I am not going to date Hunter Tafft." I wanted to be perfectly clear.

"Why not? You just told me your marriage was over."

"No."

"You'd make a lovely couple. He's so distinguished."

If I banged my head against the wall, would she even notice? Probably not, and I'd get a bruise on my forehead. "No."

It would be crass to point out he was filthy rich. She did it anyway. "You'd never have to worry about the future." I didn't now. Mother was under the impression that my career as an artist would be as fleeting as summer lightning—blinding, bright, and gone in an instant.

"No."

"Don't be silly, Ellison. You need a man to look out for you. I'll call him for you."

Oh good Lord. "Please don't."

"You'll thank me later."

I wouldn't. What's more, I wouldn't be able to look Hunter Tafft in the face ever again. "I'm going to go lie down."

"I don't think you should be alone."

It was all I wanted, and I wanted it like an alcoholic wants a drink.

"We need a fourth for bridge. Why don't you get cleaned up and join us?"

I wanted the comfort of taking up my brushes and moving the swirling fear and anger from my stomach to a canvas. "I don't feel up to it."

"Of course you do." Mother locked her gaze on me. Caught in her sights, I did what I always do. I squirmed and hemmed and hawed and wished somewhere along the line I'd developed enough backbone to stand up to her.

"It will do you good. We'll see you at two."

Things I would rather have done than play bridge included triple bogeying the eighth hole, listening to Mother's exhaustive explanation of the principles of defensive bidding, and playing doubles with Stephie Marks. Stephie established herself on the court, created a mental circle of approximately two feet, then didn't move beyond it. Playing doubles with her was like playing singles on an extra large court with an obstacle in the center. Unfortunately, it's easier to cheat fate than disappoint Mother. At precisely two o'clock, I walked into the card room at the country club. From her seat at the table, Mother gave me her best what's-Ellison-wearing look. The expression includes narrowed eyes, pursed lips, a tilted chin, and the expectation of disappointment. I wore a sunny yellow Lilly shift printed with orange baboons and green squirrels, a matching lime sweater around my shoulders, and green sandals with a sedate heel.

She couldn't complain. I was on time, appropriately dressed with my hair combed into the French twist she preferred. I offered her a pinched expression that might pass for a smile.

"Darling girl, I heard y'all had the most appalling morning." Bitty Sue Foster beamed up at me. With her deep tan, surfeit of teeth and cotton ball hair, Bitty Sue's smile could be rather blinding. I blinked. "Your momma said y'all didn't want to be alone." Bitty Sue was from Savannah and forty years of living in Kansas City had done nothing to erase her accent. "I'm so glad we had an open seat."

Lorna Michaels reached out and trapped my wrist in her roped hand. With its pointy nails, it looked like a turkey vulture's talon. "You must tell us all about it. You'll feel better."
She'd feel better dining out on a firsthand account of how I found a murdered Madeline Harper floating in the swimming pool. In that moment, murder seemed like a completely reasonable way to handle problems. I could slip cyanide into Mother's five o'clock gin and tonic or maybe I could toss a toaster into her bubble bath or...I didn't know. Never having contemplated murder before, I wasn't terribly creative.
I offered a bare bones description of my morning while Mother fanned the cards in the center of the table. We all picked one. I drew the two of clubs. The lowest card possible. My luck continued.

Mother's ace of diamonds won the deal. I shuffled the second deck—white with the country club's crest in red (like blood on fresh fallen snow)—and wished I was somewhere else. Death Valley in July. Northern Canada in January. The police station in my swimsuit.

Bitty Sue offered me another blinding smile. "Powers tells me he sold another passel of your paintings to collectors on the coasts."

"Yes, ma'am."

"Isn't that fine? He says you're in high demand."

Mother snorted. She blamed painting for the death of my marriage.

She wasn't wrong.

The trouble between Henry and me started when my art became more than just a profitable hobby. The first tax return was a fluke. Women don't make more money than their banker husbands. When it happened two years in a row, Henry developed an interest in handcuffs and floggers. I didn't. Mother told me to give up painting and save my marriage. It was the one and only time I've stood my ground.

I paint. I am obscenely well paid for my paintings. Powers says the real money will be in lithographs. What neither Powers nor Henry understands is that I don't paint for money. I never have. I paint because if I didn't have a way to channel all my feelings, I'd go mad.

Bitty Sue took in Mother's narrowed eyes and changed the subject. "My son sold another Picasso. Powers doesn't like me bragging on him but he's a mighty fine art dealer, isn't he Ellison?"

"The best." Powers Foster was better than a good art dealer. He was a prescient one. He could identify new talent long before his competition saw their promise. He belonged in New York clubbing with Andy Warhol and Bianca Jagger. With his effete manners, erupting pocket squares, and tendency to call everyone darling, he'd be a huge hit. Instead, he lived in Kansas City. Bitty Sue demanded it. Powers wasn't any better at standing up to his mother than I was to mine.

It was amazing we got any bridge in. We were the most popular people at the club. Audrey Miles was the first to interrupt us. She simpered over and asked in that breathless way of hers if I was all right.

"I heard..." She covered her mouth with her hand as if she

didn't want anyone to see her say the words. "I heard she was murdered." She sounded as insipid and vague as Mia Farrow in *Gatsby*. No wonder Gibson cheated on her with Madeline. Too bad he couldn't hold Madeline's interest. She moved on to greener pastures—namely Henry—and Gib filed for divorce. Why couldn't Audrey have been the one to find Madeline? She had as much reason to want her dead as I did.

After Audrey came Tippy, then Buffy, then Georgina. Even Myra Feathers stopped by. She'd spoken to me just once since the club Christmas party, a terse demand that we replace her mink coat. All of them had the same questions, the same sympathetic frowns, the same avid gleams in their eyes. All of them made me long to be hacking my way out of a sand trap.

Women kept coming until Mother pulled out her dragon scowl, an expression so fearsome it could keep the Huns at bay. It worked a peach with country club women.

Thank God for Mother. If one more woman came sniffing around for gossip or to see how I was holding up—*you poor dear, you look a bit pale, but I suppose that's to be expected. This must be doubly upsetting for you*—I'd have asked Mother for a refresher lesson on bidding.

My friend Libba would say I'm being too hard on them. Libba has never walked into a crowded room and had every woman in it fall silent.

It's the law of the jungle. Only the strong survive and Henry's affair made me look weak. They hardly bothered to hide their satisfaction at the collapse of my marriage—*Ellison Russell might be able to paint, but she can't keep her husband happy.* They sharpened their claws. The most I could muster for any of them was a too bright smile—all teeth, no sincerity.

After Mother donned her fire-breathing face, we managed to play an uninterrupted rubber. Bitty Sue, Lorna, and Mother managed two bottles of wine as well.

When Bitty Sue went down two because she trumped her own winner, she sighed deeply. "I told Powers time and again that woman was nothing but trouble. I've always wondered why he hired her."

Mother looked from her cards and rolled her eyes. "Isn't it obvious?"

Why did they insist on talking about Madeline? I'd rather talk about Watergate. Like everyone else, I was sick to death of hearing about it, but I'd happily discuss tapes or impeachment or even G. Gordon Liddy rather than Madeline.

Besides, if Mother thought Madeline and Powers had ever been together...Well, that was about as likely as Lorna and Powers. Powers didn't date women. Obviously, Mother's observational skills had been severely handicapped by years of paying attention to only me.

I suppose I could have asked Powers to fire Madeline. He'd have done it. Keeping an artist happy is more important than keeping a part-time salesperson. But it seemed petty. If Henry hadn't taken up with Madeline, he would have found someone else. Besides, Madeline was willing to work on straight commission so Powers didn't have to pay her unless she sold something.

The next time I was dummy I escaped to the powder room. The ladies' lounge at the club is a study in wishful thinking—white on white, with glass topped lobster traps serving as end tables, Krill baskets to hide the tampons, and etchings of seashells. The white chaise lounge sported a marine blue pillow. Someone wanted to be in Nantucket, wanted to forget that we were perched on the edge of the plains, a place rich in wheat and cattle and poor in ocean vistas.

I would have stayed at the table squirming while my bladder protested the gallon of iced tea I'd sent its way if I'd known Prudence Davies was going to be there. Henry used to call her a bony-assed harpy—when he was feeling charitable. I tried not to call her anything. I tried to stay out of her way.

"Ellison, you poor dear. How are you?"

I gave her a half-hearted attempt at a smile, the kind that shakes at the corner of your lips because your muscles aren't quite up to it. "Fine."

She pulled a tube of lipstick from her purse. "I think it's so brave of you to be here."

"Brave?"

Prudence gave me her version of a crocodile smile and I thought I ought to take notes. Her smile managed to communicate actual menace. "I don't know if I'd be able to show my face if my husband was out last night with a woman who was found dead this morning."

Bony-assed harpy was far too nice a description. I lowered my lashes so she couldn't read the expression in my eyes. "How do you know Henry was out with Madeline?"

"I saw them."

"Really? They only go to the one place." My husband didn't take Madeline out for dinner or dancing. He took her to some kinky club downtown. If Prudence had seen them out together, she'd have to have been there too. Prudence in a dog collar...I'd pay to see that.

She blinked. Rapidly. Swallowed. "I mean, I heard it through the grapevine. You know."

"I do know." I tried out a crocodile smile. I even admired it in the mirror. I'd discovered the secret to menace. I had to feel it, actually mean it. I let the threat of exposure hang in the air. No more altar guild or debutante selection committee or welcome committee for new club members for dear Prudence. "I do hope you haven't been sharing that story."

Her gaze met mine in the mirror. "Of course not."

She'd told everyone she knew.

Damn it. Henry was a prize jackass, a pimple on the butt of humanity, a middle-aged man clinging to the illusions of youth and power like a capsized sailor with an inflated donut.

He was also Grace's father, and my daughter didn't need both of her parents to be murder suspects.

THREE

When I got home from bridge, a strange sedan was parked in the circle drive in front of our house. I pulled in behind it.

The driver's door opened and a familiar plaid-clad leg appeared. Apparently, Detective Jones had more questions.

His chin jerked a greeting. "Mrs. Russell."

"Detective Jones, if we're going to see each other more than once a day, you're going to have to call me Ellison. Mrs. Russell was my mother-in-law." A queen among battle axes.

He grinned. Nice eyes and a nice smile. "I don't know if we'll be seeing each other that often."

"Call me Ellison anyway." He wouldn't. It was probably against regulations.

"I'm looking for Mr. Russell. Is he at home?"

His car wasn't.

"We can check." I unlocked the front door. "Be careful. Max ate the basket that catches the mail and I haven't got around to replacing it. I slipped on a flyer yesterday and nearly broke my neck." Despite my warning, I was the one who managed to kick an envelope under the bombé chest that stands in the foyer. I stooped and collected the rest of the envelopes that were splattered like paint droplets across the floor.

"Who's Max?"

"The dog."

On cue, Max appeared at the top of the stairs and yawned. He had the look of a dog who'd been asleep in my bed. Evil beastie.

The evil beastie trotted down the stairs and gave Detective Jones' crotch an exploratory sniff.

Oh dear Lord.

To his credit, Detective Jones chuckled and scratched behind Max's ears.

Max gave himself over to bliss and leaned against the detective's legs.

I used to think Max was a good judge of character. But Max likes Henry, so my faith in his doggy judgment has been shaken.

I tossed the mail onto the chest. "If Henry's home, he'll be in his study."

Detective Jones and Max followed me down the front hallway and waited while I tapped on Henry's door. No answer. When I opened it, the smell of cold, stale air whooshed out at us.

Detective Jones stepped around me and entered. His nice eyes had narrowed. They were taking inventory. He'd had all day to investigate Madeline's death. All day to learn the details of her relationship with my husband. Maybe he'd even heard of their proclivities.

Proclivities Henry had promised to keep far from Grace. No one would guess those proclivities from Henry's study—Tabriz rug on the floor, framed diplomas on pecan-paneled walls, a solid, dependable desk suitable for a solid dependable banker, leather club chairs, a picture of Grace in a silver frame, and one of my first paintings hanging above the fireplace. I was surprised he hadn't replaced it. Probably it had been hanging there so long he didn't notice it.

The detective crossed to the desk and ran his finger across its surface. It made a track in the dust. Harriet needed to clean in here more often.

"My husband's not here." Duh.

"When did you last see him?"

I'd thought of little else on the drive home from the club. "Monday."

"Today is Thursday."

Between the two of us, we'd cornered the market on stating the obvious.

"He lives here?"

If we weren't married, Henry would be the perfect roommate. He puts his dishes in the dishwasher, replaces the milk when he uses it all, and pays the mortgage and utilities without being asked. My offer to pay half had been answered with a resounding *no* and a quiet *bitch*. "Yes."

"Is it unusual for you to go so long without seeing him?"

"No."

"Has your daughter seen him?"

"I don't recall telling you I had a daughter." I wanted to keep Grace out of this. To keep her safe. She didn't need to know about her father's sordid relationship with a dead woman.

"I'm investigating a murder. I tend to find out about things like children." His voice was as dry as the martini I planned on downing as soon as he was gone.

"My husband's a suspect?" Of course he was. I didn't need to look into Detective Jones' brown eyes to know he was calculating the odds that Henry had killed Madeline.

The detective lifted his shoulders for half of a shrug. My question didn't merit a full one.

"His mistress was murdered."

"Am I a suspect?"

The skin around his eyes crinkled like I'd said something amusing. "Do you have an alibi?"

"No." In bed. Asleep. Alone.

"Then you're a suspect."

"Would you care for a drink?"

"I'm on duty."

"It's five o'clock."

He glanced at his watch.

"So it is. I'm still on duty." Detective Jones, follower of rules and procedures. "Any idea where your husband might be?"

"Did you try the bank?"

"They say he hasn't been in today. He missed all his appointments."

Henry missed an appointment? Dread slithered down my back then detoured to my stomach where it coiled like a snake. "I really do need that drink. Perhaps you'd like an iced tea?"

Detective Jones and Max followed me to the kitchen. I poured the man a glass of tea, filled the dog's water bowl then pulled a half-empty bottle of wine out of the fridge. Definitely half-empty. No half-baked, glass half-full optimism for me. Madeline and Henry had been seen together last night at their kinky club. Now Madeline was dead.

Admittedly, I'd fantasized about her death. Those fantasies usually included a falling piano or flash lightning on the golf course while she clutched her nine iron or three bottles of valium and a scrawled note that read *I'm sorry*. I'd never once imagined her floating in the club pool.

Madeline had been murdered and Henry was missing. I took a large sip of liebfraumilch.

My daughter chose that moment to appear in the kitchen doorway. She did it with a nonchalance that suggested real planning. Grace crossed her arms, leaned against the doorframe and took in Detective Jones' plaid pants and the shrewd look in his eyes. She would see the shrewdness straight off. She wouldn't be fooled into thinking his eyes were nice.

I cleared my throat. "Grace, this is Detective Jones. Detective, my daughter, Grace Russell."

"Nice to meet you, Miss Russell."

On the surface, Grace seemed unimpressed. She didn't ask why he was sipping tea in our kitchen. "Nice to meet you too." She turned her gaze toward me. "What's up, Mom?"

She knew. Of course, she knew. Everyone knew. Looking at the deliberately bored expression on her face, I hated whoever had killed Madeline. I hated them for bringing a homicide detective into Grace's home. I hated Madeline for getting herself murdered. My feelings toward Henry went deeper than hate. If he could have kept his willy in his pants, we wouldn't be murder suspects and Grace's eyes wouldn't look haunted and defiant at the same time.

"You know your mother found Madeline Harper's body this morning?"

"I know." The teenage girls' grapevine was every bit as effective as their mothers' and their grandmothers'. "Are you okay, Mom?"

Of all the people who'd asked me that question today, Grace was the first to care about the answer. Maybe the second—Detective Jones had seemed genuinely sincere when he asked. But that was a lifetime ago. "I'm fine."

"When is the last time you saw your father?" Detective Jones asked.

"Yesterday."

Max yawned, bored by questions that didn't involve a ball or a treat or chasing a squirrel. He curled up in his favorite spot (essentially wherever he was most in the way) and eyed the man who was questioning my daughter.

"At what time?"

"Around five or so."

"Do you know where he is now?"

She abandoned the doorway and entered the kitchen, crossed to the island and poured herself a glass of tea, took a sip then squeezed in a slice of lemon. "He packed a bag. He said he had a business trip."

The dread coiled in my stomach lifted its hooded head, ready to strike. I tried to drown it with another swig of wine. Getting wet just annoyed it.

"Do you know where he went?" Detective Jones asked.

Grace raised her eyebrows to the middle of her forehead. Short wrinkles marred her smooth skin. She rubbed her nose. "Los Angeles."

We all paused to consider the ramifications. Detective Jones probably thought about my husband getting off a plane in Los Angeles and boarding one to Brazil or Argentina or some other country where men were macho and it was easy to disappear. I didn't think that. I looked at the late afternoon sunshine shafting golden through the window onto Grace and thought appearances could be deceiving. My angelic daughter was lying.

"Did he say why?" Detective Jones asked.

She shook her head. "No."

"May I use your phone?"

"Of course." I nodded to the wall phone with the stretched out cord.

"The one in the study?"

"Of course."

The angelic, lying stranger who'd replaced my daughter disappeared when Detective Jones left the kitchen. I leveled my gaze on Grace.

She swallowed. "You won't tell?"

That she'd just lied to a police officer to protect her father? No. I wouldn't tell.

"Where did he go?" I asked.

She inspected her cuticles.

"Grace..."

She rolled her eyes. Sighed with more drama than Streisand in *The Way We Were,* before giving in. "He said he had a lead on a new investment. Maybe he went to New York."

An investment? In New York? Henry owned a local bank. What the hell was going on? Then again, Henry could be holed up at a local hotel or on his way to Quebec or Paris or Bermuda. Who knew? Unlike Grace, Henry could tell a convincing lie.

"Did he ask you to lie for him?"

"Of course not." Again with the raised eyebrows and itchy nose. She was so bad at lying she ought to give it up.

I'd deal with her later. I was too angry with Henry to think clearly. My son-of-a-bitch husband had asked his teenage daughter to lie to me. Instead, she'd lied to the police.

Grace went to the refrigerator, opened the door, and surveyed its contents. "I know what you're thinking."

I doubted it. I was thinking about using some of Henry's kinky toys on him. A bullwhip sounded about right. "Oh?"

"You're thinking Dad lied to me."

I wasn't going to argue the point. Not with Detective Jones just down the hall. My gaze turned toward the door.

"You should be nicer to him."

My gaze returned to Grace's foraging back. Be nicer to my cheating, lying, on-the-run husband? Not likely. "Pardon me?"

She turned, a container of chutney chicken salad clasped in her hand. "Did you think I meant Dad?"

"Who else?"

"Detective Jones. He could make our lives difficult." She cracked the lid of the container, sniffed, and wrinkled her nose. "You don't need to be nicer to Dad. In fact..." she pivoted so I saw only her back, "you should divorce him."

I closed my eyes for half a second, no more. When I opened them, sunlight still streamed through the windows, the copper pots hanging from the rack still gleamed, and the exposed brick wall still looked the way it always did—just a little wrong—too much scarlet, not enough crimson. My kitchen was the same. It was my world that was off-kilter.

My daughter took a deep breath, one that hunched her shoulders, then she turned to face me. "I love Dad, but I don't see why you're still married to him."

This was not a conversation I wanted to have with a detective in the house. To be fair, it wasn't a conversation I wanted have without a detective in the house. "It's complicated."

My daughter, who was never at a loss for a smart reply, bit her lip. Her chin quivered. She scrubbed at her face with the back of her free hand. "You're not staying married because of me, are you?"

Yes.

I couldn't tell her that. Not when her knuckles were white around the chicken salad and unshed tears glimmered against her lashes. I took a sip of wine, swallowed around the lump in my throat, rubbed the tip of my nose, and lied.

"Of course not. It's complicated."

"It's not complicated. You sleep in different rooms. You barely speak to each other. When you do, it's as if you're talking to strangers. Unless you're painting, you look miserable. You never smile."

"I smile all the time."

Grace tossed her hair. "Gritting your teeth and pursing your lips isn't smiling. Dad never smiles either. Why do you want to live like that? You both deserve to be with people who make you happy."

The wine bottle definitely didn't look half-empty anymore. Not remotely. Especially not after I poured myself another glass. "I thought most kids wanted their parents to stay together." That's what the counselor had said, and the child psychologist, and the shrink.

The sound Grace made was a cross between a sob and a guffaw. "You're always worried about everyone else. Don't be." She dredged up a shaky smile. "Besides, there's Christmas math."

"Christmas math?"

"Christmas. Birthdays. Any holiday that involves gifts. Divorced parents mean twice the loot."

It was my turn to swipe at a tear clinging to my lashes. Grace cared as much about loot as I did about football. Not at all. My arms ached to hug her. To create a circle where nothing could hurt her. I wished we were one of those families that actually expressed emotion. One that yelled and sobbed and laughed and hugged—all over spilled milk. We weren't. I took a step forward. Brushed a strand of hair away from Grace's face then dropped a dry kiss on the top of her head. "Don't worry about your father and me. We'll figure things out."

She sniffled. "The cop is cute."

I laughed. A strangled, choking kind of laugh. The kind of laugh that escapes your lips when you realize your daughter feels responsible for your unhappiness. "I suppose."

"You should go for it."

"Go for what?" Detective Jones stood just outside the kitchen door.

I wondered how much he'd heard and felt a flush worthy of a teenager rise to my cheeks. "Take out." I forced my hand to remain at my side. It wanted to rub my nose. "Grace isn't in the mood for chicken salad. She wants Chinese."

"You should stay for dinner." Grace shot me a watery grin.

I glared at her. If she wasn't careful, there'd be another murder. I scanned the rack of heavy copper pots that hung above the stove. Surely one of them would do as a weapon.

Detective Jones offered her an amused smile. "Thank you for the invitation, but I can't stay."

"Another time?" she asked.

The man flushed.

I took the container from my daughter's hands and put it back in the fridge. "Detective Jones has a job to do. I'm sure he's very busy." I was also sure he didn't dine with suspects. It was probably against the rules. Besides, he had to go track down my cheating, lying, on-the-run-but-please-God-not-a-murderer husband.

FOUR

We stood around the kitchen island and wondered what to say next. Grace examined her nails, I examined the level of wine in my glass, and Detective Jones examined the painting hanging above the breakfast table.

What are you supposed to say to a man who thinks you—or your husband—has committed a murder? "Did you talk to Roger?"

"Roger Harper? I did."

Was I imagining the disapproval in his voice? Surely Roger was a suspect too?

The phone rang and Grace lunged for the receiver. "Hello."

She listened for a moment then turned to me. "I'm going to take this in your room." She handed me the phone and disappeared. When I heard her pick up the bedroom extension, I hung up the receiver.

"Ellie, are you here?" a welcome voice called from the front hall.

"In the kitchen," I replied.

"Your husband?" Detective Jones asked.

"A friend."

"He has a key?" Disapproval was writ clearly across the detective's face. Let him disapprove. It was none of his business who did or did not have a key to my house. Powers didn't. He just didn't bother with the doorbell.

"He's like family."

Powers Foster—all long legs and pointy elbows, effortless

charm and affected elegance—exploded into the kitchen. "You poor darling. I just heard. How are you? Are you all right?"

Another person who cared about the answer. That made three. I glanced at Detective Jones, and the censure that had settled onto his face, and scratched him from the sincere caring list. That made two. I walked into Powers' open arms for an exuberant hug, pulling away only when my throat began to swell.

"Where's Harriet?"

I was ridiculously grateful for a question that had nothing to do with murder or my marriage. "She went to visit her mother."

"Did she leave you anything besides curried chicken salad?" He wrinkled his nose. "I doubt it. I'm taking you and Grace out to dinner. I heard about the most marvelous new place. It's a créperie. They're so uppity they only speak French. *Jambon et fromage pour moi.*"

Only he pronounced it *jam bone ate from age pore moi.*

Powers' attempts to amuse me were usually more clever than a bad French accent. I tried for a polite smile but couldn't quite manage it.

Detective Jones cleared his throat and Powers pretended to notice him. I wasn't fooled. The last time Powers failed to notice an attractive man within a half-second of entering a room Eisenhower was in office.

Detective Jones repeated Powers' sentence with an accent worthy of the sixteenth arrondissement. *"Je voudrais un crêpe de jambon et fromage s'il vous plait."*

Powers locked his spring green gaze on the detective and assessed. He began with the detective's polished loafers then moved his gaze slowly up the detective's plaid clad legs. It lingered on Detective Jones' broad chest and shoulders until it finally reached his face. Usually when Powers blatantly checked out another man, he was met with squirming or flushing or an angry glare.

Detective Jones responded with an amused smile.

"Powers Foster." He stuck out his hand. "And you are?"

The policeman shook Powers' hand. "A homicide detective."

Powers grinned at me. "If I'd known detectives were so delectable I would have told Madeline to get herself knocked off years ago. Where are you from, Homicide Detective?"

"San Francisco."

"Really?" Powers wet his lips with the tip of his tongue. "Why did you leave?"

"I didn't fit in."

Powers fluttered his eyelashes. "Oh?"

Of course Detective Jones, follower of rules, hadn't fit in with the Haight-Ashbury vibe. He'd come to the Midwest where people were as dependable as the sun rising in the east. "The lifestyle was a little too free and easy for me," he said.

"What a heartbreaking shame. Free and easy is my motto." Powers raised an inviting brow. "You might even call it a personal manifesto."

Detective Jones' lips quirked. "You knew Mrs. Harper?" Somehow, I liked him better for not being threatened by Powers' come on.

"She worked for me. Part-time."

"You must be the art dealer."

"Guilty as charged."

Max chose that moment to get up, stretch, and sidle toward Powers. The two shared a love-hate relationship. Max loved Powers. Powers hated Max. It wasn't personal. Powers hated any animal that might shed on his navy pants.

"When did you last see her?" Detective Jones asked.

Powers shifted, trying to keep the center island between Max and his pants. "Am I a suspect?"

"Please answer the question."

Powers sidestepped Max. "Ellison, be a darling and call the beast."

"He just wants you to pet him." Watching Powers try to avoid my dog was much more entertaining than his bad French accent.

"Max." Detective Jones' voice had the ring of authority. "Come."

My dog trotted to his side.

"Sit."

Max sat.

Powers sighed. "My hero."

"When did you last see Mrs. Harper?" Powers' hero repeated.

Powers waved an insouciant hand. "I don't know. The whole point of having Madeline in the office was that I didn't have to be."

"Was she a good employee? Reliable?"

"Heavens no. Ellison, my darling, vino? Or maybe you'd like to make me a martini?"

If anyone was going to drink a martini, it would be me. I poured him a glass of wine.

"If she wasn't a good employee why did you keep her?"

Powers sipped. "Madeline wanted a job that didn't interfere with her life. One that she could use as an excuse when she didn't want to do something and ditch when she did."

Detective Jones' eyes narrowed to slits worthy of Dirty Harry. Better than Dirty Harry. Detective Jones was a real cop and he didn't need a gun to look menacing. "That doesn't answer my question."

Powers' left eye twitched. I bet he didn't find Detective Jones quite so attractive now. Or maybe he did. He was looking at the policeman like I look at chocolates. Delicious, delectable, and hard to stop after that first taste.

"She worked for peanuts and gave good phone."

Detective Jones lifted a brow. "Gave good phone?"

"A hefty portion of my business comes from the coasts. Someone has to answer the phones."

"The coasts?"

Powers nodded. "A movie tanks and the producer needs to sell his Lichtenstein but he doesn't want all of L.A. to know, so he calls me. Same thing for New York. The heiress who's burned through her fortune doesn't want Park Avenue to know she's broke so she calls me and her grandmother's Monet goes to California. I need the right person to answer the phone."

"Why you?"

Powers' eyelashes fluttered again. "I'm very discreet."

"I'm sure. You represent Mrs. Russell?"

"I do."

"For how long?"

What did my paintings have to do with Madeline's murder? I opened my mouth to ask but was interrupted by the ring of the doorbell.

"Gracie, would you get that?" I called up the stairs.

The resentful trudge of teenage feet answered me.

A moment later, Hunter Tafft sauntered into my kitchen as if he owned it. He was self-assured. He was prematurely silver-haired. He was more polished than Mother's sterling. He leaned over and brushed his lips across my cheek. "Ellison, how are you?"

I didn't answer. Couldn't. What was he doing here?

"Your mother asked me to come over. She said you needed a lawyer."

There was going to be another murder. Justifiable homicide. Mother should pick out her casket. Why in the hell hadn't he called first? If he thought I was a legally challenged damsel in distress just waiting for an attorney in a white Mercedes to ride up and save me, he was wrong.

Hunter greeted Powers with the slightest of nods. Powers' answering nod was even smaller. Brief jerks of their chins said everything they didn't say out loud. They were willing to acknowledge each other socially. Barely. I wondered if there was a story there. Did Hunter feel threatened by Powers' preferences? Did Powers feel threatened by Hunter's perfect hair? Maybe a bit of both?

Hunter turned his attention on Detective Jones. "I don't believe we've met."

"I don't believe we have." The expression I was fast coming to associate with disapproval settled on Detective Jones' face. He leaned back against the kitchen counter.

The skin around Hunter's eyes tightened. "You are?"

"Detective Jones."

Hunter showed off his gleaming teeth. Blinded by their brightness, I wasn't sure if his smile was genuine or not.

"I don't believe I caught your first name," Hunter said. The smile was definitely manufactured.

"I don't believe you did."

They assessed. Not like Powers had assessed. Nope, this assessment had more to do with who could run the playground or the squad room or the boardroom. My kitchen was so filled with testosterone it was hard to breathe.

Powers fanned himself. Sighed. Then he patted his pockets until he found a packet of the colored cigarettes he favored. He withdrew a pink one then began patting again. "Ellison, my darling, may I smoke?"

There was no way Powers was smoking one of those nasty things in my house. The stench would linger for days. I shook my head and pointed to the back door. "Patio."

Then, ever the good hostess I tried to diffuse the tension. "Hunter is an old friend of the family's." Not my lawyer. I didn't need a lawyer. Henry needed a lawyer.

Hunter mirrored Detective Jones' lazy pose and leaned against the doorframe. "Do you have a warrant?"

"I invited him."

Hunter looked like his next question might have something to do with my intelligence—or lack thereof. I crossed my arms.

Powers gave up patting. "Do you have a match?"

"In the drawer."

He reached into the drawer and pulled out a matchbook, stared at it a moment then tossed it onto the counter. "Something you're not telling me, Ellie, darling?"

The matchbook was black with the name of a club printed in silver letters. Club K. It was almost innocuous. Almost. On closer inspection, the L in Club looked more like a riding crop than a letter. Something hung from the B's loop. Not a Q's lost squiggly or a printing error but a tiny pair of handcuffs.

I hate roller coasters. I hate the grinding terror as the cars climb ever higher. I hate the stomach-in-my-throat feeling of the world collapsing as I hurtle toward the earth. I hate worrying that the kid in front of me is going to vomit and that I will be covered in cotton candy-pink sick. Looking at the matchbook, I felt that way— as if the world was disintegrating, as if I was flying toward an unknown landing that was sure to be painful. Hell, I might even be the one to vomit.

I'd seen a matchbook like it before. Once. That Henry would have brought another one home and left it where Grace might find it...I blinked to clear my vision of a deep shade—perylene red.

"May I see those?" Detective Jones held out his palm.

I nodded.

He waited for me to hand them to him. He could wait forever. I wasn't touching them. My arms remained firmly crossed.

When he realized I wasn't moving, he picked them up, raised a brow.

"My husband's."

"What are those?" Hunter demanded.

"Matches." Detective Jones and I spoke in unison.

Hunter tilted his silver head. "From where?"

"Club K," I admitted.

"Where?" God bless a man who slept with half the women in the city without the aid of a riding crop or cuffs.

"Club Kink." My voice was so soft I don't know how he heard me.

Hunter looked properly appalled. "How did they get here?"

I glanced at Detective Jones. His eyes actually looked nice, as if he knew what this conversation was costing me. I straightened my shoulders. "Henry."

The detective turned them in his fingers, opened them, then dropped them in his pocket.

Madeline was dead. Henry was missing. There was a kinky matchbook in the junk drawer in my kitchen.

What I needed was to paint. I needed to mix colors and feel

their weight on my brushes—the lightness of cadmium yellow, the heft of cobalt blue, the almost burdensome ballast of raw umber. I needed to take a blank canvas and transform it with light and dark, sunshine and shadow. There's no hiding behind a polite smile on canvas. No biting your tongue. No pretending. There's only color and truth and form.

I wanted them all out of my house. I wanted it more than I wanted chocolate or another glass of wine or the end of the worst day ever. I crossed my arms over my chest and looked at the ceiling.

Hunter got the hint. "Shall I count on seeing you tomorrow?" Somehow he moved both Powers and Detective Jones toward the front hallway by simply shifting that way himself.

The police detective paused mid-step. "You'll let me know if you hear from Mr. Russell?"

"The créperie, darling. I absolutely insist." Powers pinned me with his green gaze. "Later this week? Promise?"

"I promise."

Three unconvinced men stared at me. "I promise all of you."

How was I to know I'd regret every one of those promises?

FIVE

The thing about having the worst day ever is that you're pretty much guaranteed that the next one will be better.

The thing about glass half-full thinking is that it will bite you in the ass every time. Or it will stick out its leg, trip you, then laugh when you land on your aforementioned ass.

I tripped. Then again, who expects to find a body on their front stoop? At least this one wasn't dead. It moaned when I fell on it. Maybe because my knee landed in the near vicinity of the place men least like to feel knees. The body belonged to Roger Harper, Madeline's husband.

The smell of gin wafting from Roger's body was enough to make my eyes water. The sight of his car parked on my hostas was enough to make me cry.

I nudged him with the tip of my shoe, and I wasn't gentle about it.

He groaned.

I nudged again. "Get up."

He groaned again.

His wife was dead. Murdered. He was upset. That didn't give him leave to sleep on my front steps—or crush my hostas.

I stepped over Roger's gin-soaked carcass and peered through the open window of his Jag. The keys were still in the ignition. The car stank of gin and cigarettes and grief. I got in, backed the car off my flattened shrubbery and parked it at the curb.

When I climbed my front steps, Roger was still groaning and still not moving.

A drunk man was draped across my front stoop. The homes association would disapprove—to put it mildly. My neighbors would have coronaries. They were probably calling to complain even now.

I prodded again then tried a bribe. "If you get up, I'll make you coffee." I'd even make him my super-secret hangover cure. Although, if I told Roger what was in it, he might opt to spend the day heaped in front of my door. "Coffee," I crooned.

Roger muttered something unintelligible then choked on a sob.

He was crying. I considered leaving him there. It would be so easy to get in my car and drive away from Roger's grief and the drama it promised. I fingered my keys, gazed longingly at my TR6, but opened the front door instead.

Somehow, with a combination of pushing, prodding, begging, and bribing, I got him inside.

Max stared at us from the top of the stairs, his doggy eyebrows raised as if to say, *Didn't you just leave? What in blazes are you doing back so quickly? I was planning on taking a nap on your forbidden but fabulously comfortable bed.* Then his lips curled. He must have caught scent of Roger because with a snort of canine disgust he turned and disappeared down the hall.

I led Roger to a stool at my kitchen counter, then made coffee. When Mr. Coffee finished dripping, I poured him a huge mug and began assembling the ingredients for my hangover cure.

Roger took a sip of coffee, grimaced then dropped his head to his arms.

He didn't move when I started the blender—spinach, carrots, apples, raw ginger, five aspirin, Sprite, and a raw egg—the recipe for relief.

When I put a glass of super-secret down next to him, he ignored it.

"Drink it," I directed.

Roger lifted the glass to his nose and sniffed. "What is it?"

"A cure."

A small sip passed his pale lips and he looked like he might vomit.

"It's better to drink it quickly."

He glared at me with blood-shot eyes but took another sip. His green-tinged skin transitioned from a delicate celadon to the approximate shade of over-cooked peas.

"Just do it," I said.

He drank. Drained the glass. Gasped. "Water."

I was ready with a glass.

He gulped it down.

I took the glass from his shaking hand, refilled it and gave it back to him.

"Thank you," he croaked. "What was in that?"

"It's better if you don't know. More coffee?"

Roger shook his head then looked as if he regretted moving. "No, thank you."

"You'll feel better in thirty minutes or so." Then I could send him on his way. The last thing I needed was Madeline's husband convalescing in my kitchen.

He rolled his eyes then winced as if even that hurt.

I called and rescheduled my appointment with Hunter, emptied the dishwasher, and wrote the grocery list. Roger still looked like death warmed over, completely incapable of making it to the front door, much less pouring himself into his car and driving away, so I retrieved yesterday's mail from the front hall and opened it over the trashcan.

Junk. The electric bill. More junk. Henry's credit card statement. My fingers itched to open it. Instead, I tossed it onto the counter. I didn't need to see his credit card bill to know my husband spent an unconscionable amount of money on his hobby.

Roger lifted his head. Slowly. As if his skull and the piddling brain inside weighed a hundred pounds. His mouth worked but no words came out.

"More coffee?" I asked.

He nodded and I served him a fresh mug.

He drank, stared at the brick wall, rubbed his temples. "I never thought a woman like Madeline would look at me. Then she married me and I felt like the luckiest man in the world."

Or unluckiest. It's all about perspective. From my perspective, discussing Madeline with me was a gaff exceeded only by parking on my hostas. I'd rather discuss Roger's views on Nixon's impeachment than talk about Madeline.

"I loved her." His face crumpled. It deflated as if the man inside his body had departed and the remaining husk was in the first stages of collapse.

"I'm sorry." Never were words more meaningless. I cringed as soon as they left my lips. This was why I should have left him rotting on my front steps. Unfettered grief. If *Thou shall not air dirty laundry in public* was the Walford family's first commandment, *Thou shall not make a spectacle of thyself by displaying emotion* was the second. We didn't do raw emotion or drama or storms of tears. I had no idea how to handle anguish. Still, I had to offer some comfort. I lifted my hand to pat his shoulder but couldn't quite bring myself to touch him.

Fortunately, he didn't notice my hand hovering over his shoulder like a confused UFO. "She'd been acting so strangely lately."

Lately? In my opinion, the strange behavior dated back to when she started hopping into bed with other women's husbands. It definitely began when she started letting my husband tie her up and flog her.

He gulped at his coffee. Coughed. Rubbed his eyes with the back of his hand. "Do you know who might have killed her?"

Was he asking if I had? Perhaps he thought Henry had finally gone too far. "No idea."

"She had a secret. She said things were going to change. I thought maybe she meant to break things off with Henry."

The poor man. He should have just filed for divorce. It wasn't like there were children to protect. Perhaps if he'd stood up for himself, Madeline would have respected him. He sniffled and wiped his nose on the back of his hand. Perhaps respect was too strong a word.

"Did she say anything to Henry?"

His assumption that Henry and I spoke was almost funny. Aside from social obligations and the odd comment about needing to buy coffee or laundry detergent, we had nothing to say to each other. "No."

"I went through her things."

I swear Henry's credit card statement fluttered its eyelashes. It winked. It smiled its best come-hither smile.

I forced my gaze to Roger's red-rimmed watery blue eyes.

"I found this."

For the second time in less than a day, a man tossed a book of Club K matches onto my kitchen counter.

"I went there last night." He dropped his gaze. "I didn't know..."

He didn't know?

Roger shuddered. "I tried to talk to the owner. A woman. She was busy." His Adam's apple bobbed. "She said I should come back this morning and she'd talk to me."

My heart stuttered. Surely, he wouldn't ask.

"Will you go with me? Please?"

I poured myself coffee I didn't want or need so I could clutch the warmth of the mug. "Isn't this a matter for the police?"

Roger raked his hand through long strands of thinning hair that barely covered his naked scalp. His throat worked its way around another swallow. "This isn't about her death. It's about why she..." His head dropped to his hands.

The poor man. He'd loved her and she'd cheated on him with my husband. At least Henry and I were well on our way to complete indifference when he first started cheating. I knew why Henry had strayed. He needed to dominate and I was unable to submit. Silly me. I wanted us to be equal in marriage. Equality goes out the window when one partner has a riding crop and cuffs and the other is on her knees.

I tried it. Once. In hopes of saving our marriage. I donned the black silk stockings and black lace garter and the high-heeled shoes and nothing else. I even let him blindfold me. Then I held out my wrists and let him bind me. I even knelt.

He'd turned on loud music. Blinded and half-deaf, I'd still sensed him walking circles around me and my body had tightened with anticipated dread.

When the riding crop slapped against my skin, I didn't feel fear or desire or pain or pleasure. Instead, I'd balled my hands together and spit out the safe word as if it was poison.

"You said you'd try." Henry sounded like a petulant child.

"And you said you'd love, honor, and cherish me."

I struggled to get off the floor.

"I am."

"By hitting me with a riding crop?"

I stumbled to my feet and thrust my cuffed wrists out so he could unlock me. I didn't see the connection between love and hitting me with a riding crop.

"You said you'd obey."

"When?"

"In our vows when we got married."

"I did not. We took that part out." But that was back when Henry didn't feel threatened by a wife who made more money than he did, by the thinning of his hair or the thickening of his waist.

"Women want a man who takes charge."

He wasn't a man, he was a Neanderthal. "I want a partner."

"I want you to do this, Ellison." He tried to sound masterful and dominant and in-charge.

I didn't need to *see* him to know he was a man afraid of his own mortality. A man who turned to kink as a way to convince himself he was still virile. Why couldn't he just buy a damned Porsche? I shook my head. "I can't."

It meant the end. Not of our marriage. The marriage we kept going—for Grace's sake. But it was the end of Ellison and Henry, of growing old together, of happily ever after.

After that, Henry embraced the idea of open marriage like water embraces wetness.

I painted more than ever. For a while, the hopeful pinks and greens and yellows on my canvases turned dark. Powers raised an eyebrow, made sympathetic noises, then sold the paintings for more money than ever.

I knew why Henry's and my story ended the way it did. Money. Ego. Fear. The heartbroken man at my kitchen counter had no idea why Madeline had done what she'd done.

I could have told Roger my theory—that Madeline enjoyed being punished because she knew she'd left a trail of reprehensible acts behind her. I could have told him what I knew—that knowing why doesn't make things better. It just makes them clearer. I kept my lips sealed and shook my head.

"Please? I can't go alone."

He shouldn't go at all. Well actually, he should. He should go home. He should go to the office or the country club. He and his ridiculous request should go somewhere other than my kitchen.

He wiped his eyes with hands that still shook despite my super-secret cure. Then his shoulders began to shake. "Please?"

Oh dear Lord. More drama. Roger Harper was crying at my kitchen counter. "I have a luncheon planned this afternoon."

He choked on a sob.

"It won't change anything," I said.

"It will. I know it will."

I tried to reason with him. "Nothing you find will change anything. There are some things you don't want to know."

"I went there. The things I saw..." He rubbed his face, still a near indescribable shade of green. "I have to know why."

"What makes you think this woman has the answer?"

"She said she did."

Well, if a dominatrix said so, it must be true. "Roger, it's a terrible idea."

Tears ran freely down his sunken cheeks and his shoulders didn't just shake, they convulsed. His sobs attracted Max. The dog appeared in the doorway, his head cocked as he tried to decipher the unfamiliar sound of a man barely treading water in a bottomless pool of anguish.

Of all the things my mother taught me—how to plan a party, how to begin with the silverware on the outside and work my way in, how to smile sweetly when I wanted to rage—why hadn't she showed me how to handle a crying man?

Visiting Club K was the very last thing on earth I wanted to do. It was contrary to my better judgment. It was something I could never undo, sure to be chock full of sights I could never unsee. But poor, gin-soaked Roger looked as if he was about to collapse with grief. Spending an awkward hour with a dominatrix was a small thing to bring him solace. At the very least, it would get him out of my kitchen. Silently calling myself ten kinds of fool, I nodded. "All right, I'll go with you. But I have to be home by noon and you have to shower first."

SIX

I parked Roger's car in front of a warehouse and wished with all my too-soft heart that I'd found a spine and stayed home. If the hung-over husband of my father's dead mistress asked Mother to go to a club where spanking passed as recreation and handcuffs replaced tennis bracelets as a status symbol, she'd laugh in his face then eject him from her kitchen, not drive him to the club. Certainly she wouldn't knock on the door. For the first time in my life, I thought it might be nice to be more like Mother.

Get in. Get Roger's answers. Get out. Preferably in five minutes or less. That was the plan.

I rapped on the steel door a second time and prayed no one would hear or that no one was there. Like so many of my prayers, it went unanswered.

A woman with hooded eyes and sharp cheekbones opened the door, took one look at my seersucker dress, curled her glossy lip and said, "We don't need any Girl Scout cookies."

"I'm not selling any." A rude, leather-clad woman with hair that could do with some conditioner and lips that glistened blood red was as good a reason to leave as any. I turned on my heel.

Roger caught my elbow. "Please. Don't go."

I felt distinctly less inclined to indulge him now that he wasn't sobbing in my kitchen. I pulled my arm loose. "I'm taking your car. If you stay, you'll have to call a cab."

"Please, Ellison." He looked as lost and lonely as a bottle bobbing in the ocean. One whose message was slowly disintegrating.

"Let me guess." The woman drew out the ess sound. "You must be Ellison Russell."

The air around me stilled.

She continued, "You're exactly as Henry described. Country club pretty with an expression that could form icicles on eaves in August. I didn't ever expect to see you here."

My faithless husband had talked about me to a dominatrix. I shuddered. "I didn't ever expect to be here." Could she know where Henry was? Did I care enough to ask? I didn't. But Grace cared. "Have you seen my husband?"

"Every inch." Her hands measured those inches. Correctly.

My hand tightened around the handle of my purse. I wanted to swing it at her head. Two things stopped me. First off, the purse was a Nantucket Lightship signed by José Reyes. It wasn't just a handbag, it was a piece of handcrafted art and I didn't want to damage the weaving or scrimshaw against the blades of her cheeks. Second, she was obviously trying to get a rise out of me. I wouldn't give her the satisfaction. "That's not what I meant."

"Oh?" She fluttered her eyelashes.

"He's left town. Do you know where he went?"

"Not a clue."

I doubted she'd tell me if she did know. I borrowed the voice Mother saves for waiters who bring her tepid coffee. "Mr. Harper wants to ask you a few questions about his wife. Do you have a clue about her?"

She curled her kewpie doll lips again and stood back. "Come in."

Why couldn't we just stand on the sidewalk while the woman in the leather bustier told Roger his wife had worn a dog collar and liked it?

Roger, fool that he was, stepped inside. Fool that I am, I followed him. Maybe it was prurient curiosity. If so, I wasn't willing to admit it, even to myself.

The place reeked of stale cigarettes, spilled liquor, and sex. Murky light filtered through shuttered second-story windows then glanced off a brick wall dotted with cuffs and shackles.

"Lovely place you have here," I said. Sarcasm—another lesson learned at Mother's knee, and a tactic best used when losing an argument. Also useful when the urge to run screaming from a warehouse filled with torture equipment is overwhelming. Mother probably didn't know about that use.

"What is that?" Roger pointed to a terrifying looking apparatus—padded, a bit bigger than a door, able to tilt like a lounge chair next to the pool. It had sections—key sections—cut out of the middle so that once someone was restrained, their bits would hang out the other side.

"A Berkley horse." She smiled at it as if it was an adorable child who'd just presented her with a bouquet of flowers. Then her gaze cut to Roger. "A favorite of your wife." Her smile lost its indulgent softness when she looked at me. "And your husband."

Next to me, Roger gasped. His skin, which had finally regained the color of skin on the drive over, reverted to green. The shade was reminiscent of cream of asparagus soup. "Henry tied my wife to that thing?" His red-rimmed eyes didn't look horrified. They looked curious.

"He did."

"And then?"

She ran the tip of her of tongue across the front of her teeth. "Then he whipped her or flogged her or caned her."

"Why?" Roger's green skin glazed with sweat and his throat worked as if he had more to say but couldn't bring himself to utter the words.

"She liked it. They both did. He would have one of his other subs sit on the front side of the Berkley and pleasure Madeline while he whipped her. The combination of pleasure and pain was..." She paused to find the right word. "Delectable."

Other subs? What the hell? She wanted me to ask. I could tell. I sealed my lips.

Roger sank onto a piece of leather. I couldn't imagine what it was for, didn't want to.

His head fell to his hands. "I don't understand."

"It's simple." Mistress K's voice was soft, sibilant. "What part don't you understand? The part where Henry shackled Madeline to the Berkley? The part where he flogged her? Or the part where she loved every second of it?" She stepped so close to Roger that his knees touched her legs. "She wanted someone to take charge."

Roger turned his head away, stared at the wall of manacles. "You're lying."

Mistress K's laugh was gentle. She reached out, hooked a pointed fingernail under Roger's chin, and turned his head so he was forced to look at her. "Don't you ever want someone to take charge? To let them take responsibility?" she asked. "Wouldn't it feel good to replace the pain in your heart with the sting of leather on your body?"

Why didn't he tell her to go to hell? I would. Roger sighed as if she'd described a dream vacation, not an intimate encounter with a flogger.

With just the pressure of her finger under his chin, she made him stand and drew him closer to her. Didn't the idiot man know the story of the spider and the fly?

"Roger!"

They both looked at me as if they'd forgotten I was there.

"What the hell are you doing? You came here for answers not to let some woman whip you."

She answered me with a smile worthy of a lion on Wild Kingdom—right before it tried to eat Marlin Perkins' co-host Jim. "Perhaps the whip is the answer. Perhaps Roger needs to feel it to understand why Madeline loved it so."

Oh. Dear. Lord. "Roger you're the CFO of a publicly traded company. You're vice president of your country club. You're a deacon in your church. You can't mean to let this woman tie you to that thing."

I might as well have talked to the brick wall. Roger took a tentative step toward the Berkley.

"I can take away the pain, Roger. I can take away the sorrow."

Each word was low and seductive and venomous. "I can take away the guilt."

Guilt? What guilt? Had Roger killed Madeline? He couldn't have. He didn't have the force of character to kill a mouse, much less Madeline.

"Take off your shirt, Roger." Her voice was still low, still seductive, but I heard iron beneath the velvet.

Roger, the idiot, unbuttoned the first button.

"Why are you doing this?" I demanded.

Roger didn't seem to hear me. It was as if he'd gotten lost in his own head and only Mistress K's voice could reach him.

"He wants to know why. I'm going to show him."

"Do you have to work at being a bitch or does it come naturally?"

She smiled as if I'd paid her a compliment. "It's all natural."

Roger unbuttoned the rest of the buttons and shrugged out of his shirt. His forearms and neck were tanned from golf. His torso was ghostly white. Mistress K ran her fingernail down his chest, raising goose bumps. I looked away.

She led him to the Berkley, helped him lean into it, lifted his right arm and shackled him.

"Roger, have you lost your mind?" My voice was loud enough to echo through the empty warehouse, but it wasn't loud enough to reach Roger. He didn't acknowledge that I'd spoken.

Mistress K shackled his left arm then gently patted his bare shoulder.

I took a reluctant step toward them. "He lost his wife. He's lost in his grief. You can't do this to him."

The woman in leather raised an eyebrow, daring me to stop her.

"You're a sadist."

"You say the nicest things." She circled the Berkley, looking at Roger from all angles. "Of course, I'm nowhere near as sadistic as your husband. He manipulates his subs better than anyone I've ever seen."

There it was again. Subs. Plural.

"Roger," she said, "do you know what a safe word is?"

He shook his head.

"If you don't like what I do to you, if you want me to stop, you say the safe word. Do you understand?"

He nodded.

Dear merciful Lord, the man had rocks for brains.

Mistress K cut her gaze to me for a half-second then said to Roger, "Your safe word is 'seersucker.' Say it."

Roger said it.

"Let him go."

She snorted.

"You can beat him bloody when he's not grieving, but right now he's not in his right mind."

"He wants to submit. Just look at him."

I looked. I saw a man leaned against a padded board, unable to move his arms and without the strength of will or character to lift his head. I saw a broken man, not a submissive one. "You're wrong."

"She's right." Roger's voice was raw with emotion.

Who was I to argue? He was a grown man. A grown idiot.

Mistress K laughed. At me. "The look on your face." She smiled as if recalling a fond memory. "It's funny, because Henry's so twisted. He played his subs off against each other until they'd do anything to please him. Depraved things."

"How many did he have?" I hated myself for asking.

Her smile was pure evil. "Your husband had three subs. Two now that Madeline's gone—Kitty and Prudence. I wonder if he'll add another." Then she turned her attention to Roger. "Are you ready?"

I had to get out of there. Immediately. If the man was stupid enough to put himself in her power, he deserved what he got. "I'm taking his car. Getting him home is your problem."

"You're not staying?" She blinked at me, her expression as wide-eyed and innocent as a kitten's. Bitch.

Leaving Roger to his fate, I headed for the door.

I was almost there when her voice stopped me. "Henry's been coming here for almost two years. He said you wouldn't let him touch you."

Not when he wanted to touch me with the end of a crop. Not when he was spending his free time tying up Madeline...or Kitty or Prudence. I took another step toward the door.

"I was wondering," she called, "what you do for sex?"

Sadistic bitch. I kept walking.

SEVEN

I drove without paying any attention to the road. I was more than half-tempted to turn around, go back, and drag Roger out of Mistress K's lair. Except...he *wanted* to be there. *Wanted* to be tied to that awful device. *Wanted* her to flog him.

Just like Madeline and Prudence and Kitty wanted it.

Mistress K had described what they did with Henry as depraved. What did depravity mean to a woman willing to take a belt to a man who'd just lost his wife?

Madeline was dead. Henry was missing. And Madeline's grieving husband was currently willingly bound to a torture device. Was that what she meant by manipulation?

Madeline Harper. Prudence Davies—it had to be her. After all, how many women named Prudence could frequent Club K? And Kitty? If Henry had followed his country club pattern, it was Kitty Ballew.

Why had my husband felt the need to screw my bridge group? My former bridge group. I found a new one after that fateful Christmas party.

The trees flashed by, a haze of green lost among grass and shrubs and melting speed. The car purred like a satisfied cat. Roger Harper might have the spinal strength of an earthworm and the mental acuity of a sheep but his Jag was cherry. I blew through my third yellow light.

A siren sounded and I glanced into Roger's rearview mirror. An unmarked police car followed me.

I swallowed a curse word, pulled over, and dug my driver's license out of my billfold.

Detective Jones sauntered up to my window. No plaid pants today. Instead, he wore a navy suit. He looked like a banker. Too bad I don't like bankers—haven't in a while.

The window rolled down smoothly. Of course it did. Everything about Roger's car was smooth. "I didn't know homicide detectives pulled people over for traffic violations."

"Do you know how fast you were going, Mrs. Russell?" He peered down at me with his nice eyes.

"No idea. I thought I asked you to call me Ellison."

"You've been driving like a bat out of hell since you left that club."

I frowned. "You've been following me?"

"Not exactly. I went down to Club K to talk to the owner and saw you leave. You looked shaky so I wanted to make sure you got home safely."

That was rather sweet. Almost worth a smile. Unfortunately, I was fresh out of them.

"Is this your husband's car?"

"Roger's."

"Roger as in Roger Harper?"

I nodded.

"Why are you driving his car?"

There was something I didn't want to explain. *Because I left him to the not-so-tender ministrations of a sadistic woman in a leather corset* didn't exactly cast me in the best light. I should have argued with them more. I would have if he hadn't seemed to want what Mistress K offered.

"Where is Mr. Harper?"

"At Club K." A vision of Roger tied to the Berkley flashed in front of my eyes. My imagination—damn it to hell—filled in the parts I'd missed. His pants were gone and red welts crisscrossed his milky white buttocks. I rubbed my eyes to erase the picture. "He wanted to stay."

Detective Jones opened his mouth as if to speak then closed it. Perhaps he too was imagining the things that could happen to a human jellyfish at a place where inflicting pain was a prized skill. He bit his lip and shook his head. "Are you sure you're all right?"

His eyes really were nice, a deep shade of honest brown.

"I'm sure," I lied. I was the opposite of all right. I thought I'd been helping Roger when I agreed to go with him to Club K. I thought he needed answers. I had no idea he'd discover a latent need to experience pain. Worse, I'd discovered my husband had been playing slap (literally) and tickle with not one but three women. The whole sordid morning of shameful revelations made my stomach churn. I needed an antacid and my paints and I needed them now. "Am I getting a ticket?"

A tiny furrow formed between his eyebrows and he rubbed it away with the pad of his thumb. "Not from me. Slow down. Be careful. I'd hate to see you get hurt."

Again rather sweet. Again worthy of a smile. At least a small one. I had none available. I drove the rest of the way home at a sedate pace. My mood, black is the new black, lightened to charcoal grey. I might have glanced in the rearview more than once—more than five times—but didn't see Detective Jones behind me. I was almost disappointed.

I was driving by the entrance to the club when I remembered. Lunch.

Damn.

It wasn't that I didn't want to see my friends. I did. But, I wanted to paint and think and be alone more.

I glanced at my watch. I was already late, but I could hardly cancel now. Swallowing a sigh that seemed to rise from my toes, I turned the car around and drove it up the club's winding drive.

EIGHT

The ladies' dining room at the club was decorated in shades as soft and delicate as watercolors in the rain. Small white-linen topped tables were set for two or four and the scent of roses perfumed the air. Crossing its threshold meant the reminder of simpler times— when ladies lunched, when husbands honored their vows, when Madeline Harper didn't float in the pool.

Three women had already taken their seats. I knew they waited for me with the barely contained excitement of four year-olds on Christmas morning so I lingered at the door. They'd want to hear all about Madeline and, now that I knew *all* about Madeline, I didn't want to talk about her.

I wanted to talk about Kitty and Prudence. Had one of them killed Madeline?

I walked to the table.

Jinx looked up from the menu. "Great dress. I love seersucker."

"Thank you." It was a relief to be around women for whom seersucker was a fabric and not a safe word. I sank into my chair.

Libba half rose from her chair to wave at the waiter, a soft-spoken man named Frank who'd worked at the club for years. "A glass of liebfraumilch for Mrs. Russell. Bring a bottle." Then she directed her attention at me. "You look like you need it. Do you want to tell us about finding Madeline?"

I tried to smile but my mouth felt stiff. I was reminded of Grace's description—gritted teeth and pursed lips. I gave up the effort. "Surely there's something more interesting to talk about."

Daisy choked on a sip of wine. "More interesting than how Madeline Harper came to be floating in our pool?" She looked around the table then frowned. "It's still not open. I imagine the children are just desperate. And swim team? It's almost impossible to borrow practice time from another club. Do you have any idea when the police will remove the crime tape?"

Did she think ending up in a police interview room gave me some kind of insider status? "None," I said.

Jinx rimmed the edge of her wine glass with the tip of her finger. "There's some talk of draining the water and refilling." At least she didn't pretend grief for Madeline.

Then again, Daisy was more worried about swim team than murder. And Libba? Well, she just wanted Frank to bring us a bottle of wine.

Where was he anyway?

My fingers tightened around the imagined stem of a glass. "It's not like Madeline infected the water."

Libba nodded. "That's what I said. Besides, do you have any idea how much it costs to fill the pool?"

"How much?" asked Jinx.

Libba stared at a banal painting of flowers as if it might provide a figure. "A lot."

Frank put a glass in front of me then poured a tiny amount of wine for Libba. She tasted it, nodded and then, finally, he filled my glass. I took a grateful sip. First a drunken man on my stoop, then a dominatrix and her toys, and finally the thoroughly unpleasant revelation that my husband's cheating had reached heretofore-unimagined levels. What a morning. I *deserved* a glass of wine.

"Have you ladies had a chance to look at the menu?" Frank asked.

I didn't need to look. "A cup of gazpacho and the wedge salad served together." I handed him the heavy menu printed with elaborate script.

I knew Libba, Jinx, and Daisy's orders before they spoke. Frank probably did too. A club sandwich, a house salad with the dressing on the side, and a grilled chicken breast with a side of cottage cheese. Adventurous eaters we were not.

Apparently, Kitty, Prudence, and Madeline had cornered the *adventurous* market.

I examined my cuticles, gathered my courage and, as soon as Frank disappeared to the kitchen with our order, asked, "Have you heard anything about Prudence Davies seeing anyone?"

Daisy snorted. "Prudence? She's so desperate, she'd sell her grandmother's pearls for a man."

"I think it's sad." Libba smoothed the napkin in her lap. "I always say men can smell desperation. Prudence reeks."

Had she sniffed recently? I took a fortifying sip of wine. "What about Kitty Ballew? Have you heard any whispers about her stepping out on John?"

Daisy carefully placed her glass of wine on the table. So carefully, I couldn't but wonder how many glasses she had. "Why do you ask?"

Three Lilly-clad women stared at me expectantly.

I stared back.

I hadn't really considered that my friends would want to know *why*. I'd just assumed they'd welcome the opportunity to gossip about women we didn't particularly like. I scratched the end of my nose. "No reason."

Libba rolled her eyes. "Liar."

I scratched again and tried to think of a more compelling reason than *because*. I'd grown accustomed to thinking of Henry cheating on me with Madeline. Any pain associated with that infidelity had long since worn down like the nub of an eraser on a number two pencil. But Prudence Davies? With her long face and long teeth, the woman looked like a horse wearing lipstick. Kitty Ballew had no chin and all the warmth of a pit viper. If Henry was going to cheat, why couldn't he do it with more attractive women?

My fingers crumpled my napkin. What the hell was I thinking? Would I be any less horrified if Henry chose women who looked like Lauren Hutton or the Charlie girl? I would. How shallow did that make me? I pictured a saucer, a pretty one with pale pink bouquets tied with soft yellow bows but absolutely no depth to it.

Libba cleared her throat. My friends were waiting for the truth.

Something bubbled with the wine in my stomach. I ignored it and lifted an admonishing finger. If I wanted information from them, I was going to have to offer some of my own. "Not a word. Not a whisper."

Daisy traced an x over her heart.

Jinx leaned forward. "Not a word. Not a whisper."

Libba nodded.

I swallowed. How could my mouth be so dry? "It seems that Henry has taken up with them."

Libba's eyebrows rose to her hairline. "Both of them?"

"Did Madeline know?" asked Jinx. A second later, she yelped then bent to rub her shin. Apparently, Libba or Daisy had kicked her under the table. They shouldn't have. The assumption that Madeline would care more about Henry's infidelities than I did was completely reasonable. After all, I'd convinced our little corner of the world—and myself—I didn't give a damn what my husband did.

I reached past my wine glass, closed my fingers around a sweating water goblet and lifted it to my lips for a long, slow drink. "She knew." I traded the water for wine. Sipped. "They..." Words failed me.

"You don't mean?" Daisy's pretty face was a study in shock. Her jaw hung slack, her eyes were wide and beneath her rouge, her cheeks paled.

I nodded.

"Together?" Jinx squeaked.

"You promised." My gaze traveled from stunned expression to stunned expression. "Not a word. Not a whisper." Had I made a mistake? Mother would tell me there's no such thing as a secret among four. I hoped she was wrong.

"How did you find out?" Libba asked.

"Never mind that." I tucked a stray lock of hair behind my ear.

There was no way I was telling them about Mistress K or Roger on the Berkley horse. "Did you see Prudence or Kitty the night Madeline died?"

My friends froze, one with a glass of wine halfway to her lips, another in the process of smoothing her hair and the third lining up her silverware to her own exacting specifications.

Daisy thawed first. "I saw Kitty and John. The chef fixed that special lobster dinner and you know how Martin is about lobster. Kitty and John were there." She tilted her head to the side and closed her eyes. "I didn't see Prudence."

"What time did they leave?" I asked.

"Let me think." Daisy caught the tip of her small chin between her thumb and the knuckle of her first finger. "We arrived around seven. We sat with the Strattons. Did you know their oldest son has decided to go to law school?"

Libba drummed her fingers on the table. "Back to the point, Daisy."

"Oh. Sorry. We had dinner with the Strattons. I swear George Stratton ate five of those little corn biscuits. If I were Marianne, I'd be worried about his health."

"Daisy!"

"Sorry, Libba. I just have to think it through."

"Can you think it through without biscuits?"

Daisy narrowed her eyes. "I'll try."

"The biscuits *are* good," said Jinx.

I gave her a look cold enough to freeze a water hazard.

Her hands fluttered before returning to the stem of her glass. "Well, they are."

Oh dear Lord. "I think we can all agree the biscuits are delicious. But Daisy was going to tell us about Kitty Ballew. Daisy?"

"Well, we were there with the Strattons..."

Next to me, Libba growled.

Daisy sniffed and turned her pert nose away from Libba's disapproval. "Kitty and John were having dinner with his parents. Laura Ballew looked like she was sucking lemons."

"She should have had a biscuit instead," Jinx muttered.

Libba and I ignored her. Daisy tittered.

"And?" Libba demanded.

"John and his father were doing their best to kill a bottle of scotch."

"What about Kitty?" I asked.

"She looked so miserable I almost felt sorry for her."

There was a moment of silence as we considered just how miserable Kitty would have to look before one of us was moved to pity.

"Seriously," Daisy insisted.

"Did anything happen?"

"We had dinner. The lobster was a little tough."

"That's it?" Libba demanded.

"We danced. They had this fabulous little Latin jazz trio."

"Did the Ballews stay to dance?" I asked.

Daisy grabbed her chin again.

"John did but not with Kitty. He danced with his mother and then he danced with Audrey Miles. I remember because she had on a dress with a twirly skirt and every time he spun her, she flashed the dining room."

My fingers tightened on the edge of the table. "And then?"

"We left."

"Were the Ballews still there?"

Daisy closed her eyes. "John senior was at the table with a bottle. John junior was dancing with his mother. I don't remember where Kitty was." Her mouth formed a small circle. "You don't suppose she was murdering Madeline?"

"No." I shook my head. "Not during a club party." I hadn't learned much. If Henry and Madeline had been at Club K with Prudence then Kitty might have arrived late.

We fell silent as Frank put our food in front of us.

"I'm a suspect in Madeline's murder."

"How thrilling," said Jinx. "Quit kicking me!"

Daisy raised a brow and Libba looked guilty.

"It's not thrilling. It's terrifying. I need to find out if Kitty or Prudence had anything to do with it."

"Well..." Jinx paused for effect. "I heard Prudence has been having some financial troubles."

We all stared at her. Prudence's divorce settlement was legendary. Jinx examined her manicure.

"Spill," Libba demanded.

Jinx held her hand out and tilted it until the light caught the sheen on her nails then her lips curled into a smile. "Sally Watkins asked her to go to Vail in August and she said she couldn't afford it."

More likely she couldn't afford to leave Henry alone with Madeline and Kitty. But now—

Madeleine was dead and Kitty wasn't real competition for my husband's undivided attention.

"I love Vail," said Daisy.

"Focus." Libba tapped the edge of the table with the tip of her finger. "We're not talking about vacations we're talking about— Ouch!"

"Prudence," Jinx said, her voice was unnaturally loud, "I was just telling the girls how disappointed Sally was that you couldn't go to Vail with her." She offered up a polite smile.

Prudence's smile was less cordial. Narrowed eyes, a curled lip, and a laser beam glare don't make for polite. "Really? Perhaps you should go. I'm sure Alan wouldn't miss you."

It was a weak jab. Alan would miss Jinx like crazy.

"What brings you to the club, Prudence?" I asked. It sounded so much nicer than what I was thinking—*What do you want, you bony-assed harpy?*

"Just lunch," she replied then she caught the tip of her finger between her teeth and tilted her head to the side. "Ellison, I'm trying to get hold of Henry. The bank says he's not in today." She removed the finger from her mouth and attempted a smile. "Do you know where I might reach him?" I'd believe vinegar. Honey, especially honey from Prudence, made me nervous.

"What do you want with Ellison's husband?" Libba asked.

Prudence's smile disappeared. "I'm buying an apartment in New York. Henry's handling the loan."

As lies went, it wasn't half bad. But Henry's bank didn't loan outside its footprint.

"He told Grace he was going to New York. Maybe he's working on your loan from there."

"Really?" She looked as if she'd just swallowed a whole bottle of cod liver oil. "New York? If you talk to him, would you have him call me? Please?"

Across the table, Libba choked on a sip of wine.

Prudence really was unbelievable. I shook my head. "Your best bet is to leave a message at the bank."

She opened her mouth as if she meant to speak but Frank appeared with a large tray of food. "Who has the club sandwich?" he asked.

"Me." Libba waved at him.

Prudence attempted another smile. Did she honestly think she was fooling any of us? We were more likely to believe she'd shot a twenty-seven on the back nine than that she'd suddenly become pleasant.

"Please, Ellison. If you hear from him?"

I gave her a smile as sincere as the one she'd offered me then nodded.

"Thank you." She turned and marched out of the dining room.

We waited until luncheon was served and Frank disappeared back into the kitchen before saying a word.

"She did it," said Jinx. "I feel it in my bones. She killed Madeline. You should tell the police about her and Henry."

"And Kitty," Libba offered.

"And Madeline," Daisy added.

I brought my wine glass to my lips. Telling Detective Jones about Prudence and Kitty meant telling him all about Henry's preferences—that he preferred a horse-faced woman to his own wife, that he only found me attractive if he could humiliate me, that

I was about as desirable as a flat tennis ball. I scratched my nose. "I will."

Libba crossed her arms and leaned back against the polished cherry of the dining chair. "Don't try lying to the police. You're terrible at it."

"How can you tell I'm lying?"

Slowly, deliberately, she lifted her hand to her face and scratched her nose.

If my friends could determine my tell, chances were good Detective Jones could too. I needed to find something to do with my hands when my nose itched. Especially since I had a sinking feeling I'd be lying a lot in the coming days.

NINE

When I got home from lunch, I parked Roger's car on the street, hid his keys under the floor mat and strolled up the drive, stopping to examine my flattened hostas. Mother was sure to notice and when she did, she'd want a full explanation. The thought of telling her about finding Roger Harper drunk on my front stoop or, even worse, about my ill-considered trip to Club K sent me walking past the front door to the garden shed. Perhaps some fertilizer would help.

A sleepy-eyed Max met me in the backyard.

I scratched behind his ear and he leaned into me as if he needed my support to stay upright. "What are you doing out?"

Of course, he didn't answer. He just yawned, a huge one that afforded me a full view down his doggy throat.

Max wasn't supposed to be out alone. His relentless pursuit of squirrels and rabbits had led him over and under fences. We'd replaced the Johnson's hydrangeas and the Smith's lavender and our own boxwoods more than once. It led to a house rule—*Max shall not be left unattended in the backyard.* Grace was usually pretty good about keeping an eye on him. I wondered where she was.

The back door stood open. I stepped into the kitchen and called her name.

She didn't answer.

I walked into the front hall and yelled louder, "Grace."

Nothing.

The door to my husband's study was ajar. Had he come home?

If he had, I had quite a bit I wanted to say to him. "Henry?"

I heard something. The shift of weight on old floorboards? The creak of an old house? What I didn't hear was the sound of my husband's voice. A slow shiver traveled the length of my spine.

"Max," I called the dog to my side. He didn't come. I glanced over my shoulder. He'd followed me into the kitchen and collapsed on the floor.

The shiver turned into a shudder and my chest felt tight, too small to contain the beating of my heart.

I took a tiny step backward and then a larger one.

Too little, too late. A figure exploded out of the study. Black shirt, black pants, a bit of hosiery covering the face and the dull glint of a brass fireplace poker arcing toward me.

Love's Baby Soft and Chanel No. 5 duked it out above my nose. Grace, Mother, and an appalling headache. I groaned.

"Mom!" Grace sounded like she'd been crying.

I forced my eyes open, caught a quick glimpse of her tear-stained face leaning over me then closed them again. "Too much light."

Love's Baby Soft released my hand. The sound of curtains being yanked shut and a light switch being flipped followed. Meanwhile, a gentle jasmine and rose scented hand grazed my forehead. Things must be awful if Mother was being gentle.

"Max?" My poor dog.

"At the vet having his stomach pumped. It will take more than a handful of valium to slow that disaster on four legs down." Mother wasn't one of his fans. She hadn't been since he chewed through the handle of her Hermés bag. "May I just say that burglar alarms are unaffected by sleeping pills."

Mother's version of I told you so. She'd been after us for years to install an alarm, and I'd blithely promised that Max was better protection.

I slitted my eyes. "Where am I?"

"The hospital," Grace said. Her voice was thick as if she had a cold or a throat clogged with tears.

I struggled to sit, winced as a screwdriver lanced my brain, then decided that lying back on three or four pillows—even flat hospital pillows—was just fine. "What happened?"

"Someone broke into your house."

I knew that. I raised my hand to my head and felt a lump the size of a sugar melon. My skull knew that.

"How did I get here?"

"Harriet found you and called an ambulance. Then Grace came home, saw you being loaded in and called me." Mother's voice barely masked her outrage. Obviously, she thought Harriet's first call should have been to her.

"What did they take?"

"They tore up Dad's office. Detective Jones says they were looking for something."

My aching brain supplied me with a vision of Henry's perfectly ordered study in shambles. Books ripped from the shelves, desk drawers emptied onto the carpet, his collection of Toby jugs shattered. That I wouldn't mind. The faces leer, they're creepy, and I've never understood why he's so enamored with them. In my imagination, the hinged painting that hid the safe hung open as did the safe itself. "Did they find it?"

"We don't know." Grace shook her head. "When you're better, Detective Jones wants you to look."

"Gracie, be an angel and run down to the café and get me a coffee with extra cream." Mother opened her purse and produced a bill. "Do you want anything, Ellison?"

"Water."

"No need to buy that." She handed me a plastic cup with a bendy straw and I took a grateful sip.

When the door closed behind Grace, Mother took her chair, settling in next to me.

I gave the cup back to her and closed my eyes. A clear indication I was ready for a nap or painkillers or both. There ought to be some fabulous painkillers in a hospital. Why hadn't they given me any?

"What's going on?" Mother asked.

All the sarcastic things I could say limped through my brain but I didn't feel up to starting an argument. I shrugged. Even that hurt my head.

"I mean it, Ellison, what's going on?"

"Someone murdered Madeline."

"Yes, but why are they breaking into your house?"

"I don't know." I didn't.

"This is all so upsetting."

She didn't know the half of it...or what was it called when there were three people? She didn't know the ménage of it. Henry made four. She didn't know the orgy of it. I giggled. A hysterical, deranged giggle. I swallowed it before she had me moved to the psych ward.

"This isn't remotely amusing." A barber could shave ten clients whistle clean with just the tone of her voice.

"Mother, I'm tired and I'm in pain. Do we have to discuss this now?"

"You wouldn't believe the things people are saying."

I didn't want to know.

She told me anyway. "They're saying you and Roger Harper killed Madeline and Henry. They're saying you swapped partners. They're saying he spent the night at your house last night."

He did. Passed out on the front stoop. I moaned. Not from pain, but from the sick-making thought of me and Roger together. What a nightmare.

"I insist you tell me what is going on." Again with the razor blade voice.

"There's nothing between Roger Harper and me."

"Then why is his car parked in front of your house?"

"It's a long story."

"I have time."

For a half-second, I was tempted to tell her everything. About

Henry and Madeline and Prudence and Kitty. About Roger. About Club K. She'd believe me. Then she'd tell everyone she knew. She'd tell them to protect my reputation—and hers. Ultimately *everyone*—including Grace—would know what a twisted, depraved man Henry Russell really was.

"Roger got drunk and passed out on my front steps last night. I found him this morning."

"Why did he come to your house?"

"I don't know. Because I found Madeline? Because Madeline and Henry were having an affair?" I shrugged again. Regretted it again. Winced.

"That slut had affairs with half the men at the club. Why did she have to get herself murdered when she was fucking Henry?"

My jaw dropped to my chest. Mother had dropped an f-bomb. I hadn't realized she knew the word, much less how to use it correctly in a sentence. That and she knew all about Madeline? True, after the coatroom, everyone knew about Madeline and Henry. But Madeline and Carter Ross? Madeline and Miles Porter? Madeline and Gibson Thorne? Those were affairs of the shorter-lived more discreet variety. How did Mother know?

"Close your mouth, Ellison, the flies will buzz in."

I snapped my lips together.

Mother sat up ramrod straight and her eyes narrowed like a general reviewing his troops. Or her lone soldier. "This is what you are going to do. You are going to spend the night in the hospital. Grace can stay with me." She wagged her finger in front of my face. "Do not argue. If you're in the hospital, no one will blame you for missing Madeline's funeral."

Mother's plan had merit.

"When you do leave, you will go see Hunter."

That part of the plan wasn't as good.

"You will begin divorce proceedings."

She gave me a half-second to argue. I didn't. There was no point in explaining that Hunter didn't practice that kind of law. Besides, the general idea was good.

"Day after tomorrow, you will go to the pool. Wear that light grey linen caftan. It makes you look sallow." She raised a finger to halt the objection on my lips. "I'm sorry, dear, but it does. You will accept everyone's sympathy. You might see if you can manage tears." She patted my hand. "Don't worry, we'll get through this and then we'll get your life straightened out."

Except for the part where I sat around the pool and solicited sympathy—and the "we" part of straightening out my life—her plan wasn't half-bad.

TEN

Hospitals are terrible places. Especially if you have a concussion. Someone comes and pokes and prods and shines a light in your eyes every two hours all night long. Sleep is as fractured as a broken mirror. When you finally wake up in a room the color of under-cooked oatmeal, you feel raw and gritty as if you never closed your eyes at all.

I wanted to snap at the nurse who asked how "we" were feeling. Wanted to say I didn't know about her but I felt like shit and I couldn't wait to get the hell out of her hospital. Instead, I went the polite route and asked for a cup of coffee.

She consulted her chart. "It doesn't say anything about limitations. I'll have to ask the doctor."

About coffee? "Please. I'm quite sure a cup of coffee would make me feel much better."

"Dr. Simmons saw you at 6:30 this morning."

I knew that. I was there when he woke me up.

"He's in clinic now. When's he's done, I'll ask him if you can have some."

I had to get out of there. Immediately. "How long will that be?"

Her smile was fiendish. "An hour or two."

An hour? Or two? That was just cruel, especially since I lacked the energy to argue with her. If the blonde woman—I squinted to read her nametag—Nurse Sally decided on a career change, I could introduce her to a dominatrix who'd truly appreciate her ability to torture.

The door behind her opened and Mother breezed in, resplendent in a black Chanel suit, Ferragamo pumps, and the

Hermés bag we bought to replace the one Max ate. The most attractive part of her ensemble was the Styrofoam cup with the plastic lid. She glided across the room and put it in my grateful hands.

"We're not sure Mrs. Russell can have coffee," Nurse Sally objected.

Mother raised a brow. "We? I'm quite sure my daughter can have all the coffee she wants."

I loosened the lid and took a sip. Hot and delicious with just the right amount of cream. I sighed. "Thank you, Mother." Sometimes Frances Walford was rather fabulous.

"Visiting hours don't begin for—" Nurse Sally checked her watch, "—another thirty minutes."

Nurse Sally had Mother's attention. She just didn't know she didn't want it.

"I applaud your attention to following picayune rules, Nurse—" Mother squinted "—Sally. I'll be sure and mention that at the next board meeting." Mother waved a hand, erasing every rule she ever disliked with one swipe. "Those rules don't apply to me."

Nurse Sally opened and closed her mouth like a goldfish deprived of water. Finally, unable to find a suitable response, she huffed and disappeared into the hallway.

Mother settled into the ugly chair next to the bed. "How are you feeling?"

I held up the coffee cup. "Better now."

Mother's not much of a talker first thing in the morning. We shared a moment of companionable silence while I sipped.

A short moment. "Grace tells me that Henry has disappeared."

I took another bracing sip of heaven in a cup then nodded.

"Where is he?"

I heard the questions she wasn't asking. *Has he left you? Is it your fault? What did you do?* I heard the silent comments. *This never would have happened if you gave up painting. Your daughter is suffering. You're a bad wife.*

The view outside the window was suddenly captivating. I

stared at the cars whizzing by, wished I was in one of them, then admitted, "I don't know."

Mother sniffed then looked at her watch.

"You may want to get that nurse to help you with your hair."

I reached up and felt the snarls. Nurse Sally was a coffee-withholding sadist who, if the expression on her face when she left the room was any indication, had been mortally offended by Mother's comments. I didn't want her anywhere near my aching head.

"Is my purse here? There's a comb in my purse."

Mother pulled a tortoise shell comb out of her handbag and gave it to me. I put it down on the bed next to me. Coffee first. Life is all about priorities.

"Powers called. Five times. The man is beside himself with worry."

"How does he even know I'm here?"

"Darling, half the neighborhood gathered 'round to watch the police tramp in and out of your house and see you loaded into the ambulance. I imagine everyone in town knows you're in the hospital."

"Why didn't he just call me?"

"I had them put the phone on do not disturb. Otherwise you'd have been up all night with phone calls."

Better phone calls than nurses who talked to me as if I was a fractious three-year-old. I took another sip of coffee.

"I'd like to leave this afternoon."

Mother shook her head. Vehemently.

"We decided. You stay until tomorrow."

She'd decided. I wanted to go home.

"What if the doctor clears me?"

"David won't do that. I've already spoken with him." She leaned forward, patted my free hand. "The day will pass quickly. I know Powers is going to come and see you. Grace will be here tonight when she's done babysitting." She reached into her purse again, pulled out lipstick and a compact of pressed powder, then laid them on the bed next to the comb. "Hunter might even stop by."

I opened my mouth to object.

Mother took a second look at her watch then stood. "I must fly. I've got an errand or two to run before the funeral." She paused at the door. "Really, dear, a bit of powder wouldn't be amiss. The lipstick too."

She disappeared before I could throw the comb at her.

The door opened again almost immediately and I tightened my hand round my coffee. Nurse Sally would not take it from me.

Except, it wasn't Nurse Sally. It was a woman whose corkscrew curls had somehow been corralled into an updo. She wore a stylish black linen pantsuit and wouldn't have looked out of place sitting at a bridge table at the club. I almost didn't recognize Mistress K without her leather corset and flogger. Where was Nurse Sally when I needed her?

"I stopped by your house and the housekeeper said you were here."

Mistress K knew where I lived? Where Grace lived? Henry had a lot to answer for. "What do you want?"

"You sent a cop to my club."

Her expression reminded me of Mrs. Carlson, my fifth grade teacher. She enjoyed rapping knuckles with rulers, delighted in humiliating children who spoke without raising their hands, kept a switch in the corner of her room even though the principal had forbidden her from using it. The one time she caught me out, she made me spread my hands across the desk. The wooden ruler hovered above them, the anticipation of pain more terrible than the pain itself. I swallowed, looked her in the eye and said, "*I wouldn't.*"

"Oh?" Mrs. Carlson smiled, an evil, sadistic curl of her thin lips, and then she brought the ruler down on my knuckles. The sound, wood and metal connecting with skin and bone, made me cringe. The sharp pain brought tears to my eyes. Blood welled across three or four of my fingers.

I stood, stumbled my way to the principal's office and

demanded that she call my mother. Mrs. Carlson was gone before the end of the day.

The woman standing in my hospital room could be Mrs. Carlson's daughter. I swallowed, looked her in the eye and said, "I didn't send anyone."

She must have heard the challenge in my response. Something dark and angry flashed in her eyes and her fingers twitched as if they were searching for a flogger or a ruler. "Then how did he know to come?"

"Blame Henry."

"Henry is out of town."

Yes, I knew that. I'd even gone into her hellhole club to try and find out where he was. "He left one of your matchbooks in our kitchen drawer. We found it while a homicide detective was there."

She raised a disbelieving brow. "Henry doesn't smoke. Why would he have a matchbook?"

"I don't know but there's no other way a matchbook from your club could make its way into my house."

We stared at each other. A battle of wills. The seconds ticked by. Finally, she smiled a predator's smile. I didn't know if she was ceding a tie or if she thought she'd won. "It's ironic."

"What?"

"You were worried I'd hurt Roger and you're the one who ended up in the hospital." The menace in her voice was clear. She held her hand out, examined her blood red manicure. "He came back. Last night. He wanted his belt."

I closed my eyes. I wanted to cover my ears and chant la-la-la at the top of my lungs.

"I gave him the belt. Then I gave him the flogger and then he asked me to go to Madeline's funeral with him."

Roger asked a date to his wife's funeral? Not just a date, but the woman who'd spent last evening...I shuddered. Oh, to be a fly on the wall in church this morning. I couldn't help it, I laughed.

"I imagine any number of people will be surprised to see me there."

She might be a sadistic bitch but at least she had a sense of humor. "I imagine you're right." I took a swig of coffee. How well had Mistress K known my missing husband? "You told me that Henry played mind games with his..." What was I supposed to call them?

"Submissives," she provided. The Big, Bad Dominatrix was playing a game of her own.

I pulled a metaphorical red cloak tightly around me and took comfort in the fact that in every version of the story, Red wins. "Has it occurred to you that Prudence or Kitty might have killed Madeline?"

She shrugged. Madeline's death wasn't her problem unless it brought Detective Jones to her door. "If so, why did Henry disappear?"

"No idea. You said he played them against each other. With Madeline gone, won't one of them take her place on that apparatus?"

"It's called a Berkley horse."

Who cared what it was called? "Isn't that motive for murder?"

She tilted her head to the side, regarded me with eyes that looked as if they'd seen every depravity known to man. Old eyes. Tired eyes. Wise eyes. "Henry really was wrong about you."

Like I needed reminding that my husband had discussed me with a dominatrix. He was so divorced. "Don't you have a funeral to get to?"

"Roger will save me a seat." Her lips quirked. "Don't you want to know what Henry said about you?"

Of course I did. "No."

"Do you want my advice?"

Life coaching from a dominatrix. It sounded like the title of a *Cosmo* article. Maybe a whole series of articles.

"No."

"Suit yourself." She walked to the door and grasped the handle. A welcome indication she was going to leave. She stopped and looked over her shoulder. "The people who come to my club are there because they want to be. Some of them even need to be. I'd prefer not to see the police there again."

"I didn't send them."

"I believe you." There was another flash in her eyes. "Just make sure you never do."

She was gone before I could think of a zingy comeback. Then again, I wasn't as sharp as usual. I had a head injury and a night of no sleep. It was barely nine and I'd already had to deal with a sadistic nurse, a match-making mother, and a dominatrix who tossed veiled threats like children tossed water balloons on a July afternoon.

Did Mistress K have something to do with Madeline's death? Had I just been conversing with a murderess? Just because she hadn't knocked me in the head didn't mean she hadn't drugged Madeline and dumped her in a pool.

Somehow, I couldn't see Mistress K dragging Madeline to the country club to drown her. That particular twist seemed more worthy of Prudence or Kitty or any one of the wronged wives who discovered open marriages were less attractive in practice than they were in the pages of a magazine.

Could it be Henry? Lord knows the murder was cold and dispassionate enough. Was Henry a murderer?

Was he a cheating low-life? Definitely.

An arrogant prick? Unquestionably.

A cold-blooded killer? Doubtful. Maybe it was all a tragic accident. Perhaps she'd overdosed and he'd panicked. Except Henry didn't panic. He was all about control and clear thinking. If Madeline overdosed while she was with him, he'd dump her in an emergency room not a pool. It couldn't be Henry. It just couldn't.

My thoughts skated figure eights—endless loops that led nowhere. Right in the center of one of the loops, a horrible thought held up its hand and bounced in its seat like a third-grader who wants his teacher to call on him. I skated past—once, twice, twenty times. I skated until the thought vibrated in my aching brain. I skated until there was no denying it.

I didn't want Henry to have murdered Madeline so I was ignoring anything—everything—that suggested he did.

ELEVEN

I'd been reduced to watching game shows. *The Price is Right, Let's Make a Deal*, and *Match Game 74*. That Brett Somers was a funny woman. Charles Nelson Riley was no slouch either.

The phone rang, loud enough for me to miss Gene Rayburn's Dumb Dora question, loud enough to make me long for a painkiller. Who had made it past the steel curtain of my mother's no call list?

I answered it.

"Ellie, honey, that you?"

"It's me, Daddy."

"Are you okay, sugar?"

My throat swelled with all the things I wanted to say and never would. *Come home. Protect me. I need you.* "I'm fine."

"You're not fine. You're in the hospital and your mother is fit to be tied. She hasn't been this upset since she found out what your sister's husband did for a living."

Wow. That was saying something. Mother's head had levitated from her shoulders when she found out about Marjorie's fiancé. *Words* had been exchanged. Mother was that upset and I hadn't even guessed? Then again, my head hurt like sin and Mother is hard to read.

"How are you really feeling?"

I should have repeated the lie and told him I was fine. Instead my eyes filled and the fears that I'd been keeping at bay snuck past my defenses. What if Grace had come home and interrupted the burglar instead of me? What if I'd died and Henry made Grace's

THE DEEP END 77

new mother wear a dog collar around the house? What if Henry murdered Madeline? "I've been better."

"I'm cutting my trip short. I'll be home tonight."

The week he spent in Carmel playing golf with his cronies had to be his favorite time of year. After all, one thousand eight hundred and fifty six miles separated him from Mother. He could drink scotch, smoke cigars, and eat bacon—all the things forbidden by his cardiologist. All the things Mother kept out of their house. "You don't need to do that, Daddy."

"Of course I do. We're going to get this mess straightened out and no one is going to lay another finger on you or Grace. I promise."

What he didn't say—*if that son-of-a-bitch husband of yours had anything to do with this, I'll kill him*—made it from California to Missouri loud and clear.

Maybe it's true. Maybe a girl's father is the only man she can ever count on. "Thank you," I said. Two little words to express infinite gratitude.

"Keep your chin up, Ellie. You have any idea where Henry is?" Daddy really was going to kill him, I could hear it in his voice.

"No idea."

"Well, you let me know if you hear anything. When you get to feeling better, we'll play a round."

The only time Daddy asked me to play golf was when he wanted to discuss something serious. Maybe if he didn't murder Henry, he had the name of a good divorce attorney.

"I'd like that."

"I'll be home soon, sugar."

When I hung up the phone, I felt marginally better. That lasted all of thirty seconds.

Prudence burst into my room with all the subtly of a tsunami. "Where is he?"

"Who?"

"Henry!"

I studied her from my nest of pillows. She wore a dark dress that didn't suit with an Hermes scarf tied around her neck. Her skin was pale with the exception of two spots of high color on her cheeks. Bad make-up or emotion?

My fingers inched toward the nurse's call button. "I already told you, I don't know where he is."

"I expected him to be back for Madeline's funeral."

If I'd thought about it, I would have expected him too. Not that I'd admit that to Prudence. "Why?"

The spots on her cheeks grew brighter. "Don't play dumb."

But playing dumb was surprisingly fun. "You seem awfully worried about his whereabouts. Surely there's a bank in New York that will loan you money."

"What?" She looked at me as if the bump on my head had loosened my brains. "What are you talking about?"

"The apartment. The one you're buying in New York."

"Oh. That." She ran her fingers through her hair. A mistake. Between the color of her cheeks and the mess atop her head, she looked like an escapee from the psych floor.

I closed my fingers around the call button just in case she actually was psychotic then said, "I know everything."

She staggered as if I'd just hit her with a fireplace poker and her hand clutched her chest as if she was having a heart attack.

I knew she'd been boinking my husband. I hadn't expected such a strong reaction when I confronted her. Had she done it? Had she killed Madeline?

Prudence lowered herself into a chair and fumbled with her pocketbook. She withdrew a pack of cigarettes and lit one.

"Please don't. Put it out." Already the smell had sent my stomach into a series of somersaults. It wasn't doing my head any favors either.

She jabbed the cigarette into an ashtray. "I need to talk to Henry."

Had they killed Madeline together? Had Henry left Prudence holding the proverbial bag? "You were at that club the night Madeline died."

Her lip curled. "What of it?"

I tightened my grip on the call button. "You were one of the last people to see her alive."

She stood. "I don't have to listen to this."

"Where did she go?"

Prudence marched toward the door then stopped and turned to glare at me. "I have no idea."

I might have believed her but she scratched her nose.

She'd been gone no more than a minute when Powers, bright as a firecracker on the Fourth of July and twice as loud, burst into my hospital room.

"Darling, I've been positively fixated on seeing you all morning but I had to go to that dreadful service. Are you all right? Does your head hurt? Did you see the brute that did this to you? You must tell me everything."

Too many questions. I asked one of my own. "Where does one find a fuchsia tie?"

"At the snootiest boutique in Manhattan, so be careful what you say about it."

"You wore a fuchsia tie to Madeline's funeral?"

Powers' lower lip worked its way forward and his forehead puckered. "It wasn't *really* a funeral. More of a memorial service."

"What do you mean?"

"Apparently the police haven't released her body. No body, no funeral." He fingered his tie. "No one even noticed this lovely."

I'd imagine not. Not when Roger took Mistress K as his date.

He threw himself into the chair, stretched out his legs and crossed his ankles. "I don't want to talk about my tie or the service. I want to talk about you. Are you all right?"

"I'm fine."

"You're sure? You don't look all right. Is there no one here who can help you with your hair?" He sounded way too much like Mother.

I patted the rat's nest. Turns out, combing through it was remarkably painful. Every tug on every snarl brought tears to my eyes. "My hair is fine. Tell me about the memorial service."

"It was packed. Standing room only. I bet half the people there just wanted to make sure she was actually dead. The other half wanted to see who showed up." His brows rose and his eyes sparkled. "You'll never believe what happened."

"Roger brought a date."

He screwed up his face, stuck out his tongue, and his gaze cut to the phone. "Who have you been talking to?"

"No one. Lucky guess. Tell me more."

"Do you remember the part in *The Wizard of Oz* when the witch is dead and the Munchkins start singing? Think that kind of happiness. I swear every woman there was ready to break into song. Maybe a few of the men too."

"I thought men liked Madeline." I knew men liked Madeline.

Ever dramatic, Powers looked over his shoulder then lowered his voice. "Not to speak ill of the dead..."

This was going to be good.

"But she wasn't above a spot of blackmail."

That I knew. That everyone knew. She'd tried to blackmail Topper Buckley a couple of years back and it had backfired. Badly. He told everyone he knew, including his wife, that he'd made a terrible mistake with Madeline and that she was a lousy lay...not sure if he told his wife that part. At any rate, Madeline was furious and everyone else quietly cheered and made sure the Buckleys were invited to more parties. "Old news."

He waved one of his long fingers like a metronome and smiled a smile worthy of Mephistopheles. "The new scuttlebutt is that she was blackmailing Stanton Wilde and Prudence Davies."

The scuttlebutt was wrong. Whatever nasty bit of information Madeline had on Stanton Wilde was anyone's guess. Maybe he cheated on his taxes or his wife but he wasn't cheating with Prudence. Henry was cheating with Prudence. Poor Prudence. If anyone found out Madeline had been going to Club K, she'd toss her hair and invite them to join her there. If anyone found out about Prudence, she'd be ruined—kicked out of the altar guild and the Junior League.

"Did you see her there?" I asked.

"Prudence?" He nodded. "She had on the most God-awful dress you ever saw and she turned positively green when Roger came down the aisle with his date." He rubbed his chin. "I wonder if Pru has designs on him. Rich widower and all."

I doubted it. She probably hadn't expected to see the owner of Club K walking down the aisle with him or that her two lives might intersect beneath the apse of St. Michael's Episcopal.

"What about Kitty Ballew?"

"She was there with John. She looked pale but then again, when doesn't she? Dreadful hat." He tilted his head to the side. "Do you know something? Spill."

Clever, urbane Powers, who belonged in New York and stayed in Kansas City to keep Bitty Sue happy, loved a scandal. I wasn't going to provide him with one.

"I don't know a thing." I ignored the itch on the tip of my nose.

He stared at me, probably searching for tells. I stared at the truly awful watercolor someone had hung on the wall and thought about the seventh hole at Pebble Beach. The view of the Pacific was awe-inspiring.

After a moment, he ceded defeat. "Everyone was speculating on who killed her."

"Who's the lead suspect?"

Powers flushed and his grape green gaze dropped from my face to his lap.

I was the lead suspect. At least among the country club set. My breath whooshed out of my chest and I collapsed against the stack of pillows behind me.

"No one blames you. Everyone thinks she had it coming."

"I didn't kill her."

"Of course you didn't." He reached forward and patted my hand then his nose twitched.

Oh dear Lord. If Powers didn't believe in my innocence, what hope had I that anyone else would? If Detective Jones didn't catch the murderer, I'd spend the rest of my life under a cloud of suspicion.

Powers gave me a second pat. "It's not like you're the only suspect. There was a large contingent who thought Roger finally cracked. I can tell you, bringing a date to his wife's funeral did nothing to change their minds." Powers stared at the buffed sheen of his nails. "There's a fair number who think that Henry did it."

The coffee stopped bubbling and started churning. Poor Grace. Both her parents were murder suspects—at least in the eyes of her friends' parents. "I have to find out who killed Madeline."

"Isn't that a job for the delectable detective?"

It was. If Roger, Henry, and I were the prime suspects, he had a problem. I hadn't killed Madeline. I was ninety-nine percent sure Roger hadn't either. I was really, really hoping that Henry had a valid reason for disappearing the morning after his mistress's body was found floating in a pool. If Prudence or Kitty or any of the other wives at the club had drugged then drowned Madeline, I didn't like his chances of catching them. Any one of them could disappear behind a wall of waspy silence and expensive lawyers. "I'm going to do it anyway."

"Ells, is that wise?" Powers shook his blond mane. "Madeline was murdered. I think you should retire to your atelier and paint."

Nurse Sally walked in before I could tell him what I thought of his idea. She peeled back my eyelids, half-blinded me with a pen light, wrote cryptic notes on my chart then asked how *we* were feeling.

"Fine."

She nodded and walked out.

"Who *was* that?"

"Nurse Sally."

"Nonsense. That was the Zodiac Killer in disguise. Are you well enough to get out of here?"

"I think so."

"Then why are you still here?"

An excellent question. The only thing keeping me in a hospital bed and a rear vented gown was Mother's edict. In the face of another night with Nurse Sally, risking Mother's wrath by deviating from her plan didn't seem so terrible. In fact, I didn't particularly care if she got angry. I wanted out.

I paused. Not caring about Mother's reaction was totally new.

"Well?" Powers drummed his fingers on his leg.

"I don't know. Mother wants me to stay."

He rolled his eyes. "You're a grown woman, you're a mother, hell, you're a murder suspect, decide what *you* want."

He was right. About everything. What I wanted was to go home. "Would you please find Nurse Sally and ask her about discharge papers?"

He grinned. "Atta girl."

"You say that now. Wait 'til Mother has a coronary."

"I'll deny everything."

I raised a brow. "You think she'll believe you?"

"It doesn't matter if she believes me or not, she'll still blame you."

He wasn't wrong and I didn't care.

Besides, her reaction to me leaving the hospital ahead of schedule would be small potatoes compared to what she'd do when she found out I was going to try to find out who'd killed Madeline. Mother's head would levitate from her shoulders again. It might even spin. Or she could go full on dragon with flames shooting from her eyes and mouth.

I was willing to risk it.

TWELVE

Powers drove me home. He even agreed to escort me inside. Although that might have had something to do with Detective Jones' sedan parked in the drive and not concern for my welfare.

A policeman in a blue uniform blocked my entrance. He even told me I'd have to leave because it was a crime scene.

Not likely. I was done with being bossed around. The insecurities that came with tangled hair, a make-up free face, and the mish-mash of clothes I'd worn home were nothing in the face of my newfound resolve. I said in my best Frances Walford voice, "I live here."

He actually took a step backward. Maybe I'd achieved a certain gravitas or maybe he thought I was a recently escaped lunatic. Either way, I swept past him.

Detective Jones met me in the foyer. No plaid pants today but the nice brown eyes were the same. The slow-burn smile was new. The combination was tingle inducing. "Mrs. Russell, we weren't expecting you."

"Ellison," I corrected.

Next to me, Powers grinned like a freshman girl in love with the senior quarterback. Then, coyly pretending disinterest, he picked up the mail lying on the bombé chest and perused the light bill, the phone bill, and the latest issue of *Architectural Digest*.

I scowled, a good dark scowl to make up for all the sweetness emanating from Powers. The expression also hid unwelcome flutters in the general vicinity of my stomach.

I brushed past Detective Jones and peeked into my husband's study.

Lying in my hospital bed, I'd imagined a shambles. That was too tame a word to describe it. So were havoc, bedlam, and unholy mess. It was a certifiable disaster area. Every book had been pulled from its shelf, the desk drawers—their locks jimmied and broken— had been upended on the floor, most of the chairs were overturned and Henry's files had been tossed about like confetti on New Year's Eve. The Toby mugs had survived unscathed. They leered at me from their display case. The damned things were insured. If a burglar was going to destroy Henry's office, was it too much to ask to shatter a few of the horrible things? Apparently so.

Everything—*everything*—was dusted with gray powder. I stepped inside for a closer look and my stomach dropped like an elevator with a cut cable. "Has Harriet quit yet?" I didn't want to think about cleaning it up without her.

"Pardon me?" said Detective Jones,

"My housekeeper. Has she quit yet?"

"I don't think so. She saw us dusting for fingerprints, mumbled something under her breath and walked out."

It wasn't too hard to figure out what she was mumbling. Either she was phrasing her resignation or her case for a large bonus.

The curtain rod had fallen and the curtains were in heaps on the floor. They too were covered with a fine layer of powder. "You tested the drapes for fingerprints?"

Detective Jones eyed the mound of fabric. "No. The dust travels."

That was an understatement. I gazed at the chaos with the kind of wonder usually reserved for the Grand Canyon, the Great Pyramids, or an octogenarian shooting a hole-in-one.

Despite the utter havoc, my painting still hung on the wall. My adversary, whoever he or she was, wasn't all that smart. "The burglar didn't go for the safe."

"The safe?" Detective Jones and Powers spoke as one.

"You don't think Henry kept one of my paintings up because

he liked it, do you? It's hinged." I tiptoed through the wreckage and swung the painting away from the wall.

"Can you open it?" Detective Jones asked.

Damn it. The concussion had obviously affected my mental faculties. I should have kept my mouth shut. I should have lingered in the doorway and sighed over the wreckage, anything but bring their attention to the wall safe. Who knew what secrets it held? "I can't." I jammed my hands in my pockets and ignored the itch at the end of my nose. "This is Henry's safe. I don't have the combination."

What in the hell did Henry have in there? His favorite kinky toys or Polaroids of Madeline tied up at Club K or a signed confession? Whatever it was, I didn't want to share it with Detective Jones.

"We'll have to have it opened."

They would? Oh dear Lord. Why? Was that standard procedure for a burglary? Damn. Damn. Damn.

"You'll need a search warrant for that." Hunter Tafft lounged in the doorway looking like a movie star version of a lawyer—Gregory Peck as Atticus Finch or Cary Grant as...well...anybody. I've never been so glad to see anyone.

He smiled at me, showing off his dimple and brilliant teeth. "I stopped by the hospital and they said you'd come home."

Detective Jones grimaced. Hunter raised an insouciant brow. Powers looked like he wanted a comfortable seat, preferably one that reclined, a tub of popcorn and maybe some Milk Duds.

I just wanted them all out of my house so I could open Henry's safe. I also wanted aspirin, a blistering hot shower and an extra-large bottle of extra-strength crème rinse for the tangles in my hair.

"Is Mr. Tafft representing you?" Detective Jones asked.

He was if it meant keeping the police out of Henry's safe. "Yes," I replied.

Detective Jones scowled, Hunter smirked, Powers' fingers closed around imagined popcorn, and I sank into the nearest chair.

It was really too bad I picked a chair that had been damaged when the burglar destroyed Henry's study. When I sank, the chair sank with me.

I hit the floor with a crash that sent my brain waves spiking like...spikes. For a moment, the pain blinded me. When I did see, I didn't see stars, I saw planets and supernovas and whole galaxies. My eyes welled with tears and the three men who just a moment ago had looked like they were ready to argue to the end of time sprang into action.

Detective Jones extended his hand and hauled me off the floor then Powers daubed a handkerchief under my eyes. Hunter murmured something soothing.

Tears spilled over my lashes and ran down my cheeks. I sniffled and tried to ignore the ache in my jaw. Easier said than done when my head hurt, my house—or at least one room of it—was destroyed, Henry was missing, and I was a murder suspect. I *deserved* a breakdown. I just didn't want a cop with nice eyes, the man Mother had selected to be my second husband, or Powers around when it started. As soon as they were gone, I'd let go. I'd cry. Not the delicate tears of which Mother might approve. I was going to bawl, great big gut-wrenching sobs. My nose would run like a fire hydrant being tested and my face would turn a shade just shy of red cinnabar. It was the kind of crying best done in solitude and I could hardly wait. I swallowed the sob that had lodged itself in my throat, snatched the hanky out of Powers' hand and blew my nose. It sounded like a bullhorn.

Three men began to shift and squirm and gaze longingly at the door. I gazed at it too, hoping they'd get the hint and leave. Detective Jones actually took a step toward the door just as Harriet barged through it.

If she noticed my distress, she gave no indication. Instead, righteous indignation radiated from her pores. In fact, a halo of it surrounded her. She planted her hands on her hips. "I hope you don't expect me to clean this up."

I had. She was the housekeeper. Cleaning was part of her job description. I'd even planned to slip an extra hundred into her pay envelope. In the face of her withering anger, I made a noncommittal noise deep in my throat and blew my nose again. Later, without an audience, I'd discuss restoring order to Henry's study with her. Not now. Not with her anger and my headache and Powers' avid interest.

Blustering at me wasn't enough. She rounded on Detective Jones. "If you think I'm going downtown to be fingerprinted like some criminal you're wrong."

He offered her a placating smile. "We need your fingerprints strictly to eliminate them. No one thinks you're a criminal."

She harrumphed, focused her baleful gaze on Powers and pursed her lips. "Don't you even think of smoking in this house." She wagged a finger beneath his nose.

Powers actually retreated, then crossed his hands over his heart. "I wouldn't dream."

Harriet harrumphed again. "Someone did. This room reeked when I got home yesterday." Then she glanced at Hunter. Apparently unable to find fault, she returned her attention to me. "No one ate the chicken salad. There are orphans starving in Africa and all that chicken salad went to waste."

How in the name of all that is holy had I hired someone whose personality so closely resembled Mother's? Unreasonable anger? Check. Taking said anger out on whoever was unfortunate enough to be close by? Check. Blaming world hunger on me? Check. Although with Mother, it was the orphans in Bulgaria who were starving.

At the ripe age of six, I offered to send the orphans my Brussels sprouts. Mother was not amused. I sat at the table staring at sodden green lumps until bedtime. I thought I'd won until they were served to me for breakfast. Somehow, I forced the cold, slimy, dirty-sock-tasting pellets down my throat. Then I vomited on Mother's new pumps. While her feet were in them. She wasn't amused by that either.

I should have stuffed Harriet's chicken salad down the disposal. Between finding bodies, escorting Roger Harper to a kinky club, and being hospitalized, I hadn't gotten around to it.

"This is your housekeeper?" Hunter asked. He sounded appalled.

I nodded.

"And I am your lawyer?"

I nodded again.

"I have the authority to act on your behalf?"

"I suppose."

"Excellent." He looked at Harriet standing there with steam rising from her ears. "Mrs. Russell no longer needs your services. You may go."

Hard to say who was more shocked—Harriet or me. I gasped. She clutched at her heart.

Detective Jones looked uncomfortable. Powers looked like he wanted an imaginary soda to wash down his imaginary popcorn. Hunter, damn him straight to hell, crossed his arms and leaned against the doorframe.

The first thing we do, let's kill all the lawyers. Shakespeare had the right idea. I scanned the room for a weapon. The fireplace poker was sadly missing. Then I tried to shoot flames from my eyes like Mother. I might have achieved a cinder.

Hunter flicked it from the sleeve of his immaculate navy blazer.

"He can't fire you, Harriet." I glared in his direction. I couldn't manage without Harriet. I didn't clean. I was a terrible cook. The last time I did laundry, I turned all Henry's white boxer shorts pink. If Harriet left, my impending breakdown might last longer than the hour or two I'd originally planned. It might last a day or two—or a week or two. Damn Hunter Tafft and the Mercedes he rode in on. What gave him the right to fire my staff?

One of my housekeeper's hands was still splayed over her heaving left breast. Her other hand raked through her hair. Getting fired had only increased the amount of steam curling from her ears. Her face was an undiluted cadmium red. "You're right. He can't fire me." Her eyes narrowed to slits. "I quit."

Sweet nine-pound baby Jesus.

She stomped out of the room, a study in righteous indignation and injured pride. All because we called for Gung Pao instead of eating her chicken salad. She put grapes in her chicken salad. I hate grapes in chicken salad. And nuts. I hate nuts in chicken salad. Harriet sometimes added cashews. It was just wrong. I wouldn't miss her chicken salad.

I would miss her.

Maybe I could offer her more money to stay. I'd make it up to her...

Wait a minute. What was I thinking? Where was the new improved Ellison? The one who walked out of the hospital only an hour ago? Faced with a trashed study and the prospect of dirty laundry the new Ellison caved? Absolutely not. I took a deep breath, sent another glare in Hunter's direction, then began to write a mental list of requirements for my next housekeeper.

Whoever she might be, she would be a purist. She'd add nothing to her chicken salad but celery. She wouldn't yell, she wouldn't complain when she had to clean the bathrooms, and steam wouldn't rise from her ears when she got mad. All around, she'd be better. Yeah, right. Those kinds of housekeepers were just waiting around for me to hire them. In my dreams.

I rounded on Hunter, lifted a finger and poked him in his very pompous, very interfering, very solid chest. "You are going to conduct all the interviews to replace her."

His unruffled expression faltered. Good. The man was damn lucky that Detective Jones had presumably taken my entire fireplace set into evidence. I bet I could do real damage with that miniature shovel. Hunter ran a finger under his collar. "If you gentlemen will excuse us, I need to speak with my client."

Detective Jones looked from Hunter to me and back again. His lips tightened, almost as if he was trying not to laugh. I swear I heard him mutter, "Your funeral." Then he headed for the door. "Hope you feel better, Mrs. Russell."

"Thank you, detective."

Putting aside his imaginary snacks, Powers followed him into the front hall and I got to glare at Hunter in privacy.

"She'd forgotten who worked for whom," he said.

"Be that as it may, she cooked, she cleaned, she did the grocery shopping and the laundry and the ironing—"

"We'll find you a housekeeper who does all that without scolding you."

I flushed and focused my gaze on him.

Mother was delusional. Chiseled jaw, charming smile, twinkling eyes. Bleh. No way would I ever find Hunter Tafft remotely attractive. No wonder my sister dumped him in high school for Tuck Bancroft.

"I was trying to help," he said.

"You want to help?" I asked.

He nodded. "I do."

"Then you," my voice rose an octave or two, "can clean this mess up."

Hunter Tafft gave me a not-going-to-happen roll of his eyes then stuck his perfectly coiffed silver head into the hallway. "Are you going to be much longer, Detective Jones? Mrs. Russell wants to start cleaning up."

"We're done here," Detective Jones' voice carried from the hallway.

"Ellie, I must fly. I'll call you later," Powers called. "You still owe me a dinner at the créperie."

The click of the front door closing echoed through the house.

I opened my mouth to suggest that Hunter join them and he held up his finger for silence.

Arrogant much?

He crossed to the drapeless front windows and watched them drive away.

"Are you going to open the safe or not?" he asked.

I froze for half a second then I swiped at the end of my nose. "I don't have the combination."

His smile still charmed, his eyes still twinkled, but his voice sounded as hard as the business end of a nine iron. "It's a bad idea to lie to your lawyer."

I rolled my eyes. "It's a bad idea to fire other people's staff."

"What's in the safe, Ellison?"

It's hard to pretend disinterest when you're dying to know something, but I tried. My shoulders lifted then dropped. "No idea."

"Wouldn't you like to know before the detective gets himself a warrant?"

Of course I would. "Isn't that evidence tampering?"

"Only if you actually tamper with the evidence. Nothing wrong with looking at it. I'd like to know what I'm dealing with."

"I didn't kill Madeline."

"There may be something in Henry's safe that proves that."

I trusted a charming, handsome man once. I glanced around Henry's destroyed office. It hadn't turned out well. "I don't have the combination."

He shrugged. "Suit yourself." He glanced at his watch. "Are you all right to be here alone?"

"Fine."

His gaze settled on the locked safe. "I guess I should go."

I didn't argue.

He left. I watched him drive away then I locked the front door. I went to the kitchen and checked the lock on the back door. Someone had made coffee. I drank a cup, took two aspirins, and watched the minute hand on the oven drag.

When fifteen minutes had passed, I went to the mudroom and dug out a pair of gloves. Then I returned to the study.

I stood in front of the safe and thought about all the reasons I shouldn't open it. I wasn't so sure Hunter was right about evidence tampering. It was a huge violation of Henry's privacy and I wasn't one hundred percent certain I wanted to know what was hidden within. None of that mattered because I needed to know. My fingers spun the dial and I peered inside.

Pandora's Box held fewer evils.

THIRTEEN

I stared into Henry's safe and contemplated bound stacks of hundred dollar bills. Thirty of them. Three hundred thousand dollars. What in the hell? What was Henry doing with that kind of money? In cash. That much money should be invested—unless it had to remain hidden.

A queasy, *oh shit* feeling took hold of my stomach.

I closed my eyes, counted to ten, and prayed that my head injury had conjured the obscene number of hundreds into Henry's safe. When I opened my lids, the cash was still there. Neatly stacked. Uniformly green. Utterly wrong.

I pushed the money aside.

Large, innocuous-looking envelopes rested against the back of the safe. They were held upright by Henry's gun and a box of bullets.

I pushed the gun aside and my fingers closed on an envelope. I pulled it toward me and read the name scrawled on its face. James Kensington—husband, father, stockbroker, scratch golfer. I loosened the flap and pulled out photographs and a strip of negatives.

James and Madeline would have been bad enough. James and Madeline and another man was infinitely worse. James' wife Lydia would take everything he had—the kids, the house, the vacation home in Vail, the stock portfolio. I shoved the pictures back into the envelope with clumsy fingers.

Back when Henry and I got along, we'd often played mixed doubles with James and Lydia. James had a strong backhand.

Apparently, he liked a strong backhand. Count that among the things I wished never to know. I rubbed my eyes and reached for another envelope.

Evan Platt, the club tennis champion. With shaking fingers, I opened his envelope and withdrew a photograph. A naked Evan was on his hands and knees with a bit in his mouth. Somehow—and the how didn't bear thinking about—someone had attached a horse's tail to his hindquarters. I stuffed the photograph back in the envelope.

Next was Arch Archer's. I didn't open that one, or Spencer Wilde's, or any of the others. I saw these people regularly. At the club. At parties. On the golf course. I didn't want to know what they did in the bedroom. I didn't want to know about their predilection for fetishes or kinky toys or pain or ménage.

So many envelopes. So many names. The queasiness in my stomach shifted to full on nausea. My husband was a blackmailer. There could be no other explanation for the ridiculous amount of cash or for the retina burning contents of the envelopes. Henry and Madeline had cooked up some kind of scheme using sex.

While the people on the pages of *Cosmo* might be open about their sexual experiences, the old guard in Kansas City was not, especially not when those experiences included handcuffs or whips or Berkley horses. I had to believe that the men and women whose names appeared on the envelopes had paid small fortunes to keep the pictures hidden from their business associates and more importantly, from their spouses.

Like an alcoholic reaching for another drink, I couldn't stop myself from reaching for another handful of envelopes. I read the names through a haze of disbelief. Stanford Reemes—a judge. What the hell had he been thinking? Baker Carmichael—the managing partner in the city's largest law firm. Harrington Walford.

Harrington Walford?

Daddy?

My stomach, already upset, fell faster and harder than a kid doing a cannonball off the high dive. Everything I'd ever known or counted on plummeted with it. Henry's destroyed study swirled around me in a dizzying whirl of fingerprint dust, emptied drawers and books with bent pages.

My husband was blackmailing my father. I leaned my head against the wall, waited for the world to stop spinning and tried to wrap my brain around the idea.

Hunter's voice played louder in my head than Grace played her Rolling Stones albums—*It's only evidence tampering if you actually tamper.*

I shoved the envelopes that didn't matter back into the safe and slammed its door shut. The clash of metal on metal echoed through the room and my brain. The envelope with my father's name remained clutched in my hands and I wished for January's cold winds and a blazing fire suitable for burning things I never wanted to see. I could have found charcoal and lighter fluid and barbequed the envelope, but the effort to locate even matches seemed overwhelming.

Instead, I dragged myself upstairs to my room and settled onto the edge of my bed. I dropped the envelope to the floor, stripped off my gloves and lowered my aching head into my hands. What in the hell was I supposed to do? Was it really evidence tampering if I knew Daddy had been in California when Madeline was murdered? Did Mother know?

Christ in a Cadillac.

Had Mother killed Madeline? She couldn't have. If Mother killed someone, she wouldn't leave the body in the one place her daughter was sure to find it.

I listed to the side until my cheek touched the pillow. The lavender scented linen was smooth and cool and comforting against my skin and I closed my eyes. Just for a minute. Then my eyes started to leak. I let them. I finally allowed myself to cry.

I cried because my head hurt. I cried because everyone I knew was a murder suspect—including me. I cried because my husband was a blackmailer. Most of all, I cried because I'd been wrong—a girl couldn't count on her Daddy.

I wallowed in misery for a full fifteen minutes before I got up and stashed the envelope with my father's name on it in my safe. Then I got back into bed and cried myself to sleep.

The ring of the telephone woke me and I lifted one lid and squinted at the clock on my bedside table. Three hours of uninterrupted rest. I pulled a pillow over my head and cursed whoever was calling. When I was asleep, I didn't have to face the repulsive fact that my husband was a blackmailer who made his money by targeting our friends. When I was asleep, I didn't have to think about what the envelope with my father's name on it might hold. If I thought about that, I'd convince myself there'd been a mistake. I'd have to look inside just to prove myself right. And if I was wrong, the photos could never be unseen.

I ignored the phone and landed a couple of good hard thumps of my fist against the uncaring mattress then dragged myself into the bathroom and stared at the mirror. The woman looking back at me had puffy, splotchy skin, crazy hair, and a look of desperation usually reserved for the squirrels and rabbits Max chased through the neighborhood. I stuck my tongue out at her.

A shower helped—at least with the splotchy skin and tangled hair. I checked the mirror again. My eyes seemed marginally less panicked.

Paint clothes or a sundress? Paint clothes beckoned. Escaping to a world where the feel of paint moving on canvas outweighed reality held real appeal. So did changing the locks. I straightened my shoulders and chose the sundress.

I went downstairs, found the yellow pages and flipped through it until I found the number for a locksmith. Yale locks weren't enough. I wanted deadbolts. I called, agreed to pay a ridiculous premium for same-day, after-hours service then ruffled the pages of the book until the entries for burglar alarms lay open before me.

Henry and Madeline had been blackmailing half the country club roster. Had their victims known who was extorting money from them? If they did, it seemed quite possible that the people whose names appeared on those envelopes would be coming to get them.

Of course, the easiest, safest thing for me to do would be to miraculously find the combination to Henry's safe and turn the files over to Detective Jones. What about my father's envelope? Did I give it to Daddy and swear I'd never looked inside? Did I burn it and pretend it never existed? Did I turn it over to Detective Jones? Did I call the alarm company and figure it out later?

I lifted the receiver but the sound of the dial tone was drowned out by four happy feet racing toward the kitchen. Max burst in and I hung up the phone to give him an apologetic scratch behind the ears then a shoulder rub. Poor dog. He'd been drugged, had his stomach pumped, and then I'd forgotten he was at the vet.

My father followed him into the kitchen. Either embarrassment or disappointment somersaulted my stomach. I wasn't sure which. Daddy looked the same—tall, salt and pepper hair, laugh lines at the corners of his eyes, distinguished. But everything was different. What was I supposed to say? *Did you? How could you? Hello?*

He pulled me into an encompassing hug, kissed the top of my head, and stroked my hair. I rested my forehead against his shoulder. Yes, he'd done something terrible but he was my father, the man who'd taught me how to ride a bike, the man who insisted I should go to art school if I wanted, the man I'd lie to protect. Was this how Julie Nixon felt when she crisscrossed the country declaring her father's innocence even as his guilt was obvious to all?

I searched for words, any words. Unfortunately, my stash of nouns and verbs and adjectives had somehow gotten locked in the upstairs safe with the envelope bearing my father's name.

Grace saved me. She traipsed into the kitchen as if murder and blackmail and being beaned with a fireplace poker were of no consequence. "Hey, Mom. How are you feeling?"

I extricated myself from my father's arms and held mine out to my daughter. "Fine."

Grace let me hug her. Fiercely. Briefly. Then she pulled away. "Just wait 'til Granna gets hold of you."

My father cleared his throat. "Your mother was counting on your spending another night in the hospital."

"I didn't want to," I said.

They both stared. Even Max stared.

"Granna had a plan."

I shrugged. "She didn't consult me before she made it."

Daddy rubbed the back of his neck. "You're sure this is the time you want to pick a fight with your mother?"

"I'm not picking a fight. I'm just doing what I want to do."

"You never do that," said Grace. "Well, almost never."

What was I teaching my daughter? I tightened my hold on the kitchen counter. I didn't want to raise a woman who gave up everything she wanted to please others. I stared at her. She was strong and independent despite my poor example. "I'd say it's about time I started."

My father combed his fingers through the silver strands of his hair. He was probably wishing he'd stayed in California. "Have you heard from Henry?" he asked.

I searched his face for some clue that he was concerned about the envelope I'd stolen from Henry's safe. His brows lowered and a wrinkle appeared at the top of his nose. He looked angry not worried.

"No," I replied.

"Your mother and Grace tell me you're thinking about a divorce."

"I am."

He covered his mouth with his hand as if hiding his scowl could disguise his dislike of Henry from me...or Grace. "You've talked to Hunter Tafft?"

"Not about my divorce."

"About the murder?"

If only. "Not really."

"Well then, what did you talk about?" Daddy asked.

"He fired Harriet."

No one said a word. We all pondered the unlikely possibility that I'd be able to keep a house running without help.

"Why did he do that?"

"Harriet lost her temper over the mess in Henry's office."

"It must be a real mess."

I closed my eyes and visualized the fallen walls of Jericho. Or, given that it was Henry, Sodom and Gomorrah after God did his wrath thing. "Terrible."

Daddy inched toward the door. "I'll take a look."

"I'll come with you."

"No, no. Don't get up. Gracie, get your mom a glass of iced tea. I'll just go look around."

Had I been wrong? Did he know Henry was the man who'd been blackmailing him? Could I just ask him? Yeah, right. *Daddy, did you do it with Madeline Harper? Was my son-of-a-bitch husband blackmailing you?* All things being equal I didn't particularly want an answer to the first question. The answer to the second question, I already knew. I didn't need to hear it from my father's lips. Unless Daddy didn't know Henry was the blackmailer...

Just thinking about it made my head hurt worse.

Daddy disappeared down the hallway and Grace deposited a glass of iced tea on the counter in front of me.

"Have you heard from your father?" I asked.

"No." She didn't twitch or scratch her nose or try to look honest and forthright. She was telling the truth.

"I'm sorry he disappeared like this, Grace."

She rolled her eyes. "It's not your fault, Mom."

"That's not what I meant."

She served up a second eye roll. "Yeah, I know. Did Mr. Tafft really fire Harriet?"

"Sort of. He fired her. I told her she wasn't fired. Then she quit."

"So...um...what are we going to do for food?"

"I can cook." Boiled eggs. Jell-O. Frozen pizza.

She shuddered. "So we're going to eat out a lot?"

"Yep. Although, I'd like to try and grill burgers." Any excuse to light a fire.

Grace shook her head. "I don't think so, Mom. It's not like there's a shortage of hockey pucks."

Burn a roast or two and your family will never let you forget it. "So what do you want for dinner?"

"Tacos."

"Tacos?" Daddy stood in the door. "Your mother just got out of the hospital. She needs something better than tacos. I'll take you girls to the club for dinner. Ellie, go grab your purse."

"I don't feel up to the club."

My father stared at me as if I was a stranger. Maybe I was. I'd never before said no to his plans. "You do look a little pale, sugar. How about I go pick something up for you?"

"That would be nice."

"I want tacos," Grace repeated.

"Tacos are fine, Daddy."

He delivered them thirty minutes later.

Grace and I ate then settled onto the couch in the family room to watch television.

I shifted against the cushions. I was too antsy to sit. There was too much to think about to waste time watching Michael Douglas speed through the *Streets of San Francisco*.

"Go." Grace knew me well.

"You're sure?"

"You're just going to fidget and sigh and drive me nuts. Go."

I went. I climbed the stairs to what had once been a third floor ballroom. Now it was my studio. I breathed in the comforting smells of paint and gesso and turpentine and felt the coil in my stomach begin to unwind.

The canvas on my easel was an impossibility. Hopeful daubs of paint from a woman who had disappeared. A stranger who'd never dreamed of finding a body. Someone who'd never imagined the depths of her husband's betrayal or that he might be a blackmailer. A woman who'd never considered tampering with evidence.

That woman was gone.

Fortunately, there was another prepped canvas. With the last rays of daylight, I began to paint.

FOURTEEN

I woke to the usual early morning sounds of my house—the white noise, the ceiling fan, occasional voices of runners as they passed by on the sidewalk outside. The sounds were the same. Everything else had changed. All things being equal, I preferred life the old way.

Just a few days ago, Madeline was playing kinky games with my husband and I wasn't under suspicion of murder. I missed being blissfully ignorant of Henry's other dalliances. I *really* missed not knowing that my husband was blackmailing half the people we knew—including my father.

I clutched a pillow to my chest, stared into the darkness and wished I didn't know what I did. But, once bitten, Eve's apple cannot be returned to the tree. It hardly seemed fair. I hadn't plucked the damn fruit. I'd had it shoved into my hands then down my throat.

What I wanted was a return to my life—a life without sordid revelations or soul-chilling disasters. My life might not have been perfect but it had been comfortable with reliable rhythms and certainties. I wanted a return to those rhythms, to a routine that made sense.

Watching the sun rise made sense. Swimming made sense.

I dragged myself out of bed, downed a quick cup of coffee, and drove to the club.

I didn't let myself think about Madeline's water-soaked body when I dove into the water. I just held my breath for the length of the pool. Of course there was no corpse in my lane. I exhaled, and then I swam.

Arms and legs cutting through water shouldn't be cathartic, but it was. I saw the remains of the night. I smelled chlorine. I heard water and birdsong welcoming the coming dawn. Each lap washed away a layer of pain or fear or anger. By the time the sky over the seventh green began to lighten, I felt graceful, peaceful, even quiet.

Then I saw the man standing at the edge of the pool.

I pretended I didn't. I even tried to swim more laps. The motions that had been smooth and fluid felt choppy and out of sync. I gave up and swam to where Detective Jones stood waiting for me with his arms crossed and a look of disapproval settled firmly on his face.

"I'm surprised you're here, Mrs. Russell," he said.

I rested my arms on the lip of the pool and stared up at him. "I swim every morning."

He scowled at me. "The last time you swam you found a body."

"The time before that I didn't."

"Still I'd think you'd want to avoid swimming in this pool."

Where else was I going to swim? We didn't have a pool in our backyard and even if we did, it wouldn't be big enough to swim laps. It's hard to shrug in the water, but I did it anyway.

"Have you forgotten that Madeline Harper was murdered?" he asked. "Swimming alone might not be wise."

Of course I hadn't forgotten about Madeline's death. The thought of her body laid out on the pool deck followed me around like a balloon on a string. "No one wants to murder me."

"How do you know?"

I wasn't into kinky sex—or blackmail. I shrugged. "If the murderer wanted me dead, he or she would have finished me off when I was unconscious in my foyer."

"Do you know for certain the murderer and the burglar are the same person?"

"I don't believe in coincidences." Besides, it stretched the bounds of credulity to believe otherwise. A cool breeze ruffled across my wet shoulders and I shivered. "Speaking of coincidences, how is it you're wandering around the pool deck this morning?"

Detective Jones stared out at the golf course where black trees turned lavender with the sunrise. "We have a car drive by your house every hour or so."

My heart stuttered in my chest. How was I supposed to barbeque Daddy's envelope if the police were watching my house? What if I'd tried to do it last night? I swallowed. "Why?"

Stupid question. Madeline had been my husband's mistress. My husband was missing. Someone had hit me over the head with a fireplace poker and tossed Henry's office. Clearly someone at the Russell house was involved. It just wasn't me.

Apparently Detective Jones found my question as stupid as I did. He didn't answer it. Instead he asked, "Hunter Tafft is your lawyer?"

"He is." Until I found a better one.

"He's a corporate attorney."

It was hardly my fault that Mother couldn't find any handsome criminal attorneys with impeccable backgrounds on short notice. "He's still a lawyer."

"You ought to have a criminal lawyer."

Was he threatening me? He didn't sound like it. He sounded almost like he was worried for me. "Am I still a suspect?"

The smile he gave me was wry. It crinkled the skin around his eyes. I was suddenly aware that when he looked down at me he saw wet hair, skin naked of any make-up, and cleavage.

"You haven't been officially eliminated," he said.

"I didn't kill Madeline." How many murderers declared their innocence?

"Did Roger Harper kill her?"

I shook my head. "I don't think so."

"Did your husband kill Ms. Harper?" he asked.

"No!"

His eyebrows rose. "You sound sure."

Detective Jones was lying. I didn't sound sure, I sounded desperate.

"I am sure." Somehow, I kept my voice from squeaking. Henry hadn't killed Madeline. One of their blackmail victims had. I was going to have to go through the safe and make a list of the names on the envelopes. I was going to have to figure out who committed murder.

His lips quirked. "It wasn't you. It wasn't Mr. Harper. And it wasn't Mr. Russell. So, who was it?"

"Someone else." The water lapping against my skin was icy—or maybe that was the temperature of my blood as it struggled to pump through my veins.

He crossed his arms over his chest. "Why did this mystery assailant kill her?"

My heart, already dealing with frosty blood, beat faster. He could probably see it thudding in my chest. "How would I know?"

He looked down at me with his nice brown eyes and his sandy hair and his movie actor good-looking face and said, "That's the thing, Mrs. Russell. I think you do know. I think you're protecting someone."

I swallowed. Hard. Then I reviewed the neat row of lounge chairs next to the pool. They were fascinating and if I didn't look Detective Jones in the eye, he wouldn't be able to read my expression.

"Who are you protecting?" he repeated.

I'd started out protecting Grace. I didn't want her to suffer for her father's choices. Now I was protecting my father too. There was no way I was going to tell Detective Jones about Henry and Madeline's blackmail scheme. "If I knew who killed her, I'd tell you."

The light around us was a soft lemon yellow, certainly bright enough for me to see the concern in Detective Jones' eyes. We stared at each other for a moment. That moment stretched and bent and wrapped us in a delicate bubble made up of gentle light and birdsong and the touch of a breeze.

He cleared his throat and shattered the bubble. Then he glanced around the empty pool deck and scowled. "Withholding evidence can get you into trouble with the law. It can also get you killed."

I shifted my focus from his face to his shoes. Nice conservative shoes. Loafers. They were paired with nice conservative khaki pants and a nice conservative blue blazer. And then I was looking at his face again. He really was handsome. I returned my gaze to his shoes.

"Tell me what you know." His voice was as soft as the breeze on my shoulders.

I almost did. It was so tempting to tell him everything—about Kitty and Prudence, about Madeline and the money and the pictures. A robin landed on the pool deck—not three feet from us. It tilted its head as if it too wanted to know what I knew. I took a deep breath and shooed it away. I couldn't saddle Grace with being the daughter of a depraved, kinky blackmailer. That kind of thing tends to follow one through life. The people we knew might forgive her a murderous father—no one had liked Madeline—but they wouldn't forgive her a father who'd blackmailed his friends. I shook my head. "I don't know anything."

Detective Jones took a step backward. Away from the pool...and me. He frowned. "Until I catch the killer, you shouldn't swim alone...Ellison."

And then Detective Jones turned on his heel and walked away.

I drove home, drank half a pot of coffee, donned clothes already destroyed by paint, and stood in the doorway to Henry's office.

The doorbell rang at precisely nine o'clock. I know that because I was staring at a miraculously unbroken clock and wondering how one went about cleaning up Armageddon when I heard it.

Max met me at the door. I opened it to a woman with frizzy hennaed hair somehow contained by a barrette Grace would have snubbed as babyish at age five. The orange hair clashed with the fuchsia of her cardigan and the deep purple of her dress—all the colors of a lurid sunset. "Good morning, Mr. Tafft sent me," she said.

I stared at her. Then I stared at a beat up, emerald green VW Beetle with a light blue driver's side door. Its engine still knocked like it couldn't decide if it wanted to start up again and move to a neighborhood where the ladies walking their dogs on the sidewalk didn't stop and gawk.

She squinted at the piece of paper she held in her right hand then her left hand dove down the front of her dress. It emerged seconds later with a pair of readers. She positioned them on her nose, glanced at the paper, then glanced at me in my ratty clothes and said, "You are Mrs. Russell?"

"I am." I nodded. "And you are?"

"Agatha DeLucci. You can call me Aggie. Everyone does."

Why would I call her anything? And why had Hunter sent her to me? "How may I help you?" I asked. It seemed more polite than asking *what the hell are you doing here?*

She shook her orange haloed head at my slowness. Earrings the size of tennis balls jangled. "Mr. Tafft sent me."

That part I got. "Why did Mr. Tafft send you?"

"He said you needed a housekeeper."

Max chose that moment to bury his nose in her crotch and sniff. I grabbed his collar and hauled him backward. "I apologize. Max is...friendly."

She chuckled. "I don't mind. Do you?"

Did I mind that Max insisted on sniffing visitors' bits? I did. "Pardon me?"

"Do you need a housekeeper?"

"I do."

"Then I'm your gal. Mr. Tafft told me about the job last night and I said I was willing to give it a go. He said you'd had a break-in and I should start by cleaning up Mr. Russell's study."

Hunter Tafft had hired a new housekeeper without consulting me? Of all the arrogant, high-handed men I'd ever met, he was the absolute worst. I ought to apologize to Aggie DeLucci for the misunderstanding and send her on her way. Except she'd uttered magical words—*I should start by cleaning up Mr. Russell's study.*

"How do you know Mr. Tafft?" I asked.

"My husband used to do some work for him."

I closed my eyes and tried to imagine what the husband of a woman who wore purple muumuus did for Hunter. My imagination wasn't that good. "What kind of work?"

"My husband was an investigator."

"Was?"

She ran a finger under her eyes. "The cancer got him."

"I'm terribly sorry."

She sniffled then offered me a lopsided attempt at a smile. "He had a good go."

"How long has he been gone?"

"Three months."

Hunter had sent me a recently widowed woman in need of work. How was I supposed to send her away? "Do you cook?" I asked.

She grinned. The expression transformed her. She had the smile of a child who hasn't yet been knocked on their ass by life. "I'm a great cook."

"Can you make chicken salad?"

She tilted her head, probably wondering if I'd lost my mind. I hadn't. I had criteria.

"I make a chicken salad that will bring tears to your eyes," she said.

"What do you put in it?"

Her head tilted further. "Chicken."

"And what else?"

Her brow wrinkled. "Celery."

"And what else?" She was now regarding me as if I was *that* eccentric woman, the one who wore a period costume to a cocktail party—or a purple muumuu to a job interview. "Mayonnaise."

"And?"

"Nothing. I suppose if you're one of those people who like

grapes or nuts I could add them." She sniffed.

"I'm not."

"Then why are you asking? If I did add them and you didn't like them, you could tell me not to."

A novel concept. One that never worked with Harriet. "You're right. Do you have references?"

She regarded me with washed out blue eyes surrounded by heavy mascara. Her eyelids were coated with fuchsia and purple shadow. The makeup, the sadness, and the determination were at odds with her hopeful smile. Aggie DeLucci had taken plenty of knocks in her life. Her eyes told me she'd gotten up each time and asked for more. Her smile told me she hadn't given up on people. "Mr. Tafft said he'd be my reference."

She was totally inappropriate. Her hair. Her attire. Her makeup. Mother would have a coronary, and if I hired her, Hunter might smirk at me. I didn't care. I liked her. "Well, Aggie, let's give it a go."

She gifted me another one of her smiles. "Thank you, Mrs. Russell. You won't be sorry."

Her car chose that moment to emit one last knock then shudder into stillness. Mrs. Phipps from across the street had come out on her front stoop to investigate. From fifty yards away, I could see her pinched lips and raised eyebrows. "Why don't you move your car around back?" I suggested.

"Bessie? Bessie won't start for at least an hour. I can move her then." Aggie bent and picked up a carpetbag. "I've got my cleaning clothes in here. Wouldn't want to mess up my good duds."

Oh dear Lord. When Mother met Aggie, she was going to have a seizure then a stroke and only then would she indulge in a coronary. And when she was done with her histrionics, I was going to be able to tell her that her golden boy, Hunter Tafft, was responsible. I smiled and welcomed Aggie DeLucci into my home.

She followed me into the kitchen and grunted.

"Is there a problem?" I asked.

"Women who don't cook always have the best kitchens."

I didn't spend much time in kitchens. I'd have to take her word for it. "There's a room where you can change right over there." I pointed to a closed door.

Aggie nodded and took a step toward the maid's room. The phone rang. She paused then raised a questioning brow.

If she was going to be the housekeeper, she might as well answer the phone. I nodded.

She picked up the receiver. "Russell residence."

She listened for a moment then said, "The new housekeeper."

Again, she fell silent.

"I'll see if Mrs. Russell is at home." She pressed the mouthpiece into her ample bosom then whispered, "It's your mother."

I shook my head. "Not home." Harriet had never, not once, helped me duck a call from Mother. As far as I was concerned, Aggie could stay forever.

"I'm sorry, Mrs. Russell isn't in. May I take a message?" More silence ensued. "Dinner tonight at the Country Club? I'll tell Mrs. Russell when she gets in...No, I'm not sure when she'll be home."

Aggie hung up the phone then offered me a rueful smile. "It looks like you're going to have to wait to try my chicken salad. Your mother wants you to join her at the club for dinner."

What fresh hell was this? I rubbed my forehead and wondered if my headache might reappear. Then I sighed and tried to look on the bright side. I might be having dinner with Mother but at least I had a decent housekeeper.

FIFTEEN

When the doorbell rang, I answered it. After all, Aggie was busy restoring order to Henry's study.

Libba stood on the front stoop. She wore a print caftan, Dr. Scholl's sandals, a floppy straw hat, and an apologetic smile. "Hi. I thought I'd stop by and see if you wanted to go to the pool."

In all the years Libba and I have been friends she'd never done such a thing. A thing that exactly meshed with Mother's stated plan for me. I narrowed my eyes and crossed my arms over my chest. "Really?"

"Please?"

"I've already been to the pool today." And it hadn't gone as planned.

"Please?" She clasped her hands and tried on puppy-dog eyes.

"What did she promise you?"

To her credit, Libba didn't even try to play dumb. "She's chairing the benefit for Corinthian Hall this November."

My arms stayed firmly crossed.

"I'm on the invitation committee but she might have mentioned something about needing a committee chair for ambiance."

I snorted. "She bought you off with the ambiance committee?" Yes, it was more prestigious than invitations but I thought I was worth more to Libba than the opportunity to select the flowers at a gala.

Libba glanced down at her Dr. Scholl's. "She also mentioned the clean-up committee."

I shuddered. Clean-up was the worst committee possible—its members stayed after the party to make sure vases and table cloths and décor made it safely through the night when all anyone wanted to do was go home and take off their shoes.

It was a classic Frances Walford technique. Offer Libba a carrot then threaten her with a stick. Take me to the pool and she chaired ambiance. Fail and she spent a night cleaning up after a huge party.

She looked up from the study of her shoes. "Please?"

Oh sweet God of undeserved guilt. I couldn't be responsible for Libba staying at Corinthian Hall until three in the morning just to make sure that the pre-sold vases were available for pick-up first thing Sunday morning. "Fine," I sighed. "Come in while I change."

The pool was relatively quiet and we secured lounge chairs in the filtered shade of the lanai. Then came the production of positioning towels and applying suntan oil.

"You're sure we can't sit in the sun?" Libba grumbled.

I tapped my head. "Mild concussion. I probably shouldn't be here at all."

That shut her up. She probably had to keep me at the pool for at least an hour before Mother made good on her ambiance promise.

"Do you want a drink?" she asked.

I tapped my head again. "I can't."

"Iced tea?"

"Thank you."

"I'll just go get it." She headed not toward the snack bar but inside where she could procure my tea and something tall and cool with an umbrella. Poor woman. She probably needed a drink. Mother had that effect on people.

Nearby a contingent of young mothers eagle-eyed their toddlers in the baby pool. A few kids played a half-hearted game of Marco Polo in the big pool. Across the pool deck sat a woman tanned to the exact shade of roasted almonds. She wore a bikini designed for a younger woman, one who lost the top when she went cruising on a Greek shipping magnate's yacht. She also wore enormous dark glasses that hid half her face. Didn't matter. I could still feel Kitty Ballew's stare. Did she know how completely out of place she looked at a pool where women wore Lilly and kids wore Speedos? Did she care?

I glanced at my watch. I gave it two minutes before she found an excuse to come ask me where Henry was.

It took her a minute—and a good thirty seconds of that minute was devoted to tying a towel around her waist just so.

She sidled up to me. "I didn't expect to see you here." Whatever happened to *hello?* Or, better yet, *how are you?*

At least I knew where I stood. Ours would not be a friendly conversation. I looked up at her from the comfort of my lounge chair. "Libba insisted." A not so subtle reminder that Libba would be returning soon. If Kitty had a point she should make it quickly.

"Do you know where Henry is?" No dilly-dallying for Kitty. No pretend smile either. Any expression in her eyes was hidden by her glasses.

I faked a sigh. "Everyone's looking for Henry. Why do you want him?"

Kitty's lips thinned. "Who else is looking for him?"

I manufactured a yawn, barely covering it with the tips of my fingers. "Simply everyone. Such a shame about Madeline, isn't it?"

A corner of her kittenish mouth curled. "Yes. About Henry—"

"It was awful finding her in the pool." I glanced out at the water where I'd found Madeline's body. True, I'd wished horrible accidents would befall her—snake bites, lightning strikes, pattern baldness—but I never hoped to see her murdered, floating. "Do you have any idea how she got there?"

"What? Me?" She lifted her hand and covered the hollow near the base of her throat, almost as if she could feel a noose tightening. "Of course not. Why would you ask such a thing?"

"Prudence might have said..." my voice trailed to nothing.

"That bitch!" Kitty wasn't quite as cold blooded as Prudence. It was easier to fluster her.

"So you do know how Madeline got in the pool?"

"No!"

"But you saw her the night she died?"

"Yes. No. I didn't dump her in a pool."

"I have your tea." Libba breezed across the pool deck, her caftan snapping behind her. In one hand she held a glass of iced tea garnished with mint and lemon. In the other, she grasped something colorful and slushy, garnished with a bendy straw and a little paper umbrella. She wrinkled her nose at Kitty. "Are you looking for Henry, too?"

Kitty barely moved her chin.

Libba sucked on her drink. "Let me guess. An apartment in New York?"

"What?" The hand at the base of Kitty's neck shook.

"Why are you looking for my husband?"

She opened her mouth, closed it, then repeated the exercise. Really, she should have prepared a story before she traipsed over.

In the pool, the children gave up on Marco Polo and balanced on a lane rope. A lifeguard's whistle startled us all. Libba and I flinched. Kitty jumped out of her flip-flops.

"Were you with him and Madeline at Club K the night she died?"

The color leeched from Kitty's skin until she looked like an empty duffle bag, one made with cheap, poorly tanned leather. "What's Prudence been telling you? It's all lies. That woman would say anything, do anything, to get what she wants."

And Kitty wouldn't?

It seemed likely one of them had killed Madeline.

"What's Club K?" Libba asked.

Kitty's shaking hand stilled.

I shifted my gaze to Libba. "It's—"

"You just better watch out, Ellison. Look what happened to Madeline."

"Are you threatening me?"

I pushed away from the reclined back of the chaise and sat straight.

"No. Of course not. I'm just saying you swim alone."

Libba slurped up some more rum. "Sounds like a threat to me." She shook her glass, swirling the contents of her glass. "Ellison, what's the name of that police detective? He ought to know if someone's threatening you."

Did Kitty think I'd turn to Jell-O because she threatened me? Maybe the old Ellison. The new, improved Ellison said, "Jones."

Kitty took off her glasses and glared at us. "I am not threatening Ellison, and I didn't kill Madeline. I just want to know where Henry is."

Lie. Maybe a lie. Truth.

I shrugged—a new, improved shrug. Libba raised a brow.

"I didn't kill Madeline," Kitty insisted. "She got herself killed looking under rocks."

Libba took another sip of her drink. "Everyone around here does that."

Kitty perched her glasses back on her nose, hiding her eyes. "Not for money."

The conversation was headed in a horrible direction but still I asked, "How much did it take for her not to tell John about you and Henry?"

An unbecoming shade of red darkened Kitty's cheeks and she glanced at Libba. Now she worried what Libba learned? She should have thought about repercussions before she started an affair with my husband.

"I have no reason to keep Henry's secrets." I crossed my ankles. "Or yours." Maybe she'd think twice about threatening me again.

A whiff of baby oil and sweat floated toward me on the breeze.

Kitty's hand returned to guarding the base of her throat.

"I didn't have anything to gain by killing Madeline."

"No more blackmail."

"She wasn't blackmailing me." Kitty scratched the side of her nose. "Prudence is the one who wanted her dead."

Libba handed me my iced tea then tilted her head. "Prudence?"

"With Madeline out of the way there was nothing to stop her from being with Henry."

"Henry's married to Ellison."

Kitty's chin bobbed as if she was laughing, as if Libba had delivered the punch line to a joke.

She had. The joke was my marriage.

"Henry and I are getting divorced."

Kitty's brows rose above the frames of her sunglasses. Libba choked on a slurp of her tropical drink.

"He doesn't know yet."

Libba sank onto the chaise next to mine. "You're sure? What about Grace?"

I lifted my iced tea to my lips and took a sip. "Grace is fine with it."

"I guess that leaves you—" Libba pulled the umbrella out of her glass and pointed it toward Kitty, "—and Prudence to fight over him. I wonder which one of you will get him."

After one hour, thirty-three minutes and seventeen seconds of talking about my impending divorce, I convinced Libba that I'd stayed at the pool long enough to earn her the ambiance committee chairmanship.

The car doors closed and Libba turned the key in the ignition. "Blackmail?"

"I'm sorry?"

"Madeline blackmailed Kitty. Kitty lied about that."

Not a topic I wanted to pursue. It was a short jump from Madeline the blackmailer to Henry the blackmailer. "Sometimes people just scratch their noses."

Libba snorted.

"Besides, Madeline is dead. It doesn't matter anymore."

"It matters if Kitty killed her."

Libba made an excellent point. She turned the wheel and drove down my street. "She threatened you. That matters too."

Another excellent point.

She pulled the car into the drive and slowed to a stop. "What are you doing tonight?"

"Dinner with Mother and Daddy."

She nodded. "You'll be careful?"

I chose to misunderstand. "Mother's scary but she's not actually dangerous."

Libba scrunched her face. "Ha ha."

I climbed out of her car. "It's dinner at the country club. What could possibly happen?"

Famous last words.

SIXTEEN

Henry once accused me of pausing in doorways so I could make a grand entrance. Just goes to show how poorly he understood me. I pause to observe what's on the other side, to take a last quiet breath, to gather my courage.

I didn't pause in the door that led from the clubhouse to the terrace. I lingered. It was so tempting to turn around, go home, crawl into my jammies and watch Kojak. I sighed. Appearances must be maintained—for Mother's sake, for Grace's sake and I supposed, for mine too.

In Africa, lions cull the herd. In the jungle, jaguars kill the very young or the very old. At the country club, members winnow the weak.

Outside, in the hunting grounds, enormous pots of cadmium red geraniums and black wrought iron furniture created an oh-so-civilized killing field. The combatants wore crisp linen and printed cotton and needlepoint belts through the loops of their khakis. The fabric covered a cache of metaphorical weapons—poison-tipped arrows and swords and razor-edged knives. I wasn't about to be winnowed. Not by men who wore gingham. Not by women whose most important decision of the day was the color of their nail polish. I straightened my shoulders, and passed through the door.

I walked straight to the table, careful not to stare—or even glance—at the people whose names were on envelopes in Henry's safe. I might have half-stumbled when I passed Kitty and John Ballew's table but that wasn't because of a name on an envelope. It had more to do with the way she glared at me.

Daddy stood as I approached. Of course, Daddy's envelope wasn't in Henry's safe. It was in mine until I could figure out how to destroy it. In the meantime, I had to figure out how to look him in the eye.

I tried. The expression pasted on my face was excruciatingly polite. It rivaled Mother's. She might be furious with me for leaving the hospital early but no one near us would ever know. "Your father thought it would be fun to dine *al fresco*."

"Great fun," I muttered through locked teeth and clenched lips.

Daddy pulled out my chair.

I sat and a waiter appeared like a genie rubbed from a bottle to lay a napkin in my lap. "A Tom Collins for you this evening, Mrs. Russell?"

"Please."

He shimmied off, a study in white-coated near magical efficiency.

Mother lifted her sunglasses and stared at my dress. "Aren't you a bit old for a halter dress?"

I gritted my teeth so hard my jaw hurt. "It's Missoni."

"Miss who?" Daddy cocked his head to the side and considered the colorful zigs and zags of the fabric. "I think you look very pretty, sugar."

"Are you wearing a bra?" Mother sounded scandalized.

I wasn't. Bras were as passé as poodle skirts. I usually wore one anyway, but the Missoni didn't allow for any extraneous straps. Instead, I'd slapped Band-aids across my nipples and hoped Mother wouldn't notice. I should have hoped for world peace. It was more likely than Mother missing any detail of my appearance. "No."

Mother sat back in her chair, raised her martini to her thinned lips and drank deeply.

A ruddy pink stained Daddy's tanned cheeks. I don't suppose any father wants to hear his wife and daughter discuss breasts or bras. He looked out at the view of the golf course, not at me, certainly not at my braless chest. "I still think you look pretty."

Mother shot him *the* look. Poor man. If she ever discovered he'd done something worthy of blackmail her expression would make *the* look seem like the besotted gaze of young love. Where was the waiter with my drink?

Daddy took another sip of his gin and tonic. "Frances, be nice. Ellie has had a rough couple of days." His voice was so low no one but Mother and me could hear him.

Mother sniffed. "It's not like she's a serious suspect."

I ought to have claimed a headache and stayed home. I might not be a suspect but Henry was. If he ever turned up, Grace might have to live through watching her father tried for murder.

I glanced at the empty place at the table. "I thought Grace called you. She got a babysitting job and she's not coming."

"She called." Mother lifted her wine glass to her lips.

A sinking feeling took hold of my stomach. She wouldn't.

Daddy shot me a sympathetic look.

She had.

The waiter arrived with my Tom Collins. I thanked him, took a bracing drink then leaned forward and pitched my voice as low as possible. "It's bad enough you feel the need to throw him at me. Must you do it here?"

Mother's brows rose. She wasn't accustomed to me questioning her dictates. "He's a perfectly charming man and he's representing you. Why shouldn't we meet him for dinner?"

Because I was still married. Besides, the sparkle in his eyes was dangerous. What's more, I wasn't entirely sure if I trusted him. I scowled at her.

Daddy looked at Mother's raised eyebrows then at my scowl and shook his head. "It's a nice night. Why don't you girls try and get along?"

Mother sniffed. "I'm sure I don't know what I ever did that my daughters have such taste in men."

Now my brows rose. Mother had been thrilled, to-the-moon happy, when Henry asked Daddy if he could marry me. Just look how that had turned out. By contrast, she'd been less than pleased when Marjorie brought home Gregory Blake from Akron, Ohio. It helped that his family was in the rubber business. She could put a brave face on a marriage that included a rubber manufacturer from Ohio. At least until she discovered the Blakes made condoms, not tires. She'd never forgiven Marjorie.

My sister was blissfully happy. She didn't need Mother's forgiveness.

"There's a band playing tonight." Ever the peacemaker, Daddy nodded toward the microphone stand and the speakers set up in the corner of the terrace. "When they start playing, will you dance with me, Ellie?"

I'm only good at a handful of things—painting, swimming, dancing, being polite, and, until a few days ago, pleasing others. Of that handful, I only like painting, swimming, and dancing. Besides, if I concentrated on the music and the steps and what great fun it was to dine *al fresco*, I bet I could put a certain envelope clean out of my mind. "I'd love to, Daddy."

Mother snorted.

I glared at her.

She stopped inventorying everyone seated on the terrace and glared back.

By any measure, Mother's expression was scarier. Of course, she'd had decades to practice turning people to stone with just a look.

Except, the sensations inside me weren't remotely stony. They felt more like molten lava. Burning, angry feelings that demanded a stand be made. "You liked Henry."

"I did. But that was before he treated you shabbily. You'll be well rid of him."

I couldn't argue that.

"Hunter would have been a better choice."

Hunter Tafft went through women like Sherman went through Georgia. He hardly constituted a better choice. Well...maybe if you discounted Henry's floggers and whips and infidelity and blackmail. Since Mother only knew about the infidelity, I was willing to argue. "Hunter has been married three times."

Mother shrugged off my point. "Hunter hasn't met the right woman."

"He met me twenty-five years ago."

"When you were a girl. When he gets to know you as a woman, he'll fall head over heels."

"I don't want him to fall head over heels." Not that he ever would. "I've had it with marriage."

Mother paled then lifted her glass. If she didn't watch out, she'd get tipsy. Daddy reached across the table and patted my hand. And Hunter Tafft blinded us all with the white of his smile.

Hunter claimed his seat at the table then devoted the salad course to charming us all. He talked tennis. Mother fluttered her eyelashes and gave me an I-told-you-he-was-fabulous kick under the table. When the entrées were served, Hunter discussed politics and managed to agree with both my parents' differing viewpoints. During dessert, Daddy and Hunter compared notes on the golf courses they'd played. They talked about Gary Player and his win at the Masters. I knew Hunter's charm had worked on Daddy when he offered to call one of his cronies in Augusta so Hunter could play the course.

Christ in a Cadillac.

I didn't want Hunter to charm Mother. Or Daddy. Or me. I excused myself to the powder room...the pouter room. Pouting was definitely in order.

Either way, it was blessedly empty. No one was there to watch me freshen my lipstick, fluff my hair, or smooth the seams of my dress. I didn't have to face Prudence or Kitty or the wives of any of the men that Madeline and Henry had been blackmailing. When I returned to the terrace, a singer was covering *Midnight at the Oasis* and a handful of couples were swaying on the area left clear for dancing.

At the table, Hunter stood, extended a hand and asked, "Dance with me?"

Mother narrowed her eyes, daring me to say no.

Dancing, which I loved, or listening to Mother try to sell me like a handful of magic beans...tough choice.

Common sense told me close proximity to Hunter might not be the best plan. He added a charming smile to his invitation. When he smiled, the skin around his eyes crinkled. Damn him. He was nearly irresistible. He led me to the dance floor before I could think to tell him no.

His hand at my waist felt warm. He used it to pull me closer. "It's nice to see your parents."

I made a noncommittal sort of sound.

"It's nicer to see you." He drew me closer to the crisp cotton covering his chest.

It was definitely better to talk about Mother and Daddy than me. "You charmed them."

"I tried."

"Why?"

"If we're going to spend time together, it's easier if they like me."

"You're my lawyer, not my boyfriend. It doesn't matter if they like you or not."

He opened his mouth, snapped it shut then twirled me in a circle. "What if I want more?" he asked.

I had a husband. I didn't want a boyfriend. And, if I did, I certainly didn't want a high-handed man who fired my housekeeper or tried to make decisions for me or smelled like Pierre Cardin cologne and old money. "Isn't there an ethical problem with dating your client?"

"As you've pointed out, I'm neither a criminal nor a family law attorney. I'm going to have to refer your cases to other lawyers. So, there's no problem." The skin around his eyes crinkled again. "We can spend as much time together as we want."

My throat was suddenly dry and any response I might have formed was lost in the depths of his eyes.

We danced for a moment in silence. Close enough for the

warmth of his skin to touch me, close enough to shiver when his breath tickled my ear.

Too close. I pulled away, putting precious inches between us. "Tell me about Aggie."

"Salt of the earth."

"She said she lost her husband."

He nodded. "Damn shame."

"She said he was an investigator." Someone who pried into others' affairs.

"Do you think I sent Aggie to spy on you?" The hand on my waist stiffened.

The thought had crossed my mind. "Did you?"

"I work for you. Why would I spy on you?"

Because he wanted to know what was in Henry's safe or because he thought I'd murdered Madeline? I didn't quite believe that Hunter Tafft, man about town, was truly interested in the spurned wife of a community banker. He had to have an ulterior motive. Maybe I was being too hard on him. Maybe I wasn't. "I don't trust easily."

If he'd offered me a trite lie—*you can trust me*—I would have left him on the dance floor, even if it meant walking by Kitty and John Ballew's table and, given the way Kitty was scowling at me, she'd probably stab me in the leg with a fork if I got too close.

Fortunately, Hunter didn't lie. "Having someone you care about betray you will do that."

It made me wonder who'd betrayed him. He initiated a series of turns that left me too dizzy to ask. Other dancers made room for us. They stopped to watch then clapped when he slowed us to simple steps.

The band transitioned into *Haven't Got Time for the Pain.* Hunter didn't let me go. Instead he smiled at me as if I'd passed some sort of mysterious test. "You dance well."

I should. Mother stuck me in Mrs. Goodman's dance classes when I was three and kept me there until I left for college. "You too."

At the table, Mother was beaming. Her plan was coming together. At least it appeared that way.

The poisoned arrows I'd worried about had been returned to their quivers, the swords and knives had been sheathed. Without trying, I'd found a new champion.

The evening wasn't the total disaster I'd anticipated. I closed my eyes and let myself enjoy the feeling of Hunter's hand at my waist, the breeze in my hair, and the way the music thrummed through my body.

Hunter turned me again and I opened my eyes. His face looked harder than the marble floor in the club's foyer. It even looked harder than the business end of a fireplace poker. Around us, conversations fell silent. The singer muffed the lyrics.

I followed the collective gazes of everyone on the terrace, glanced over my shoulder, and tripped. Only Hunter's hand on my waist kept me upright.

My husband lounged against the bar.

SEVENTEEN

There's a difference between dawn's lavender and dusk's lavender. At dawn, a lavender sky is pure and hopeful. At dusk, the same color makes promises that are far from innocent.

Henry was positively bathed in lavender light.

He was a philanderer, a blackmailer, possibly a murderer, and definitely my soon-to-be ex-husband, but for a half-second, I was glad to see him. Glad to know he wasn't dead and that he hadn't abandoned Grace entirely. Then his handsome features scrunched up into the smug, superior smirk that was half to blame for the death of our marriage and I wished he'd stayed missing.

"Do you want to go talk to him?" Hunter asked.

Oh dear Lord. "No." It would end in a scene. Free entertainment for everyone on the terrace with scathing reviews appearing on the phone lines first thing in the morning.

Hunter's lips quirked. "Another dance?"

"Another drink. Let's go back to the table."

Henry's expression turned dark when he realized I wasn't going to come skipping over because he'd deigned to appear. He could glower all he wanted. I wasn't one of the women who wanted to please him, and I wasn't going to go trotting over like a dutiful wife when what I really wanted to do was borrow an Oldsmobile station wagon, the country club version of a Sherman tank, and run him down.

I also wanted to find out where he'd been. While I was at it, I wanted to tell him he needed to find a new place to live—preferably someplace hot and fiery with demons and pitchforks.

Hunter escorted me back to Mother and Daddy's table.

"I'll say one thing, sugar, your life isn't dull." Daddy scowled in Henry's direction.

Unfortunately, Daddy's scowl did nothing to slow Henry's progress across the crowded terrace. Then again, given the look of furious determination on my husband's face, I doubt Mother's dragon stare would have slowed him down.

Henry reached the table and his bred-to-the-bone good manners kicked in. My husband might be the scum of the earth, but his mother had taught him to greet his elders and the lesson had stuck. "Frances, Harrington, nice to see you."

Neither of my parents responded.

"Lovely weather for June."

My parents stared at him, slightly incredulous looks on their faces.

"Where have you been?" I asked.

He lowered his chin, tilted his head and gave me another half-smile that was really a smirk. "Duluth." Then he offered the smile to my father. "Harrington, I thought you were in Carmel."

"I came home when someone attacked my daughter and put her in the hospital with a head injury." It's been said that the perfect martini involves filling a glass with gin then waving it in the general direction of Italy. Daddy's voice was dryer than that.

A slight flush stained Henry's cheeks. He didn't respond well to criticism—even implied criticism. "Obviously there's no permanent harm done. Ellison was out there dancing like she thinks she's Ginger Rogers." His eyes narrowed. "I guess that makes you Fred Astaire, Tafft."

Hunter's hand, which still rested lightly on my lower back, fisted. I stepped away from his touch.

"What do you want, Henry?" I tried to keep my voice low so the Robertsons, who were dining at the table closest to us, wouldn't hear.

"I went home and my key didn't work." He glared at me some more. "Where's Harriet?"

"She quit after your office was burglarized." No need to tell him that Hunter had fired her first.

"My office?" Amazing how much worry and concern could be imparted with two little words.

"Your office." Let him worry about the contents of the safe. I wasn't going to say a word unless he asked.

His lips thinned to nothing. "What was taken?"

"We're not sure."

"Did they open the safe?"

I hid a manufactured yawn with the tips of my fingers then waved my hand. Airily I hoped. "No, but the police are getting a subpoena to open that." Who cared if it wasn't true? My little lie was nothing compared to all the things he'd done.

There's a certain satisfaction in seeing someone you'd like to serve a strychnine cocktail go pale and stumble backward just from the force of your words.

Unfortunately, he recovered quickly. "Why did you change the locks?"

Hadn't he been listening? "The break-in."

"I want a key." He held out his hand as if he actually expected me to hand over my keys.

"No."

A moment of silence ensued. One in which Henry glared at me, my parents glared at Henry, and I glared at everyone on the terrace who was leaning forward trying to listen to our conversation. "I'm filing for a divorce. You can come get your things tomorrow."

"We're not getting divorced." Henry shifted his stare to Daddy until my father's gaze dropped.

If Henry thought he could use whatever dirt he had on Daddy to keep me in our marriage, he was delusional.

"We are." I crossed my arms over my chest. "I'll be asking for primary custody of Grace and the house."

"Dream on, Ellison." The sneer on Henry's face might have once turned my blood cold. Now I didn't care if his face froze that way. I knew things now and even if it made me as despicable as Henry, I was willing to use them against him if it meant getting custody of Grace.

I took a step closer to my husband and lowered my voice to a whisper. No one but Henry would hear what I had to say. "I know about Madeline and Kitty and Prudence and Mistress K. I know you've been blackmailing our friends. You will not fight me on this."

"Oh, I'll fight you and I'll fight dirty." His eyes cut toward my father. "You will not divorce me."

What had Daddy done? Maybe I should have looked in the envelope. Or not. I didn't want to know. Maybe I could ask Hunter to look for me. I had to find out if what he saw was covered by attorney-client privilege.

In the meantime, I didn't want Henry to see me looking the least bit concerned. I wrinkled my nose as if he'd said something funny. "We'll see. The police want to talk to you about Madeline's murder. You're a suspect."

"I didn't do it."

"That's what all guilty people say."

He puffed his chest and wagged a finger in my face. "Don't push me, Ellison."

"Or what? You'll beat Prudence and Kitty extra hard?" I searched the patio until my gaze lit on Kitty. "I hear they like it."

"Bitch." His voice was loud enough to attract the attention of the people on the terrace who weren't already trying to eavesdrop.

I straightened my shoulders, stiffened my spine, and tried to look tougher than I felt. "Come get your things tomorrow."

"This is all your fault." He spoke loud enough for everyone on the terrace and maybe even the people on the pool deck to hear.

My fault? Oh, yes—because I'd dared have a career. If I'd only squelched my one talent and done everything Henry wanted, this never would have happened. He never would have cheated on me or blackmailed half the country club or disappeared when his mistress was murdered.

Obviously, it was my fault. I didn't bother to respond. Instead,

I borrowed a move from Mother's playbook and raised my left eyebrow.

His chest deflated slightly. I wasn't reacting the way I was supposed to. I didn't try to appease him. I failed to offer up concessions. I wasn't being Ellison.

"You should call Grace," I said. "She's worried about you."

"And you weren't?" Faster than the speed of the club tennis champion's serve, Bullying Henry was replaced by Charming Henry. Charming Henry wouldn't get his way either.

"Only so far as it affects Grace."

"I told Grace where I was going." He offered up his best how-can-you-possibly-resist-me smile and held his hands out, fingers splayed, palms up.

Ah yes, Henry Russell, Father of the Year. He was easy to resist. "You told Grace to lie. Where were you, Henry?"

"Toledo." Again with a smirk.

"You just said Duluth."

"Maybe it was Provo." Henry rocked back on his heels, well pleased to have thought of three cities I knew he'd never visit.

"Have you ever considered a trip to Leavenworth?" It was nearby and the only prison I knew.

I glanced at the table. Daddy looked like his veal was doing a rumba in his stomach. Mother regarded me as if I was some new and heretofore undiscovered species. Hunter, well...He was grinning at me. The kind of grin that made half the women in Kansas City jump into bed with him and the other half want to. I grinned back—partly because Hunter's grin really was irresistible and partly because I knew it would annoy Henry.

Wow, did it.

"Don't you smile at him. Are you fucking my wife?"

So much for Charming Henry.

His voice carried, loud enough for the people inside the clubhouse to hear. Around us, forks froze in mid-air, conversations ceased. Even the lightning bugs out on the golf course stopped glowing their little behinds.

Hunter's grin disappeared. It was replaced by a stern, lawyerly expression.

By contrast, I goggled. Henry had been boinking at least three women and he was objecting to me sleeping with one man? "What if he is?"

Mother sucked in air through her teeth. Daddy reached for his drink.

"You're *my* wife."

"You're my husband and that never stopped you from—" I glanced at my parents and edited out all sorts of things they didn't need to know "—carrying on with Madeline." Or Prudence. Or Kitty. Or who knew whom else.

"Your wife and I have a strictly professional relationship," Hunter said.

"It didn't look too professional when your hand was inching toward her ass on the dance floor."

It had been? I hadn't noticed.

"Be that as it may, I'm not sleeping with your wife." He grinned again then added, "Yet."

My stomach flip-flopped, Mother choked on her martini, and Daddy looked like he'd prefer to be dining with the Khmer Rouge.

"This isn't over, Ellison."

We had the attention of the entire terrace. Above us, people in the clubhouse had discreetly gathered around the windows. We'd become a spectacle. The evening's entertainment. Fodder for gossip. *One of them probably murdered Madeline Harper but after what I saw at the club last night, it's a cinch they didn't do it together.*

I went to my chair and grabbed the thin strap of my handbag.

"You're not walking out on this." Henry was using his masterful voice. It might work at Club K but I'd had it up to my eyeballs with his...his shit.

I tried Mother's raised eyebrow trick again then reached into my bag. There wasn't much in it—a lipstick, pressed powder, keys, my driver's license, and a business card—Detective A. Jones, homicide. I gave the card to Hunter. "Would you mind going inside and calling Detective Jones? I promised to let him know when Henry turned up."

"Bitch." White lines appeared around Henry's mouth and his eyes narrowed to slits.

Hunter hesitated.

"Go," I said. "We're on the terrace at the club. What could possibly happen?"

Hunter went. Everyone on the terrace watched him walk from our table to the clubhouse's French doors and disappear through them. Then their collective gazes returned to the main event—Henry and me.

My husband glanced around the terrace, apparently realizing for the first time that we were providing a summer's worth of gossip in one night. He lowered his voice. "We have things to discuss."

We'd had things to discuss for days. Instead he'd been gallivanting across the country doing God knew what. We'd had things to discuss for the past eighteen months. I'd just refused to acknowledge that a terrible marriage was worse than no marriage. I'd kept my mouth shut and put up with infidelity and...and depravity for Grace's sake. No more. He wanted a discussion? Fine. He'd get a discussion. On my terms. "Call my lawyer."

The color drained from Henry's face. All that was left was the blazing blue of his eyes and the pale slash of his mouth. "Bitch."

"You already called me that."

Maybe Henry was used to the rules at Club K. Maybe I had too much faith in the rules of polite society. At any rate, I never saw it coming. Henry slapped me so hard my head snapped. Even through the ringing in my ears, I could hear the collective gasp of the peanut gallery. Tears filled my eyes. Anger? Embarrassment? Pain? Who knew?

My father leapt from his seat, his hands closed into tight fists. If Henry's face was the color of ice, Daddy's was like fire—flushed red with brows drawn together and teeth clenched.

A brawl at the country club? Please, God, no.

I grabbed for his arm. "Daddy, don't. It's not worth it."

My father pulled against my hold.

"Harrington," Mother's voice cut through Daddy's rage. "Don't. We'll punish him in court."

Henry's mouth hung open and deep furrows marked his forehead. If anything, he looked more shocked by the slap than the onlookers. "I...I didn't mean to do that, Ellison. I'm sorry. You shouldn't have made me so angry."

I stared at him. I shouldn't have made him so angry? I shook my head and wished that my eyes would stop leaking. "Go to hell."

Mother dipped her hand into her water goblet, caught some ice and deposited it in her napkin. Then she rose from her chair and brought it to me. I held it against my cheek.

"You will not see my daughter again." Mother's voice was emotionless, implacable. "If you come near her, we will file assault charges." She offered everyone around us an expansive wave. "I'd say we have at least sixty or seventy witnesses."

Henry opened his mouth to speak but Mother held up a finger for silence.

"You are a disgrace. You don't deserve a woman like Ellison or a daughter like Grace." Mother scanned the terrace until her glance lit upon Kitty Ballew and then her lip curled. Did she know? How could she know? "I am going to make sure they're protected from you. Forever."

Henry scowled. Deeply. Then he turned on his heel and stalked off. Shocked silence followed him.

Daddy pulled me into a one-armed hug. "Are you all right?"

I nodded, afraid that if I spoke tears would turn into sobs.

"Well, sugar, at least it can't get any worse."

I hate it when my father is wrong.

EIGHTEEN

I drove home from the club and parked behind Aggie's ailing Beetle, Bessie. An hour hadn't been enough rest for the car to start again. A whole day hadn't been enough.

Max met me at the front door with his usual crotch sniff and a doggy smile, and I led him to the backyard where he took care of his doggy business. Then I peeked into Henry's study. Aggie had accomplished more in a day than I would have in a week. Most of the dust was gone, many of the books had been returned to their shelves and the broken furniture had been moved to the corner of the room. Next I checked to see if Grace was back from babysitting. I tapped softly on her door then opened it just in case she was wearing headphones and didn't hear me.

Her empty room was plastered with posters of Davy Jones and Paul McCartney, discarded clothes covered the floor, and a stack of books wobbled precariously next to her unmade bed. If my childhood bedroom had ever approached that level of messiness, I would have been treated to a three-hour lecture on the importance of neatness then grounded for a month. I ought to say something about her room to Grace when she got home, but the energy for that particular battle simply wasn't there.

I traded the Missoni dress for a soft t-shirt and a pair of shorts then climbed the stairs to my studio. I needed the comfort that painting offered.

For the first time ever a blank canvas failed to welcome me.

I've always been able to express my feelings with paint, but now my feelings didn't want to be expressed. Perhaps they were too jumbled or too ugly. Perhaps they too were wishing I could step back in time and kick Henry in the nuts instead of tearing up like a pathetic doormat.

I sat in the shabby, comfortable easy chair I kept in the corner and stared at the walls.

Tomorrow, I'd call the divorce attorney Hunter had recommended.

Tomorrow, I'd find a way to destroy Daddy's file and maybe all the others too.

Tomorrow, I'd begin a new life.

I heard paws and feet climbing the stairs and tried to at least sit up straight. I managed to wedge myself into the corner of the chair in an approximation of having a spine.

Grace paused in the doorway to look at the blank canvas then me. The skin around her eyes looked tight and she was pale beneath her tan.

"How was babysitting?" I asked.

"I got a couple of phone calls. Are you okay?" Of course she'd heard. What passed between Henry and me was way too interesting to stay on the terrace. The story had probably scorched the phone lines.

"Fine," I lied.

"I heard you were making out with Mr. Tafft on the dance floor."

"Mr. Tafft and I danced on the dance floor."

"I heard Daddy punched you in the stomach."

I touched my cheek. "He slapped me."

"Are you okay?" she repeated.

"No. But I will be. Do you want to sit?" I nodded toward a beanbag.

Grace dragged it across the floor, stopped directly in front of me, then dropped into it and crossed her legs.

"I'm filing for divorce."

"About time," she mumbled. She sounded like she didn't care, but I searched her face, looking for signs she was upset.

There weren't any.

"Your father and I both love you very much. That will never change."

"I know, Mom." Teenagers know everything.

"Your father is coming over tomorrow to pick up his things. Please don't give him a new key to the house."

She stared at me for a moment as if I'd insulted her intelligence. "No problem."

So far so good. "You're taking this really well."

"Well, duh." She rolled her eyes. "The writing's pretty much been on the wall, even before Dad disappeared. Did he tell you where he went?"

"Not really."

Grace cocked her head so her ear almost touched her shoulder then raised a brow in a close approximation of Mother's you-don't-have-the-sense-God-gave-a-goose look. "Did you ask?"

I took a deep breath and reminded myself that all teenagers have attitude problems. Poor Grace had had a lot thrown at her. I ought to cut her a bit of slack. "Of course I asked."

"He didn't tell you?"

"First he said he'd gone to Duluth, then Toledo, and then Provo."

She snorted. "Yeah, right. I bet he doesn't even know that Provo's in Idaho."

"Utah," I corrected.

"Whatever. It looked bad, him being gone like that after Mrs. Harper's murder."

I couldn't argue that. "The police are going to want to talk to him."

She shrugged. "They have to know he's back first."

"They know."

"How?"

"I told them." Well, actually, Hunter told them but he did it on my behalf.

"How could you do that?" Grace's voice rose an octave with

each word. "What if he gets arrested?" Here was the breakdown I'd been anticipating.

"Gracie, calm down. Your dad didn't kill Mrs. Harper but the police have to talk to him to clear him." God, I hoped Henry hadn't murdered Madeline.

My daughter crossed her arms and glared at me.

"You were there when I told Detective Jones I'd let him know when I heard from your father."

"I didn't think you'd actually do it."

We stared at each other for a moment. I huddled in a chair, pretending to be strong and resolute. Grace, sitting Indian-style with a straight back and teardrops on her lashes.

She spoke first. It was barely a whisper. "What if he did it?"

"He didn't."

"Yeah, but what if he did?"

Then Grace's father would go to prison for murder and we'd muddle through. I dredged up an authoritarian voice I didn't know I had. "He didn't."

"But..."

The doorbell saved me from having to repeat what I hoped wasn't a lie for a third time. I glanced at my watch. Eleven o'clock. Way too late for social calls. "I probably ought to answer that."

She shrugged. "Whatever."

"Are you okay?"

She burrowed into the beanbag. "Yeah."

This was all Henry's fault. If he could only keep his dick in his pants...If he hadn't decided to blackmail everyone we knew...I paused on the steps. Why had Henry decided to blackmail our friends? It wasn't as if we needed the money. Did he enjoy the power? The control?

The doorbell rang again and Max and I descended the remaining stairs, went to the front door and peeked through one of the panels of glass running vertically next to it. Powers stood on the other side.

I opened the door and he swallowed me in an encompassing

hug. Then his hands closed on my shoulders and he pushed me away so he could search my face. "I was worried you might be in the hospital again. I heard that Henry beat you bloody when he caught you sneaking off onto the golf course with Hunter Tafft."

He loosed one of my shoulders and clasped my chin, turning my face from side to side. "You don't look bloody."

"He just slapped me."

"The beast. Why?"

"I made him mad."

Power's eyes lit with interest. "So you were sneaking off with Hunter."

"Of course not." I took a quick breath. "I'm going to file for divorce."

"It's about time." Powers glanced around the foyer as if he worried that Henry might be listening. "Where is he?"

"I don't know."

He pursed his lips. "Guess."

"With Prudence Davies?" I doubted if he'd go to the Ballew's. I couldn't see John welcoming him.

"No!"

"I'm afraid so."

"So he replaced Madeline already."

I shut my eyes on the image of Henry's foursome. "Not exactly."

"He was cheating on Madeline?"

The damn picture still played on my closed lids. I opened my eyes. "Not exactly."

His face lit with interest. "How delicious. Do tell." Powers has a tendency to forget that Henry's actions can affect Grace.

"Can we talk about something else?" I really didn't want my daughter to overhear a discussion of her father's...depravities.

Powers extended his lower lip in a pout.

I crossed my arms.

Powers huffed. "Fine. Did you find out where he's been?"

"He wouldn't really say."

"Did he say what was in the safe?"

I tried out the *you-don't-have-the-sense-God-gave-a-goose* look.

"Stop trying to look like your Mother. It doesn't work for you." He brushed past me and stuck his head in the study then flipped on a light. "Did you lure Harriet back? It looks almost like an office again."

"No. Aggie did that."

"Aggie? I assume that explains the jalopy in the driveway. Does she live in?"

"No. Her car wouldn't start."

"Well, she's a miracle worker."

He stepped into the study and parked himself in front of the painting that hid the safe. "I always liked this series."

"The critics didn't."

"To hell with the critics. What do the critics know? Half of them can't tell the difference between Roy Lichenstein and Stan Lee."

It wasn't remotely true—art critics can definitely distinguish pop art from comic books—but it was nice of him to say.

"Did you find the combination? I'd love to know what Henry is hiding."

"Cash and a gun."

"Really?" His spring green eyes searched my face "That's all?"

"That's all." I didn't scratch my nose. I didn't shift my weight from foot to foot. I didn't do anything to let Powers know I was lying by omission.

He shrugged. "I expected something more interesting."

"Like what?"

"Dirty pictures or cooked books or a signed confession. Who knows? It's Henry we're talking about."

Quite possibly all of those things were in the safe. I manufactured a yawn.

He glanced at his watch. "You're tired?"

I yawned again. "It's late."

He wrinkled his nose and stuck out his tongue. "Be that way."

What way? Tired and cranky with a headache, still needing to deal with a teenage girl whose parents were murder suspects? Fine, I would be. "Good night, Powers. You were a dear to stop by." I pushed him toward the front hall.

He leaned forward and kissed me on the cheek. "Are you sure you don't want me to stay? What if Henry shows up here tonight?"

If he did, Powers would be about as useful as an unstrung tennis racket.

"I'll be fine. See you in the morning."

Powers ventured outside and I locked the door behind him. Then I checked every other lock on the first floor. Finally, I trudged up the stairs.

Grace had relocated from my studio to my bedroom. She was asleep in my bed. I curled up next to her and didn't move for five hours.

I woke up in the absolute darkness, at an hour when most people were still clinging to sleep. Not me. I had too much on my mind to sleep. The thoughts trapped in my head circled and buzzed like a swarm of angry bees.

I glanced at the clock. It was only twenty minutes before my usual wake-up time. I dragged myself out of bed, brushed my teeth, then pulled on a swimsuit and a sweatshirt. Grace didn't move. Then again, she was a teenager. She wouldn't move until noon without an alarm as loud as a rock concert.

I stepped out onto the front steps, took a deep breath of humid air, climbed into my car and threw it into reverse.

Rather than glide smoothly down the drive it thumped, like I'd run over a bag of lawn clippings or a stack of kickboards.

I stopped the car before I ran over whatever it was with the front wheels too. There'd been nothing in my driveway when I came home. I got out and looked.

The reflection of my front lights off Aggie's bumper shone brightly enough for me to see a body half beneath my car. Loafers and khakis protruded from under the rear passenger door as if a well-dressed mechanic had decided to take a look at the undercarriage. A mechanic who wore no socks.

Shit. I'd run over a person. Had Roger passed out in front of my house again? Had I killed him?

I bent, grabbed a cold ankle and shook it gently. "I'm so sorry," I squeaked. "I'm going to get help."

The glint of the coin in one of the loafers caught my eye and I took a half-second to look more closely. Instead of a penny, the owner had inserted an English pence in his shoe. Only one man I knew did that.

I gasped for air and my heart raced faster than Roger's Jag.

I'd done it. I'd killed my husband.

NINETEEN

My hands were slick with panicked sweat and I fumbled with my house keys. First I couldn't find the right one. When I did, my hands shook too much to jam it into the lock. Finally, I got the door open, yanked the keys from the lock, and dropped them. They skittered across the floor and slid under the bombé chest.

To hell with the keys. I ran for the closest phone.

I picked up the receiver and called the operator. "Please me connect police," I jibbered.

"Pardon me, ma'am?"

"I need to speak with the police."

Seconds later, I was talking to someone who could help me—a woman who sounded like she fielded calls from hysterical wives who've just killed their no-good husbands all the time.

"Please, send help. I ran over my husband and," my voice squeaked as of I'd inhaled helium, "I think I killed him."

There was a pause, a long one. "Where are you, ma'am?"

I gave the woman my address.

"What's your name?"

"Ellison Russell. I know Detective Jones."

This time the pause was brief. "We have more than one officer named Jones, ma'am. Do you have a first name?"

I didn't. "He's a homicide detective. His first initial is 'A' and he has nice brown eyes."

I thought I heard a chuckle. "*That* Detective Jones...We get lots of calls for him. I'll let him know you called, Mrs. Russell. Help is on the way."

"An ambulance?"

I pictured her rolling her eyes or maybe she was waving to one of her co-workers to refill her coffee. She might even be making spirals near her temple with her index finger indicating another crazy lady had called for Detective A. Jones. "Yes, ma'am."

"Please hurry," I begged.

"Yes, ma'am."

I went back outside. From the front door, I couldn't see the body, just my car. The driver's side door hung open and the engine was still running. If Henry wasn't dead because I'd run over him, I was probably killing him with carbon monoxide from the tailpipe.

I hurried down the steps and turned off the car, turned off Carly Simon singing about a vain, cheating man she'd once thought cared for her. Then I threw up in the yard.

I was wiping my mouth on my sleeve when the first police car arrived.

Seconds later a fire truck arrived.

"Are you all right, ma'am?" a policeman asked.

I shook my head and pointed to my car.

"How did this happen?"

"He was behind my car. I didn't see him."

The police and the firemen conferred and then each one grabbed a fender. They bent their knees then lifted my TR6 off the body. Unfortunately, they deposited the car on my hostas.

Not that I cared. Much.

Another police car pulled up. Then another. I knew because I heard them. I couldn't see anything but Henry's body. Apparently, I'd held out hope there were actually two men in Kansas City pretentious enough to wear pence in their penny loafers. With my car gone, there was no doubt. My husband lay in a pool of blood on the driveway and he wasn't moving or groaning or demanding that the police arrest me for running him down. He had to be dead.

The policemen milled about like shoppers outside a store where a sale is about to start. The firemen got back in their truck and drove away.

I stared at the blood. There seemed to be an awful lot of it. Who knew there was so much blood in one body?

Oh dear Lord. I was a horrible person. An awful bitch. A witch of the first order. I was more concerned with the blood on my driveway than my dead husband. Worse, I couldn't dredge up a bit of grief. All I could do was wonder over how much he'd bled. I ought to feel something. At least guilt. I'd killed him. I was going to have to tell Grace I'd killed her father.

I struggled to breathe. The air was too heavy, and I couldn't get enough of it into my lungs. Lights danced at the edge of my vision, swirling with the blue and red strobe lights cast by the police cars and the dark stain beneath Henry's head. Then the world turned black.

The air was cool and dry as opposed to warm and damp. My head rested on something soft. I thought about opening my eyes but if I did, the lights, the car settled into my hostas like a bird in a nest, and the body would all be real. I'd killed my husband. Of all the ways I'd thought about ending Henry's miserable existence, I'd never considered backing over him while he lay prone on the driveway. My car fantasies had taken more of a run-him-down turn. They'd been fantasies. Not anything I ever planned on doing. I wasn't ready to face reality. I kept my eyes closed and listened to the voices in the room.

"I'd say a couple of hours."

"You're sure?"

"Hard to be exact in the driveway. Plus, it was a warm night. Call it a best guess until I get him to the lab."

"So she didn't kill him."

"Not with her car. It looks to me like someone bashed him on the head."

I peeked through my lashes.

Detective Jones stood in my living room wearing pressed khakis and a pristine button down. A homicide detective should have looked out of place standing there on my Mahal rug surrounded by six generations worth of antiques. He didn't. In fact, he probably fit in better than I did with my rumpled shirt, wrinkled shorts, and the faint whiff of...vomit. Oh goodie.

"Any idea what hit him?" Detective Jones asked.

The other man was older with droopy eyes and a face like a basset hound. "I'll let you know once I've had a closer look."

Detective Jones glanced my way. "You're sure she's okay?"

The basset hound man shrugged. "She fainted."

I fainted? I closed my lashes and considered that. On the surface, it seemed impossible. I wasn't the kind of woman who fainted. Except...how else could I explain waking up on the couch?

"She could have hit her head."

"The ground's soft."

A hand grazed across my forehead and my lashes fluttered. The gentle fingers on my skin paused then disappeared. No point in playing opossum now. I opened my eyes.

Detective Jones leaned over me. His expression was warm enough to melt chocolate, almost tender. It had been so long since a man looked at me like that—for a moment I forgot that Henry lay dead on the driveway. For a moment, I forgot my own name.

The basset hound man barked a cough and Detective Jones pulled away. Damn cough.

"Thanks, Meeks." Detective Jones dismissed the man. Maybe he planned on gazing at me some more. A woman could hope. Staring into Detective Jones' nice brown eyes beat the hell out of reality.

Meeks cleared his throat in a way that suggested Detective Jones was behaving like a complete idiot, then he disappeared into the hallway.

Detective Jones sat on the end of the couch. The end near my feet. Too far away for any gazing. "You want to tell me what happened?"

Not really. "I got in the car to go to the club and backed up. When I felt the back wheels run over something..." My stomach lurched at the memory. "I stopped. I got out, saw legs, and called the police."

"Tell me about last night."

"I got home from the club around ten. I think Grace got home around ten-thirty or so. Powers stopped by elevenish."

"So late?" Detective Jones raised a brow.

"He'd heard what happened at the club...sort of."

"What happened at the club?"

"Henry and I had an argument. He slapped me."

"And?"

"He stalked off. I didn't see him again."

"What did you argue about?"

I dragged my gaze away from Detective Jones and stared at the ceiling. "I told him I wanted a divorce."

Detective Jones said not a word. He sat at the end of my couch and waited for the rest of the story.

I looked at the ceiling. There was a small crack near the corner, a jagged line marring its smooth white expanse. I stared at it for a while. If I narrowed my eyes, it looked like a lightning bolt. Divine retribution.

Detective Jones remained silent.

I sighed and looked at the man sharing the couch with me. "Henry was angry and said he'd never give me a divorce."

"Why was he angry?"

Because I'd danced with another man. "Because I stood up to him." I went back to staring at the crack.

"What happened after Mr. Foster left?"

"I went to bed."

"Did you hear anything?"

"Nothing."

"Did you kill your husband?" His brown eyes had lost their warm expression. They were cold enough to freeze a pool full of water in mid-July. Cop eyes.

"I didn't mean to." My stomach flipped and twisted and rebelled, bile rose in my throat. I pointed at a trash basket. "Would you get that for me?" I asked through locked teeth. All things being equal, I preferred not to ruin my rug. I'd already ruined my life.

He put the basket on the rug near my head. "Running over him didn't kill him." He sounded almost kind.

The muscles in my abdomen loosened. "I didn't kill him?"

"He was dead before the wheels touched him."

I swallowed. "How did he die?" I knew. The basset hound man had mentioned it. Someone had bashed Henry in the head. My stomach tightened again and I reached for the trash basket.

"Detective Jones." A policeman stood in the doorway. "We found something."

"Something?" I echoed.

Detective Smith ignored me.

Detective Jones' eyes lost all their niceness and a cool mask covered the warmth of his smile. Full cop mode. He crossed to the door. "Where'd you find it?"

"The shrubs."

My poor hostas. First Roger parked his car on them, then four brawny men deposited my car among their leaves, and now the police were pawing through them. They might never recover.

They left the room and I pulled myself off the couch. I stood still for a moment, waiting for the stars to stop twinkling at the edge of my vision. The telephone and the door to the hallway vied for my attention. Call for help or find out what killed Henry? I took a step toward the door and the phone rang. Loud and shrill and intrusive. I answered it.

"May I please speak with Ellison Russell?" a voice asked.

"This is she."

"Ellison, it's Hunter. Someone called and said you needed me. Are you all right?"

I considered the question. My husband had been murdered. I was going to have to tell Grace her father was dead—the child slept like a rock but even she was going to wake up with all the commotion. My stomach felt like I'd ingested five or six cones of cotton candy then spent an hour on the Tilt-a-Whirl. Too bad the phone cord didn't reach the spot where I'd left the wastebasket. I was not all right. "No. Henry's dead."

The silence on Hunter's end of the phone was so thick and dense with thought it was almost tangible. After what seemed like an eon, he offered one word. "How?"

"Apparently someone banged him on the head." It was my turn to pause. I stared at the shiny black phone, the gloss of the walnut table it sat on, the colors of the rug. "I ran over the body." My stomach tilted with the whirl.

"Crap." Who knew Hunter Tafft swore? "Ellison, listen to me. Don't say anything to anybody. I'll be there in ten minutes."

Not a problem. No one was talking to me anyway. The police were busy and if I stayed inside, the nosy neighbors, still dressed in their nightgowns and pajamas covered by hastily pulled on seersucker robes, wouldn't be able to ask me any questions. I owed at least one of them a thank you for calling my attorney. Although, I didn't want to think about the amount of gossip required for them to know who was representing me. "Hunter, who called you?"

"I'm on my way," said my lawyer. "Don't talk to a soul."

"Who called you?" I insisted.

"Detective Jones," said Hunter. "Don't talk to him."

Then he hung up.

TWENTY

Once upon a time, I might have done as Hunter asked and stayed in the living room with my hands in my lap and my lips firmly sealed. Those days were gone. I wanted to know why Detective Jones had called my lawyer.

There were fewer flashing lights when I stepped outside, but the cluster of neighbors had grown to a clump. Their rest disturbed, they stood untouched on the outside of a tragedy. Later they'd drink an extra cup of coffee and complain about how very tired they were. They'd trade gossip like stock tips while Grace came to terms with her father's murder. I scowled at them.

They stared back at me like I was an exotic animal in a thoroughly mundane zoo. I shoved my hands in my pockets so I wouldn't gesture what I thought of their ghoulish curiosity.

A station wagon with a medical examiner's logo painted on its doors was parked next to Henry's blanket-covered body. Half of the policemen loitered nearby. The other half gathered round my flattened shrubs where a photographer took pictures. Flashes from his camera cut through the dawn.

I stood in the doorway, gnawing on my thumb knuckle, and considered. It wasn't too late. I could still go back inside, wait for Hunter, let someone else handle the nightmare unfolding in my front yard. Except someone had murdered Madeline, attacked me, and then murdered my husband. Grace might be in real danger. I descended a step, then another, then another until I was standing on the driveway.

My mouth was as dry as an unwatered sand trap. I inched

closer to the circle of policemen, discovered the camera clicked before it flashed, and learned to close my eyes in anticipation of its blinding light.

Walking with eyes closed, even inching with eyes closed, is a dangerous proposition. I tripped over a metal tent some policeman had left in the drive and opened my eyes to see asphalt rushing toward me...or me rushing toward asphalt. Bare knees and the heels of my hands took the impact.

I didn't move for a second. The sting of skinned knees rose to my eyes and they began to leak again. The embarrassment of falling in front of a gallery of pajama-clad onlookers and a healthy percentage of the police force warmed my cheeks. Not to mention Detective Jones. He raised his gaze from whatever nestled in my hostas to come help me.

He bent, clasped my elbow, and half-lifted me off the drive. "Are you okay?"

"Fine."

He released my arm, took a step backward and regarded my legs. "You ought to go inside and clean those up."

I glanced at my knees. Not one but two strawberries. Impressive ones. Knees an eight year-old boy would brag about while recounting an unlikely story about diving for a fly ball. Blood trickled down my shins.

I wasn't going back inside. I was tired of being a spectator in my own life, watching with detachment as my husband cheated and lied. I was tired of pleasing Mother because it took less energy than arguing. I was tired of abdicating responsibility. "What killed Henry?"

Detective Jones shook his head. "You really ought to go take care of those knees."

"I'm fine. What killed him?"

"A golf club."

Figured. How many times had I imagined some poor unsuspecting golf ball as Henry's head? Obviously someone else had the same fantasy. "What kind of club?"

"Golf."

"Yes. You said that. Left-handed or right-handed? What brand? Is it engraved?"

Detective Jones blinked. "You can tell by looking if a golf club is left-handed or right-handed?"

"Yes."

"Come take a look."

A three-iron lay in my hostas, its head darkened with blood. My stomach and what little was left inside it lurched. I took a deep breath and moved my gaze from the club face to the shaft and grip. Then I turned away.

"It's a left-handed club."

"Can you tell me anything else?"

Hunter's warning—*don't talk to him*—reverberated in my ears. No need to tell Detective Jones it looked like a MacGregor. My MacGregor. My golf clubs were in the trunk of my car. It would be all too easy for someone to slide an iron out of the bag then hit Henry with it. The police might think that someone was me. "I'd like to sit down."

Detective Jones led me to the front stoop and I claimed the top step. Then I rested my elbows on my thighs and let my head sink to my hands.

I expected Detective Jones to go back to the golf club in the shrubs. Instead, he sat next to me. "Where's your daughter?"

"Asleep."

He took a moment to inventory the flashing lights and policemen and vehicles in my front yard. "Through this?"

"You don't have teenagers, do you?"

"No kids."

I raised my head from my hands. "Grace could sleep through the apocalypse." The policemen around the three-iron were moving. Maybe they were going to pick it up, take it into evidence, and discover my initials engraved just beneath the grip. EWR. My ticket back to the police station. Maybe my ticket to jail. "Thank you for calling my lawyer."

Detective Jones' gaze remained fixed on the crime scene in my front yard. His body tensed. "I'd appreciate it if you didn't mention that to anyone."

"Done."

I'd found two bodies in less than a week. My husband and his mistress. Even I thought I looked guilty. Yet, he'd still called my lawyer. "Why'd you do it?"

He raised a brow.

"Why did you call Hunter Tafft for me?"

He opened his mouth. He might have answered me, but Mother and Daddy chose that moment to push past the policeman at the end of the driveway. For perhaps the first time in her adult life, Mother didn't look bandbox perfect. Backcombed hair was flattened on the left side of her head and she hadn't bothered to tuck in her shirt.

Mother charged up the drive like an enraged rhinoceros, brushing past uniformed police officers, near trampling someone in a medical examiner's uniform. "Ellison, are you all right?"

"Fine," I lied.

"You don't look fine." She stared at my bloody knees. "You look pale. Is that blood on your face?"

I glanced at my bloodied palms. "Probably."

Detective Jones stood, cleared his throat.

Mother ignored him. "Elaine Markham called me. She said the police were here."

Daddy took Detective Jones' spot on the stoop and cradled my hand as if it was something precious. "You okay, sugar?"

"Henry's dead. Murdered."

Mother's sharp intake of breath was audible above the chatter of the neighbors, the conversation of the police, the too loud beating of my heart.

Daddy wrapped his arm around my shoulders. "Who killed him?"

I shook my head. "I ran over his body."

"*Ellison!*"

All the air Mother had drawn into her lungs was expelled with one word.

"I didn't kill him. He was already dead."

Mother goggled. Scandalized. "You ran over your husband's body?"

"It was an accident. I didn't see him in the driveway."

"I just don't understand how this happened. If you had—"

"Enough." My father's voice cut through whatever list of complaints my mother had been about to begin. His gaze cut toward Detective Jones.

"Mother, Daddy, this is Detective Jones. Detectives Jones, these are my parents, Frances and Harrington Walford."

My parents stared at Detective Jones. He stared back. Mother was the first to look away. "Nice to meet you." Then, unfortunately, her gaze returned to me. "You can't stay here. You and Grace will have to move in with your father and me until the police," she inclined her head toward Detective Jones, "catch this maniac."

Move in with Mother? Getting whacked on the head again would be less painful. On the other hand, how could I make Grace stay in a house where both of her parents had been attacked? I gritted my teeth. "Thank you, Mother."

Mother's chin dropped, her eyes narrowed, and she pursed her lips. I'd deprived her of an argument she'd looked forward to winning. She rallied quickly. "Go in and pack."

"Not now."

"Pardon me?" Mother's brows, perfectly groomed arcs of disbelief, rose to her forehead.

"Grace is still asleep. She doesn't know yet. We'll come later today."

Daddy squeezed my hand, which hurt like hell.

Mother's lips thinned then she reached up to pat her perfect hairdo and discovered the flat area on the side of her head. Her hand dropped and the morning's half-light revealed an uncharacteristic flush on her cheeks.

"Ellison, I believe I'll step inside."

My father stood to make room for her to pass. I glanced at Detective Jones. His forehead was wrinkled, his lips were parted. He looked almost wistful. Almost like he wanted a battle-axe mother who never had a hair out of place. He wouldn't if he had one.

"Jones," one of the policemen shouted from his post atop my hostas, "over here."

"Excuse me." Detective Jones left me with my father.

We sat in silence, unsure of what to say. Finally, Daddy asked, "What killed him?"

"Golf club. A three-iron."

Daddy's lips quirked—so slightly I almost missed it. He wouldn't mourn Henry. I touched the cheek my husband had slapped. I wouldn't mourn him either. Mother might. Grace would.

The medical examiner chose that moment to load my husband's body into the back of his station wagon. He really was dead. In life, Henry would never have ridden in a station wagon.

"It's a left-handed club. It looks like a MacGregor."

My father and I have been playing golf together since I was old enough to swing a golf club. He knew my clubs. His gaze settled on the growing mob on the sidewalk across the street. "Lots of people play MacGregors."

"Their spouses are still alive."

"Not Madeline Harper." Daddy rubbed his hands together as if he'd discovered the secrets of cold fusion. "Roger Harper plays MacGregors."

"Is he left-handed?" I asked.

Daddy thought for a moment, probably playing through Roger's swing in his mind. Then he nodded. "He is."

I couldn't see Roger as a murderer. A man who'd willingly put himself in Mistress K's clutches didn't have the strength of character to kill two people. Did he? Did it take strength of character to commit murder? Did committing murder suggest a gaping lack of character? I shook my head, unsure of the answer.

Daddy looked like he might be ready to lay out a case against poor Roger when we were distracted by a flurry of activity at the base of the drive. A moment later, Hunter slipped past the policeman who kept the curious at bay at the bottom of the driveway.

"Your mother will be thrilled." Daddy spoke through the side of his mouth, barely moving his lips. "Although, you might want to go clean up a little. If she knows Hunter is here with you looking like...like you've had a rough morning, her head will spin."

Me? Rough morning? My husband was dead. My legs were bloodied. I'd agreed to move back to my parents' home. Frankly, seeing Mother's head spin might lend the proceedings some much-needed comic relief. I kept my seat on the front stoop.

"Harrington." Hunter acknowledged my father then turned his gaze to me. "Ellison, how are you?"

"Fine." The lie was getting easier with repetition.

Hunter rolled his eyes. "Uh huh. What happened to your knees?"

"I tripped."

Mother emerged from the house, her hair perfect, her shirt neatly tucked in to the waistband of her skirt, order restored. When she saw Hunter, her lips stretched into a smile. "Thank God Ellison had the good sense to call you."

Neither Hunter nor I corrected her about my lack of good sense.

"How much longer do you think they'll be?" She waved her hand at the policemen combing through the remains of my hostas.

"I couldn't say," Hunter replied.

She nodded as if he'd provided her with a satisfactory answer. "I believe someone ought to warn the neighbors."

Daddy, Hunter, and I blinked. I spoke. "Warn them about what?"

She sighed as if my slowness was a heavy cross to bear. "Someone needs to tell them there's a killer on the loose."

"They think it's me," I whispered. My lips barely moved.

"Yes, dear. And they'll keep on thinking it's you unless we offer them an alternative. When these policemen," she waved again, "go talk to them, don't you want your neighbors to say something besides *Henry was a terrible husband. Ellison did it. Did you know Roger Harper spent the night with her on Tuesday?*"

"Did he?" Hunter asked.

"He passed out on the front stoop. I didn't know he was here until morning."

Daddy grunted. "Man never could hold his liquor." For my father, such a weakness was unforgivable.

Mother descended the stairs. "Lovely to see you, Hunter. I hope you'll stay for breakfast."

Mother had lost her mind. If I hadn't been arrested by breakfast, I'd be comforting Grace over the loss of her father. I scowled at her.

She ignored me and swanned down the drive toward the milling mob eager for news.

Behind me, the door opened. Every muscle in my body tensed in anticipation.

"Mom, what's going on?"

There was the question I'd been dreading all morning, and I didn't have anything like a good answer. I felt as flattened as my hostas, but I stood, took my daughter's hand, and led her inside to tell her that her father was dead.

TWENTY-ONE

Telling Grace her father had been murdered was the worst experience of my life. Worse than finding him *in flagrante* in the coat closet with Madeline. Worse than swimming into Madeline's body. Worse than running over Henry's.

Grace sank onto the living room sofa as if her body was too heavy for her knees to hold. When she was sitting, she brought those knees up to her chest, wrapped her arms around them, and rocked. An egg about to crack. A girl about to shatter.

I should have spent the hours while she slept preparing, found the words to soften the blow, put aside my disbelief and fear and thought of nothing but my daughter. Too late now.

She rocked. She keened. Tears ran unchecked down her cheeks.

I had nothing to offer but the dubious comfort of my arms around her shoulders, my hands smoothing her hair, my voice whispering soft lies. *It will be all right.* It wouldn't. *He didn't feel any pain.* For all I knew it had hurt like hell. I hoped it had. *He loved you so much.* That at least was true.

I don't know how long she cried. Long enough for the bars of sunshine on the carpet to grow bright, to move from the club chair by the fireplace to the mahogany table my great-great-grandfather brought to Kansas City in a covered wagon, to the couch where we sat wrapped in grief.

I hated whoever had caused Grace so much pain, and I hated Henry for getting himself killed. Whoever was responsible had to pay. Each tear that filled Grace's reddened eyes hardened my resolve.

Finally, her sobs lessened. She crawled into my lap as if she was six instead of sixteen and rested her head on my shoulder. "What happens now?" she asked.

"Now we go and stay with your grandparents."

She shuddered. "Why?"

"I don't think it's safe for us to stay here."

Her body stiffened. "Who would do this?"

Anyone with their name on an envelope in Henry's safe. Maybe even Roger. "I don't know."

When we emerged from the living room, my parents had gone home. The policemen still poked around the remains of my hostas, and some helpful souls had lifted my car out the shrubbery and put it back on the driveway. Detective Jones had gone. Hunter had not. He stood when we entered the foyer.

Grace ignored him and trudged up the stairs. "I'll go pack."

I nodded. "I'll be up in a minute."

When Grace had disappeared upstairs, Hunter said, "The police want to talk with you again."

No surprise there. I expected nothing less. "Have they opened my trunk?" I asked.

Hunter cocked his head to the side, not sure what I was talking about.

"To my car. Did they open the trunk of my car?"

"I don't think so. Why?"

I looked at the crown moldings, I looked at the turned spindles of the banister, I looked at the stack of mail on the bombé chest. "There's a possibility," I mumbled, "that the golf club used to kill Henry is mine. My clubs are in the trunk of my car."

Hunter rubbed his chin, said nothing. Nothing. The silence lengthened like moonbeams across midnight water. Lovely, ephemeral, hiding a dark secret. His eyes, usually bright and observant stared into the middle distance, unseeing. Finally, he spoke. "You have to tell the police."

Like hell I did. I wanted to know what was in my trunk before I told them anything. "I need a cup of coffee."

Hunter followed me into the kitchen. "Detective Jones is no fool. He'll be back to look for golf clubs."

I located the filters and scooped grounds into the Mr. Coffee. Its cheery yellow and white seemed entirely inappropriate. Why didn't they make them in gray? Or black? Then again, who cared as long as it produced coffee? I pushed the button and waited for ambrosia. While the pot filled, I considered Hunter's point. It was a good one.

I would look exponentially guiltier if I said nothing and the police discovered the clubs in my car.

Damn it. Grace was upstairs crying. I ought to think about her not Henry's death or the appearance of guilt or innocence. It shouldn't matter how things appeared. I hadn't killed him. If my golf club had, my innocence wouldn't make any difference.

Appearances were what mattered.

I'd found Madeline's body. Madeline's husband and his car had spent the night at my house. My husband and I had a loud, violent fight in front of half the country club. Now he was dead. I appeared very, very guilty.

If I hadn't been whacked on the head I'd probably be drinking my coffee in jail. Did they have coffee in jail? I opened the cupboard, grabbed two mugs, filled them, handed one to Hunter then took a bracing sip. "Fine. I'll tell him." After I'd looked.

The doorbell rang. It did that way too often of late. I took another sustaining sip of coffee then headed to the foyer.

When I opened the door, a fresh-faced policeman said, "We're done for now, Mrs. Russell. Detective Jones asked me to give you his card. He wants you to call him to schedule a time to go down to the station and answer some questions. Today if possible." He held out a small, innocuous piece of paper.

Hunter reached around me and took it. "Mrs. Russell will call him shortly."

"Thank you, officer," I said.

The policeman nodded and turned his back, walked down the drive, climbed in to a police cruiser and drove away.

My yard was trampled, my hostas were a memory, and Aggie's car still sat in the drive, the colorful constant to the scene. The neighbors had given up watching my yard in favor of jobs or swim practice or a weekly tennis game. My Triumph now faced the other way. I could drive straight down the drive rather than backing up. Was there a subtle message in its position? Doubtful. With the exception of Detective Jones, the police hadn't displayed much subtlety.

"We can look in the trunk now."

I descended the front steps, walked oh-so-innocently to the trunk of my car, and pushed on the latch. Nothing happened. I pushed again, harder. Nothing. I pushed on the latch and tugged at the same time. The stubborn metal didn't budge.

Could it be locked? Had I for once actually locked my trunk? I dug in my pocket for the keys. It was empty.

Where were they? I'd started the car. I'd even run over my husband. They had to be around somewhere. Mentally, I retraced my steps. The rush up the front steps, the house key's stubborn refusal to open the door, success and then the keychain skittering across the floor.

I brushed past Hunter, who wasn't doing much but staring at me with lawyerly disapproval, and went inside. I dropped to my knees and reached an arm under the bombé chest. My hands closed on something soft. I pulled out Henry's favorite slipper. It had been missing for months. Part of the heel had been gnawed off—some of Max's best work. I reached again. This time my search yielded a letter addressed to Henry. It had not been chewed. I tossed it atop the chest with the rest of the mail and reached again. My fingers closed on something soft—a dust bunny that had grown to dust lion size. Yuck. Where were the damn keys? My hand slid across the smooth boards. There. The edge of something metal. Just out of reach.

I rested my cheek on the floor and extended my arm. Damn it.

I inched closer to the chest.

Behind me, Hunter exhaled. It sounded like the whiff of a golf club—that horrible whooshing sound no one ever wants to hear. Then it occurred to me. My head was on the floor. My ass was in the air. I'd been wiggling it, trying to get closer to the blasted keys.

Fortunately, Hunter couldn't see my face. The blood rushed to my cheeks. They were probably a lovely shade of napthol scarlet.

I lowered my whole body to the floor and reached again. My fingers closed on the keys but I didn't move. I gave my cheeks a second or two to return from the color of a Coke can to flesh tones. When I stood, I didn't so much as look at Hunter. I couldn't. Instead, I fumbled for the key to the trunk. When I had it, I hurried outside, opened the trunk and began to count.

One, two, three...all the way up to fourteen.

I wasn't that lucky. I counted again while ignoring Hunter's presence at my side.

"I count fourteen," he said.

"Me too."

"You only carry fourteen?" he asked.

My gaze flew to his face. Except, it wasn't a gaze, it was a glare. One worthy of mother. "Of course I only carry fourteen. Those are the rules."

He grinned as if I'd confirmed every supposition he had of me. I was an ass-wiggling, rule-following widow whose three-iron was mercifully in the trunk of her car and not in police evidence.

Relief washed over me—as invigorating as diving into a pool of chilly water, as satisfying as driving a shot straight down the fairway. My three-iron had been locked safely in my trunk. I grinned back. Well, for a moment anyway. Until I considered that someone had enough foresight to bring a golf club to my home to kill Henry. Then my grin faltered.

"Could it be Henry's club?" Hunter asked.

I shook my head. "Henry didn't play golf. Too many variables he couldn't control. Tennis was his game."

Hunter gazed at the clubs in my trunk. "You're a golfer?"

"I am."

"What did the two of you have in common?"

"Grace."

He stroked his chin. "So she's the reason you stayed with him."

I nodded. It didn't matter now. Henry was dead. There would be no contentious divorce, no embarrassing details aired in court, no sharing my daughter with Henry's latest girlfriend.

"The kinky stuff Henry did," Hunter's cheeks darkened a shade or two, "any lawyer would have won you full custody."

I shrugged. "Grace loved her father." Her dead father. Grace needed me, and I was yammering in the driveway. "Will you go to the police station with me?"

"Of course. When would you like to go?"

Never. "I need to move Grace to my parent's house. After that, I'm free."

"You're going too. To stay with your parents?"

I nodded then closed my eyes and saw my future. Mother wouldn't like what I wore or my hair or Grace's hair. We needed to look exactly right to welcome the flock of Bundt cake carrying women who would swoop in like a murder of crows. I would sit on the edge of the velvet-covered settee with my ankles crossed and a lace-edged handkerchief clutched in my hand. Every so often, Mother would touch her eyes—a reminder for me to dab at my own. I'd accept condolences, avoid questions, and wish I was someplace else—anyplace else—even a police station. What about Grace? If I defied Mother and went to the police station, could she handle being left alone at Mother's? I bit my thumb knuckle so hard it hurt.

"You're worried about your daughter?"

"Yeah." The understatement of the decade. Well...maybe not the decade. Maybe just the year.

"Your father said something about horses and taking her out to their place in the country for the rest of the day."

Daddy was a genius. If the outside of a horse was good for the inside of a man, it was an absolute balm for a teenage girl. Nothing could be better than fresh air and horses and thirty miles between Grace and the biddies who'd descend on Mother's house, who might be circling it this very moment, driving around the block with their Bundt cakes in the passenger seats until someone else parked so they wouldn't be the first to arrive. Maybe Grace and Daddy could spend the night out there. Maybe I could drive out and join them.

"Would you please call Detective Jones and see if we can go this afternoon?"

Hunter nodded. "Of course. What else can I do?"

Gratitude made me attempt a smile. It never reached my lips. "Figure out who murdered Henry." Of course, he wouldn't. That was Detective Jones' job. Or mine.

Hunter didn't seem to think I was joking. He rubbed his chin, surveyed the neighborhood and asked, "How did Henry get here?"

He was right. My husband's car was nowhere in sight.

"Is his car parked behind the house?" I asked.

We followed the curve of the driveway to the rear of the house. No car. No sign that Henry had been there recently. We stared at the reassuring sight of untrampled shrubs in silence.

Hunter hadn't asked the right question. It didn't matter how Henry got home—Prudence or Kitty could have easily given him a ride. The right question, the real question, was why he'd come home.

I knew the answer. Three hundred thousand dollars and a safe full of incriminating envelopes.

Before Grace and I went to Mother's, I had to do something about that answer.

TWENTY-TWO

When Max was hungry, he'd whap his bowl with a gigantic paw. If he was really hungry, he'd whap *me*. If that didn't get my attention, he'd lay his head on my knee and stare at me with amber eyes. If I still failed to fetch his kibble, he'd circle my legs like a cat, making it impossible to move in any direction but toward his dog food.

Fear and Max have a lot in common. First and foremost, they don't like being ignored.

There's no ignoring a dead husband.

Now that fear had my attention, it wanted sleepless nights and fuzzy mornings. It demanded I listen to every noise in the neighborhood and assess it for danger. It insisted I look over my shoulder—constantly.

I didn't much like its plan.

The killer's name was in Henry's safe, scrawled on an envelope, waiting to be discovered. I was sure of it. All I had to do was make a list of the names and figure out which one was a murderer. Yeah, right. When I was done, I'd fix the recession and find a new source for crude oil.

I could look at those names, I could even look inside the envelopes, and I'd still have no idea who'd killed my husband. I needed help.

Hunter Tafft stood next to me—strong, solid, and handsome as Paul Newman. I took a second to admire my undamaged hostas, sucked a large breath into my lungs, swallowed and said, "I've never given you a retainer."

"No. You haven't."

"If I give you one, everything I tell you is confidential, right?"

"It is anyway." He offered me a movie star grin, the kind the hero gives the heroine right before she melts into his arms.

I didn't have any inclination to melt, not while my husband's body was on the way to the morgue, my daughter was upstairs grieving, and the memory of my disastrous marriage still ached worse than a bad case of tennis elbow. "I'd feel better knowing everything is legal and binding. I'd like to write you a check."

He blinked. "Your mother already did."

Of course she had.

What other reason could there be for a lawyer who billed at God-knows-what an hour to sit around my house all morning? It wasn't concern for Grace or me, it was billable hours. I felt a twinge in the vicinity of my heart. Wounded pride? Wounded feelings? It didn't matter. Hunter Tafft was my lawyer—not my friend.

It was better that way. Friends drank too much wine and repeated your secrets at cocktail parties. They told you that you looked fabulous in a dress that made you look like a pregnant elephant. They borrowed your favorite sweater and forgot to return it.

The thought of Hunter Tafft in a soft, pink, angora sweater tickled some long-forgotten funny bone. A sound, somewhere between a giggle and snort, escaped me. "Come with me." I led him back into the house and Henry's study, swung the painting away from the wall, and begin to spin the dial on the safe.

"I thought you didn't know the combination." One eye narrowed. The brow above it dipped. Hunter looked even more like a lawyer when his expression was wry.

"Turns out I knew it after all."

He crossed his arms over his chest. "Lying to the police can get you into trouble."

"Pish." Someone had murdered my husband and left his body in the driveway. Lying to the police was the least of my worries.

"Pish?"

"Pish. I don't care about the police. I care about Grace. If I gave what was inside here to the police, Grace and I would have to move to Timbuktu just to escape the fall-out." I turned the dial to the last number and opened the safe.

It was all there. The money. The envelopes. The sinking dread.

I stepped aside so Hunter could peer into the abyss.

"What is all this?" he asked.

"Henry and Madeline were blackmailing everyone they knew."

"What's in the envelopes?"

I shuddered. "I only opened two. I'd say they hold proof of indiscretions."

"How many are there?"

"Twenty." Twenty not counting Daddy. As far as I was concerned, Daddy would never be counted. His envelope would remain hidden, unopened until I had a chance to destroy it. "I think one of these people probably killed Henry. We need to find out which one."

"You need to turn these over to the police."

"Look at the names."

He did.

Two judges, a congressman, four company chief executives, a philanthropist, the mayor, and a past president of the Junior League were among those whose names were listed. If I gave the envelopes to the police, I'd ruin the lives of so many innocent people. Well, maybe not innocent—but definitely influential. If I gave their files to the police, I could count Grace and myself in the number of ruined lives.

Hunter flipped through the envelopes and seemed to grasp the gravity of my situation. At least his brows drew together and his lips thinned. "What do you want me to do?"

"I want you to help me figure out who murdered my husband. Quietly."

He reached into the safe, pulled out the federal judge's envelope, and stared at the name. "I'll need Aggie."

"Aggie? My housekeeper?"

"She's a good investigator. Better than her husband was."

"If she's so good, why is she cleaning houses?"

"She got tired of digging into people's dirty laundry."

So she decided to do the laundry instead? "You're sure?" I asked. Somehow, Aggie with her knocking car and purple muumuu and dangly earrings seemed an unlikely investigator.

"Sometimes not looking the part is an asset." It was like he could read my mind, or maybe my face. "People underestimate her."

I wasn't about to argue anymore. "What next? Should we make a list of the names?"

His lips quirked. "Are you likely to forget any of them?"

Never. Not as long as I lived. "No. What should I do?"

"Take Grace to your parents. Meet me at the police station at two."

I glanced at the open safe.

"I'll close it when I leave," Hunter said. "You can count on me."

Henry said that once. My heart cannonballed into a pool of dread. Had I done the right thing telling Hunter? Fear sat quietly in the corner. It wasn't whapping me or staring at me or trying to direct my steps. I figured that was as close to the right thing as I was going to get.

The tanned skin on the back of my hand looked yellow, almost jaundiced in the fluorescent light of the interview room. It rested on a scarred table next to an empty Tab can.

On the other side of the table, Detective Jones glanced at his watch.

I shifted my gaze to the mirror that hung behind him.

After convincing me I could count on him, Hunter was late. Not *sorry I couldn't find a parking spot* late. That kind of late came and went thirty minutes ago. Hunter had passed into the realm of *is he even coming?* late.

"I'm sure you've got better things to do than sit here with me," I said. After all, the detective was investigating two murders. Surely there was a more profitable use of his time than listening to me not talk.

Detective Jones just smiled like sitting in silence was the most fascinating thing he'd done in years.

I went back to looking at my hands. I needed a manicure. Maybe some moisturizer. Where the hell was Hunter?

The silence stretched longer than the thirteenth fairway at Augusta.

"Why did you leave San Francisco, Detective Jones?" My voice startled us both.

"The job."

"Really? Were you a detective there as well? Grace is half in love with Michael Douglas. You know, on *The Streets of San Francisco.*" Look in the dictionary under idiot. You'll find my picture.

His lips quirked. "Television shows don't have much to do with reality."

He hadn't answered me. Detective Jones, man of mystery. I didn't know anything about him, not even his first name.

"Did you always want to be a policeman?" I asked.

He tilted his head as if he couldn't quite believe I was still trying to question him. He was the one with the questions. Who killed your husband? Why? Except, he wasn't asking them. He was actually waiting for my lawyer. Detective Jones was an honorable man. A man who followed rules. One who colored inside the lines.

The honorable man shrugged. "Or a lawyer."

"Why did you pick policeman?"

"I didn't like law school."

It was my turn to quirk a brow.

"My father is a professor at Stanford. He cared about education." The tone of his voice suggested he wasn't exactly open to any more questions.

I ignored his tone. "What does your father teach?"

"Politics."

"What about your mother? Does she work?"

"She's an artist."

I pondered that for a moment. "What kind?"

He laced his fingers together. "A sculptor."

"And you're a policeman..."

"Is that a question?" The detective raised a brow.

"Not exactly," I ceded. "Do you see them often?"

"No."

I felt rather like I'd dived into a pool and hit the bottom. Jarred by the sudden harshness of his voice. Almost bruised by the unforgiving hardness of his face. No more questions about his family. Got it. I picked up the empty pink can and stared at the white lettering. "What's your first name?"

He stared at me like I'd suddenly turned into Marvin the Martian from a Bugs Bunny cartoon.

"You want to know my name?"

"Seems only fair. You know mine."

"Everyone calls me Jones."

I put the can back on the table. The aluminum made a hollow sound.

"What do your parents call you?"

He mumbled.

"Pardon me?"

He mumbled again.

"Did you say Anthony?"

"No." He glanced over his shoulder at the mirror then leaned forward and whispered, "Anarchy."

I had to have misheard him. "That's not a name."

"It is in San Francisco."

No wonder he went by Jones. Detective Follow-the-Rules was named Anarchy? "How?"

"My father wears his politics on his sleeve."

Professor Jones advocated for the abolition of law. Detective Jones enforced them.

And I thought I had problems with Mother.

My fingers, quite of their own volition, reached across the

table. I stopped their progress before they touched Detective Jones' hand.

We both stared at them, my hand hovering an inch above his. It was as if some magnetic force was drawing me to touch him, to connect. My gaze traveled to his face, tanned, lean, a frame for the nicest brown eyes I'd ever seen. Those eyes looked into mine.

We sat, opposite sides of the table, our hands almost touching, our questions forgotten.

Then I remembered who we were. Detective Jones didn't need empathy from a murder suspect any more than I needed sympathy from the man who might arrest me. My husband was dead. My daughter was grieving. I pulled my hand away.

Anarchy Jones, police detective, honorable man continued to stare at me and my throat went dry.

"No more questions?" Was his voice regretful or amused?

Why couldn't I tell? I shook my head. I'd asked personal questions and learned more than I bargained for. "No."

"I have questions." He offered me a wry smile. "I don't think your lawyer will object to them."

I glanced at my watch for the umpteenth time. Where the hell was Hunter? "Go ahead."

"What does 'rah' mean?"

"Raw?"

"No. R.A.H. Rah."

"Where did you see it?"

"On the golf club that killed your husband."

R. A. H. Roger Ainsbrey Harper. Had I been wrong? Had Roger killed Madeline? Had he killed Henry?

"It's a monogram."

"Roger Harper's?"

"Yes. And probably a lot of other people's too."

"Anyone you know?"

"No." Damn it. Just Roger's.

"How did Mr. Harper feel about your husband's involvement with his wife?"

My shoulders stiffened, I folded my hands into my lap and crossed my ankles. "You'd have to ask him."

Detective Anarchy Jones' brown eyes flashed. "Two people are dead, Ellison."

"I don't think Roger killed them."

"What if you're wrong?"

What if I was? I looked at the dingy ceilings, the cream walls with paint gone sepia from too many years of cigarette smoke, the state of my cuticles. "Madeline was having an affair with my husband. I already told you that."

"You didn't tell me how you or Mr. Harper felt about it."

"Don't say a word, Ellison." Hunter stood in the door. He didn't look apologetic or sheepish or even embarrassed at being an hour late. He looked lawyerish—not a single silver hair was out of place, his tie quietly shouted *don't mess with me*, and his lips, thinned to a stern line, showed not a hint of humor.

"The golf club they found—it might belong to Roger Harper," I explained.

"Then clearly the detective should be talking to Mr. Harper and not you." Hunter glared at Detective Jones. Detective Jones glared back.

"Perhaps a question or two about last night?" Detective Jones clasped his hands behind his neck and leaned back in his chair. "To help us establish the timeline."

Hunter offered the slightest of nods.

"What time did Mr. Foster leave last night?" Anarchy asked.

"Around eleven-thirty."

"And you went directly to bed after he left?"

I nodded. "Yes."

"You didn't hear anything? No cars in the driveway, no doors closing, no voices?"

I'd fluffed my pillow then listened to Grace breathe. I hadn't heard anything else. "Nothing."

"What kind of car does your husband drive?"

"A Cadillac."

The man with the nice eyes had been replaced by the no-nonsense detective. "We found it parked around the corner from your house. Any idea why?"

It took all I had not to glance at Hunter. He knew the answer. Henry had planned on sneaking into our house, emptying the safe, and disappearing into the night. Someone had killed him instead. "No idea." My nose itched. Terribly. I squeezed my hands together and tried to look honest.

"That's not a timeline question, detective. If that's all?" It wasn't a question, and Hunter didn't wait for an answer. Instead, he clasped my elbow, hauled me out of my chair, and half-dragged me through the door. When we reached the hallway, his whisper in my ear was furious. "You are the worst liar on the face of the planet. If you can't tell the truth, don't say anything. It's a wonder that cop didn't arrest you based on your suspicious expression."

Anarchy wouldn't do that. Anarchy? The man investigating my husband's murder was no longer just Detective Jones. He was Anarchy, a man who had as many issues with his father as I had with my mother.

"What? What are you thinking about? You look like you sucked a lemon." Hunter hadn't let go of my elbow and he gave it a small shake. "Come along. I'll see you to your parent's house."

All things being equal, I wished he would have left me with Anarchy.

TWENTY-THREE

There were three Mercedes, a BMW, two Volvos, and four Cadillacs parked in front of Mother and Daddy's house. The Bundt cake brigade had arrived in full force.

I was tempted to drive right on past.

A glance in my rearview mirror at Hunter Tafft's car made me pull into the drive, throw my car in park, and hurry inside. I didn't want another lecture on lying to the police nor did I want to know the contents of the envelopes in my safe.

Bitty Sue Foster met me in the foyer. "You poor girl. How are you doin', sugar?"

I dredged up a weak attempt at a smile. "I've had better days."

"Ain't that the truth? Your momma has the ladies well in hand. Why don't you go freshen up?"

It was a nice way of telling me I looked like hell.

I snuck upstairs, powdered my nose, combed my hair and twisted it away from my face, then gave my lips a swipe of sea orchid pink. I was ready. Prisoners on their way to face a firing squad were more eager to face their fates than I was.

I tiptoed down the back stairs, the ones that would deliver me to the kitchen, and earn me another minutes' respite. Voices stopped me. Not the voices of Penelope, Mother's long-suffering housekeeper, or Frank, Penelope's husband who served as additional help when Mother entertained.

Instead, I heard Prudence Davies' unmistakable bray and Kitty Ballew's squeaky response. "I don't know, I just can't see her doing it."

"Who then?" Prudence sounded stuffy, almost as if she'd been crying.

"Maybe Roger. Maybe you." There was a pause then the click of high heels on hard wood and the gush of the tap. Whatever Kitty said next was lost behind the sound of running water.

The tone of Prudence's answer carried up the stairs although not the words themselves. Anger, sadness, outrage. Then the tap was turned off and I could hear again. "She was a bitch and she deserved what she got. But Henry? Never. I," Prudence's voice cracked, "I loved him." A sniffle followed. "You could have done it. It could have been you."

Kitty's laugh was as shrill as a lifeguard's whistle. "You'll never pin this on me."

The snip of a pair of scissors reached me. What the hell were they doing? Why hadn't Kitty denied killing Henry? Did I have it all wrong? Maybe it wasn't one of Henry's blackmail victims who'd killed him. Maybe it was Kitty or Prudence.

"I saw you looking at him last night," said Prudence. "You were furious."

"Weren't you? He disappeared and I worried. I couldn't sleep for worrying. Then when he finally comes home, he goes to the country club to see the Ice Queen and ignores us."

They called me the Ice Queen? I swallowed a hysterical giggle and considered sneaking back up the stairs, but I stayed put.

"It's always been like that."

Another snip and then Kitty said, "He didn't ignore Madeline."

Neither spoke for a moment. Were it not for the occasional sound of scissors cutting through something, I would have thought the kitchen empty.

Prudence broke the silence, her voice, thick with tears, still conveyed disdain. "You thought you'd take Madeline's place. That was never going to happen. You aren't kinky enough."

"And you are?" Kitty's voice was every bit as disdainful as Prudence's.

"I did whatever he wanted." Prudence gasped for breath as if she was struggling not to sob. "I did whatever it took to keep his attention and it wasn't enough."

Had Prudence killed Madeline? Had she killed Henry? I was frozen to the steps.

Kitty snorted. "That was Henry's genius. No matter what we did, it was never going to be enough."

"I hate her."

"Who? Madeline?"

"Ellison. She's the one who'll accept the sympathy. We're the ones who loved him."

"You ought to get yourself cleaned up," Kitty said. "You can't go back out there looking like you've been crying."

The freezer door opened and someone dug for ice, presumably for Prudence's tear-swollen eyes.

"I left my handbag in the living room." Prudence's voice was muffled.

"Then sneak upstairs and use Frances' powder. You've got to do something."

Sneak upstairs? My feet unfroze and I hurried back to the second floor then down the front steps. Better to face a full contingent of country club ladies than Prudence when she'd been crying over my husband. I paused in the doorway to survey the chattering crowd. Navy was the color of the day. Navy dresses, navy skirts paired with demure white blouses, navy pumps and even a navy suit or two. The assembled guests looked like blueberries dotting the lemon chiffon of Mother's living room. I wore black.

Mother's friends were there in force. As were mine. Together we played tennis or bridge or golf. Women I'd known since I was old enough to play tea party held delicate Spode cups and saucers in steady hands. They would offer me trite expressions of sympathy and I would feel like a fraud accepting condolences for a grief I did not feel. Any sadness in my heart was there for Grace, for the very real grief she was feeling.

Someone noticed me standing in the arched entry and the quiet conversation stilled.

Mother put her cup on a side table, stood, graceful as a perfect swan dive, then came and put her arm around my shoulders. "Look at all the people who wanted you to know they were thinking of you."

I offered up the expected sad smile. "Thank you all for coming."

Mother led me to a delicate fauteuil covered in bargello fabric in the softest shades of rose madder and Winsor lemon. Watercolor instead of acrylic or oil. The perfect frame for the picture of a grieving widow. "Sit," she instructed. "I'll get you some coffee."

Lorna was the first person to take my chair's twin. She sat, leaned forward and reached for my hand with her scarlet-tipped talon. "I'm so sorry for your loss."

Lorna's fingers were cool, dry, and despite their resemblance to a turkey vulture's, comforting. "Thank you," I murmured. "This has all been such a shock."

We chatted for a few moments then she ceded her seat to Bitty Sue. "Honey, I brought you a ham baked in Coca Cola. You won't have to worry about cooking for a week."

"Thank you, Bitty Sue." I didn't tell her I never worried about cooking. "I know we'll appreciate that."

"Powers will be here soon. He'd be here now but he had some deal he needed to close." She bent so she could whisper in my ear. "I'm not supposed to talk about it but it's another Picasso. He's doing real well selling those paintings. He hasn't asked me for help in months." She sat back in her chair, unaware she'd shocked me into silence.

Why did Powers need help—country club shorthand for money—from Bitty Sue?

She patted my knee. "Nothing else would keep him away."

Penelope wandered through the room with a stack of cucumber and watercress sandwiches on a silver tray. I beckoned her over, took a sandwich, and found my voice. "I'm sorry, Bitty Sue, I haven't eaten today."

"Oh, honey. Of course you haven't. I imagine you've been too upset to eat a bite. But you've got to keep your strength up."

I hadn't eaten because I'd lacked the opportunity not the appetite. Turns out they don't serve canapés at the station house. Still, for Bitty Sue's sake, I nibbled rather than gorged.

Laura Ballew, John Ballew's mother, Kitty's mother-in-law, was sitting next to me when Kitty entered the living room carrying a bouquet. A watery Prudence trailed after her. Laura's upper lip curled slightly. "Dana Simmons brought you some flowers from her garden and Kitty offered to arrange them."

I wasn't sure if the curled lip was for flowers from a garden rather than a florist or for the less than stellar job Kitty had done sticking them in the vase. Either way, the flowers explained the snip of the kitchen scissors. "How thoughtful of both of them," I said.

Laura's gaze was as pointed as the tip of an ice pick. "That's Kitty, always thinking of others."

Laura knew. Maybe not about the kink or the blackmailing or the orgies—but she knew about Kitty and Henry. Beneath the cool lines of her navy shift, she was seething. If Kitty had killed Henry, if she was caught and brought shame to the Ballew name, Laura might kill her before she ever saw jail.

"Were the police dreadful? Do they have any idea who did this terrible thing?" Laura's hands were clasped so tightly in her lap I could see the whites of her knuckles.

It was almost as if we were thinking the same thing.

I shook my head. "They were very kind. But—"

"Laura, Annie Bruce was just sharing her secret recipe for lemon squares. I know you've wanted it for years. Come write it down." Mother had Laura out of her chair before she had time to object. Before we had time to sidle up to the idea that Laura's daughter-in-law had killed my husband.

Barb Evans took her place. I shifted in my chair, clasped my hands in my lap and waited, unsure of how to begin a conversation with someone my husband had been blackmailing.

Who would have thought that perfectly dressed, perfectly coiffed, president of the Junior League Barb would end up as a name scrawled on an envelope in Henry's safe?

"I'm so sorry for your loss," she said.

I searched her long, tanned face for hints of irony. She had to be thrilled that the people who'd been blackmailing her were dead. She didn't look pleased or smug or even relieved. Her forehead was slightly puckered and the expression in her eyes was kind. She looked sympathetic—and sincere. "Thank you," I murmured.

"Losing a loved one is the worst sort of pain." She reached forward, clasped one of my hands in hers, gave it a squeeze then released it. "I hope you'll call me if you need anything."

Again I searched her face, this time for a hidden agenda. Did she want to get close to me so she could search for whatever proof Henry had of her indiscretions? She didn't look like a woman with an agenda. She looked like someone who meant what she said.

I crossed my ankles and wondered what she'd done to end up as a name in Henry's safe. "You're very kind."

"I'm not." She opened her handbag and withdrew a pack of cigarettes. She even withdrew one from the pack. Then she noticed the lack of ashtrays and slid the Virginia Slim back into its package. "I heard you ran over his body. You must feel terribly guilty. You shouldn't feel that way."

When I learned he was already dead, any guilt I felt had dissipated like mist in the sunshine. How do you tell someone that you don't feel the least bit guilty about running over your husband? You don't. My hands were neatly folded in my lap. The left hand, lying atop the right squeezed. *What do you feel guilty enough about to warrant blackmail?*

Mother might have some idea. She had everyone's life story committed to memory. She remembered who dated in high school, anniversaries, birthdays, and the names of all her friends' grandchildren. I didn't have to open Henry's envelope to get an idea of what had happened in Barb's life to make her feel guilty. I just had to ask Mother. Or Hunter.

One thing I could tell without Mother's input. Barb had no idea who'd been blackmailing her. Did Henry's other victims? If they didn't, who had killed Henry? Kitty? Prudence? "Where's Grace?" Barb asked.

I returned my wandering attention to the woman sitting across from me and loosed my left hand's death grip on my right. "My father took her out to the house in the country. I thought she could spend a few days up there while I get things..." My voice trailed off.

"Settled?" Barb suggested.

"Settled." It was as good a word as any for planning a funeral, dealing with the police, and discovering who killed my husband. "Thank you for being so kind."

"It's my pleasure. Sometimes we get so caught up with the little things we forget what's important." The hint of a smile touched her lips. "If you need someone to talk to when the Bundt cake brigade is gone, call me."

Three well-meaning ladies and two finger sandwiches later, Powers arrived. He wore a navy suit with a subtle chalk stripe, a positively boring tie and his pocket square was a neatly folded bit of white linen. He looked slightly green beneath his tan. Selfishly, I needed the carefree, funny Powers who could make me smile and forget. Instead, the man who collapsed into the seat next to mine looked like he'd triple bogeyed every hole on the back nine.

"Are you all right?" I asked.

He offered me a half-hearted smile. "I think that's my line."

"My husband's been murdered. I'm not all right. You?"

"I've been better."

"Anything I can do?" I patted his hand.

Powers grimaced. "Ellison, you have to stop stealing my lines."

"I wouldn't be stealing anything if you didn't look like you'd just run over your dog."

"I don't have a dog."

"Well, trust me, if you did, and you ran over it, you'd feel awful."

He leaned forward, his elbows on his knees, an odd expression in his green eyes. "So it's true? You ran over Henry?"

I might not feel guilty about running over Henry's body, but it also didn't count as one of my finest moments. "I'm afraid so."

Powers sat back. "But he was already dead." He sounded almost disappointed.

I nodded. "For hours."

"Who do you think killed him?"

I glanced at Mother. She was deep in conversation with Bitty Sue, not paying the least bit of attention to me or Powers. A good thing since speculating on your husband's murderer was well outside the prescribed bounds of polite conversation at an afternoon tea. Then I searched the room for Kitty and Prudence. Kitty wore a sour pickles expression and sat next to Laura. Prudence looked miserable, but whether that was due to Henry's death or Lorna's talons dug deep into her arm was debatable. "I have no idea."

Powers cast a glance toward Mother and Bitty Sue then lowered his voice. "I think Roger did it."

How could he think it was Roger? Then again, he didn't know all about Henry and Prudence or Henry and Kitty. "Roger?" The tone of my voice expressed my doubts.

Powers nodded, his chin moving up and down, as fast as the pistons in Roger's jag. "Who else? I think he got tired of her cheating on him."

Maybe Powers was right. The golf club that had caved in Henry's skull bore Roger's monogram. Still, I couldn't bring myself to see Roger as a murderer. "Why would he kill Henry?"

Powers raised a brow, lowered his chin, and crossed his arms, a classic don't-be-dense look.

I scowled back at him. I wasn't dense, I was doubtful. "Madeline cheated on him with half the men at the club."

"You have to admit she stayed with Henry longer than most."

I lifted my shoulders and let them drop.

Powers raised a finger and wagged it. "Mark my words, Ellison. Roger did it and I bet everything comes out in the next day or so."

He was only half right.

TWENTY-FOUR

That night Mother and I ate slices of Bitty Sue's ham, an anonymous casserole, and Bundt cake at the kitchen table.

After dinner, I called Grace. "Honey, you okay?"

She answered with a sniffle.

My heart contracted. "I can drive up there. Tonight, if you want." I ought to be with my daughter not my mother. The guilt I'd failed to feel over Henry roared into life. I'd been so busy yammering polite replies to the Bundt cake brigade I hadn't worried nearly enough about Grace. I should have. Guilt weighed on me.

"How about tomorrow?" Her voice was tiny.

"Done," I promised.

Another sniffle.

This time my heart didn't just contract, it twisted.

"Mom?"

"What is it, honey?"

"Would you bring my jods? I forgot them."

The pain in my chest loosened. If Grace was worried about riding pants, perhaps things weren't entirely dire. "Of course. Anything else?"

"We forgot food for Max."

"Is your grandfather feeding him table scraps?"

"He's in heaven."

Of course he was. All the squirrels and rabbits he could chase, no fences to worry about, and people food. He'd achieved doggy Nirvana. At least one Russell was happy.

When Grace and I hung up, Mother caught my chin between her thumb and index finger then turned my head from side to side. "You look like ten miles of bad road." She put a valium in my hand and closed my fingers around it.

"Take it," she ordered.

"But—"

"One won't hurt you. Besides, you need to rest."

I took the pill with a large glass of water and the certainty it wouldn't work. I slept without dreaming and woke at eight instead of five. Refreshed might be too strong a word, but I did feel able to face the coming day.

I shuffled downstairs for coffee.

Mother waited for me in the kitchen. "Did you sleep?"

"I did. Thank you."

"I thought we'd go pick out a casket."

"No. I'm going to the farm."

Her lips flattened. "Don't be silly, Ellison. You can't go gallivanting off to the country."

Last evening, after running over my husband's corpse, being interrogated by the police, and facing the Bundt cake brigade, I hadn't felt much like standing up to Mother. After a decent night's rest, I did. "Watch me."

Her mouth dropped open. She snapped it shut. "I don't know what's got into you lately."

Really? "I've discovered two dead bodies in a week."

"That's no excuse."

"Maybe not for you. For me it works just fine." I took a large sip of coffee and waited for an explosion.

It didn't come. Instead, Mother issued one, small, put-upon huff. Then she sniffed and wiped under her eyes as if she was about to cry.

Guilt.

Two could play at that game. "I can't believe you want me to look at caskets when Grace needs me."

"You can't bury Henry in a pine box."

I could, but we both knew I wouldn't. "You pick something. Whatever you want." She could have carte blanche at the funeral home. She could plan the funeral, pick the hymns. For all I cared she could give the eulogy. I didn't care. "I'm going to run home and pick up some things for Grace. I'll call you when I get to the farm."

Gratitude swelled somewhere in my chest when I pulled up in front of my house and saw Aggie in the driveway with a hose. At her feet, rivers of red tinged water ran into the grass and disappeared into the earth.

She didn't ask how I was or express her sympathy or rearrange her features into some warm, supportive expression she didn't feel. Not Aggie. Aggie picked up the hose and washed away my husband's blood. The woman was worth her weight in purple muumuu covered gold. When she saw me, she crimped the hose, cutting off the flow of water.

"Thank you." I managed to wave at the driveway without looking at it.

"I didn't figure you'd want to deal with this."

She was right. More than right. I tried to convey my gratitude with a smile. My cheeks were too brittle and stiff to manage the expression but Aggie seemed to understand. She smiled at me.

"I came home to pick up a pair of jodhpurs for Grace and food for Max."

"Do you need any help?" Aggie asked.

"No."

"Then I'll finish up out here."

The sound of water rinsing gore followed me into the house where the ring of the telephone greeted me.

I answered without thinking, a habitual response to its jangle. "Hello?"

"Ellison Russell?" No hello. No identification. Nothing but a woman's voice.

"Who's calling?" I asked.

"Is this Ellison Russell?" Each syllable was higher than the last, the *ell* of my last name nothing more than a squeak.

"Who's calling?"

The woman at the other end of the line took a deep breath. "This is Kathleen O'Malley. I need to speak with Ellison Russell."

"Kathleen who?"

"It's you, isn't it?"

"Yes. I'm afraid I don't know a Kathleen O'Malley."

"Yes, you do. You know me as Mistress K."

Mistress K had a name suitable for a Catholic schoolgirl? Unbidden the image of her dressed in black leather and tartan plaid popped into my brain. Oh dear Lord. "What do you want?"

"Come to Roger Harper's house. Now."

What the hell? "Why would I do that?"

"Because I told you to."

"I don't play your kinds of games, Miss O'Malley." The name tasted sweet as revenge on my lips. Miss O'Malley sounded like a typist or a third grade teacher or a secretary. So different from Mistress K who flogged grown men. "Goodbye." I hung up the phone.

It rang again within seconds.

My hand hovered over the receiver. To answer, or not to answer, that was the question. The slings and arrows of outrageous fortune had been particularly sharp of late. If I answered, would I be stuck again? If I didn't, would I wonder forever what she could possibly have wanted? Maybe she knew something about Madeline and Henry's deaths. Maybe if she needed something from me, I could find out. I picked up the handle. "Hello."

"Please. Come. I need you. Roger needs you."

I let the silence play out. No wonder my father had used it against me—I could almost hear her weighing her options.

"I'll tell you about your husband and his women."

"I only want to know if one of them killed him."

There was no answer. Apparently two could play the silence game.

No way was I losing to Kathleen O'Malley or Mistress K. I examined the cuticles of my free hand, made a mental list of the things I needed to pack, and when the silence continued to spin, I picked up the handful of ignored mail and flipped through it.

Bills. The dusty letter from beneath the bombé chest. Catalogs. Magazines. Silence.

She cleared her throat, a clear sign of weakening.

I studied a perfume advertisement. A model with killer cheekbones strode toward a private plane, a confident smile on her crimson lips. I flipped the page.

"Fine." One word, clipped and sharp as if she'd cut it with a knife.

Victory.

No need to gloat. We both knew I'd won. "I'll see you in a few minutes." I tossed the mail back onto the chest.

Out front, Aggie was still spraying. I waved to her. "I have to run a quick errand." I climbed into my car and drove the four blocks to Roger's house.

Mistress K opened the door before I had a chance to knock.

Had she trussed him so tightly she couldn't loosen the ropes? No. Her face lacked its usual surfeit of confidence. The dominatrix's forehead was wrinkled and her eyes seemed too big for their sockets.

She reached outside, closed her hand around my wrist and hauled me into the Harpers' foyer. "This way."

She pulled me toward the kitchen.

Harvest gold and pumpkin orange assaulted my retinas but what burned them was the pajama-clad body kneeling on the floor with its head in the oven.

"Oh my God." The words slipped through numbed lips. "Is it Roger?"

Mistress K bit her lower lip and nodded.

"Have you called an ambulance?"

"He's dead."

"How do you know?"

"Gas."

"Do you smell any?" I knew the answer. *No.* Madeline's oven was broken. It hadn't worked in years. She didn't cook so she'd never bothered to have it repaired.

"He wrote a note."

Sure enough, a single sheet of white paper lay on the counter. R.A.H. was embossed in gold across the top. On it, Roger had scrawled *I'm sorry.*

Bullshit. If Roger were going to kill himself, he wouldn't do it by sticking his head in a gasless oven. I bent over his body, grabbed a handful of seersucker robe, and pulled him free of the broken appliance.

His skin was cool and grey but he wasn't dead. At least I didn't think he was. "Call an ambulance."

She picked up the phone and dialed zero.

I tapped Roger on the cheek. Gently. Then with more force.

Behind me, the dominatrix snorted.

"Roger!" The tap became a slap. He didn't move. Maybe he *was* dead. I dug in my purse for my compact and yanked it open, accidentally sprinkling him with powder. Then I held the tiny mirror over his mouth and nose.

Fog.

He wasn't dead.

"Tell them to hurry," I said over my shoulder.

Mistress K rolled her eyes. Now that she wasn't dealing with a dead body by herself, her natural contempt for me had returned. "It's not like ambulances drive slowly."

"Just tell them."

"Hurry." Her voice was as flat as a deflated beach ball.

What a bitch.

She hung up the phone.

"What are you doing here, Kathleen?"

Her nostrils flared at my use of her first name. "Roger was late. I came to punish him."

That explained the leather pants and the whip that hung from her belt. It didn't come close to explaining who'd tried to kill Roger and make it look like a suicide.

"How did you get in?"

"Roger gave me a key."

Roger *wanted* to be punished. I kept my lip from curling with distaste. Barely.

Instead, I stood, picked my purse up from where I'd left it on the counter, then rooted through it until I came up with Detective A-is-for-Anarchy Jones' business card.

"What are you doing?" Kathleen asked.

"Calling the police."

The dominatrix edged toward the door.

"If you leave, I'll tell them you were here," I said. "They'll wonder why you left."

Emotions flickered across her face. First shock—her crimson lips formed a circle and her eyes grew big, then anger—brows drawn, lips thinned, then something sly, like she believed she could tell me some pretty lie and leave me to be discovered with a third body in a week. Not.

"I called you because I thought you could help. I thought maybe I could stay out of this."

Did she think I couldn't recognize cow manure? "Then you thought wrong. Someone who didn't know that oven was broken tried to stage a suicide. You're staying to talk to the police."

"If you'd just let me explain. I—"

I held up my hand. "Shush." I needed to think, not listen to her jabbering. Kathleen could have left Roger. She'd thought he was dead. No one would have found him for days. Why had she called for help? Could it be that deep beneath the leather and floggers there was a decent human being? More likely someone at her club knew she'd come here. They might wonder when Roger was reported dead.

"Do you think Kitty or Prudence could have done this?" I asked.

She stared at me.

"Kitty Ballew or Prudence Davies. Could either one have done this?"

"Maybe. But why would they?"

The murderer had staged a suicide. They'd wanted the police to believe Roger had killed Madeline and Henry and then himself. Two murders neatly tied up. The end of the investigation. Seemed like a good reason to me.

I picked up the phone and dialed the number on the card. "May I please speak with Detective Jones?"

"This is Jones."

I narrowed my eyes and glared at Mistress K who was inching toward the door. "Detective Jones, this Ellison Russell, I'm at Roger Harper's house with Kathleen O'Malley. Someone tried to kill him."

"Another body?" The voice on the other end of the phone was incredulous.

That's me. The woman who finds corpses. "He's not dead." Yet. "The ambulance is on its way."

"So am I, Mrs. Russell." He hung up.

Mrs. Russell?

Shit.

I put the receiver in the cradle, lifted it again then dialed. "Hunter, it's Ellison. I'm at Roger Harper's. Someone tried to kill him and I think you'd better come over here."

To his credit, Hunter didn't question, didn't wonder aloud about my propensity for finding bodies, didn't call me Mrs. Russell. "I'll be there in ten. If the police get there before me, don't say anything."

It was déjà vu all over again.

TWENTY-FIVE

No way had Madeline spent any time in her kitchen. She probably hadn't even known where it was. Say what you will about her non-existent morals, her sexual proclivities or her talent for causing trouble, the woman had possessed good taste. She'd had no hand in the harvest gold and pumpkin orange wallpaper or the dated cabinets. The kitchen was dreadful. Add a comatose middle-aged man in his bathrobe and a leather-clad dominatrix and it was downright awful.

I stopped noticing the walls when the ambulance arrived. I was too busy shrinking into the breakfast nook while men with blood pressure cuffs and needles and a gurney swarmed around Roger.

"Is he going to be all right?" I asked.

One of the paramedics grunted and then they all ignored me. They had a harder time ignoring the leather-clad dominatrix. Only the man monitoring Roger's vitals kept his eyes on his work, the rest ogled.

I tried to shrink further into the nook when Detective Jones arrived, but a dying Swedish ivy in a macramé hanger whapped me between the eyes. It hurt like hell. Turns out cursing in a crowded room is a fairly effective way of gathering all the attention you don't want. Lesson learned.

Kathleen O'Malley tittered, Detective Jones glared, and I closed my watering eyes and rubbed the bridge of my nose.

"Do you want to tell me what's going on?" the detective asked.

There was an option? If I didn't want to tell him, I could leave?

I'd go to the farm and move in. Grace could spend her summer in horse heaven, Max could chase varmints to his heart's content, and I could paint. If wishes were horses...

I opened my eyes to find a very stern Detective Anarchy Jones standing in front of me with his arms crossed. The fingers of his left hand drummed against his right bicep.

"Miss O'Malley stopped by to visit Roger. When she found him with his head in the oven, she called me."

The fingers drummed faster. "Why did Miss O'Malley call you?"

"You'd have to ask her."

Arms still crossed, Detective Jones turned toward Mistress K. "Why?"

Her smile was kitten sweet. "Mrs. Russell introduced me to Roger."

Oh dear Lord, what a bitch. I attempted to mimic her kittenish smile then abandoned the effort. It wasn't working and even if it did, I wouldn't look sultry or sexy, I'd look like a simpering fool. The distant, chilly smile I'd spent years perfecting at the country club slid into place. "That's not exactly correct. Mr. Harper met Miss O'Malley before I did. I did not introduce them."

"How did you meet Miss O'Malley?"

My cheeks warmed, but I kept the chilly smile on my lips. "At her club."

"That's where, not how, Mrs. Russell."

Mrs. Russell, again. I searched his face. Same dark hair, same lean cheeks, same brown eyes. Except, those eyes didn't look remotely nice anymore.

My chilly smile slipped away. "Mr. Harper wanted to see where his wife and my husband had been spending their time." My cheeks weren't warm anymore. Nope, they flamed hotter than a barbeque grill. I covered them with the tips of my fingers. "We drove there together."

Detective Jones shifted his gaze back to Miss O'Malley, Mistress K. He assessed the black leather pants, the stiletto heels, the bustier barely containing an abundance of rounded flesh, the whip on her left hip, and the flogger on her right. So did the men who were taking an unconscionably long time cleaning up after wheeling Roger to the ambulance.

My skirt, a navy wrap that reversed to a ladybug print, was long enough to cover the scabs on my knees. Coupled with a white linen camp shirt, it felt downright dowdy. I fingered the bow tied at my waist.

"I take it Mr. Harper returned to your club?"

The tip of Mistress K's pink tongue moistened her already glistening lips. "Take what you want." She tried the kitten smile again.

"Yes or no, Miss O'Malley?"

She gave up on the smile. Instead her lower lip, pouty, red, and as full as a down sofa cushion extended. "Yes." Somehow, she managed to make that one word sound like an invitation and a promise.

"Did Mrs. Russell return to your club?"

Heat rose from my toes to my hairline. How could he think such a thing? Ask such a thing?

"You're serious?" Mistress K snorted. "Look at her. Henry told me the most adventurous thing she's ever done is go to a swingers' party. Even then she left as soon as she figured it out." When Mistress K laughed her breasts looked like they might spill over the top of her bustier. "She fished their keys out of the bowl and left. Henry was furious. Well, at least until he ended up in a threesome. Then it became an amusing story."

I remembered that night and the skin-crawling realization that Henry was willing to let another man have me so long as he got access to that man's wife.

Of course, I'd walked out.

I was stodgy. I was boring. I believed in monogamy. I believed marriage should be a partnership not a power exchange. I forced myself to look into Detective Jones' brown eyes. Let him judge me, I wasn't backing down from who I was or what I believed.

His eyes were marginally nicer, almost like he felt bad for embarrassing me in front of a room full of lingering paramedics. Maybe I was wrong. Maybe he didn't feel bad. Maybe I saw pity.

I swallowed around the lump in my throat, took one very deep breath, then picked up my handbag from the breakfast table. "When I arrived here this morning, Miss O'Malley led me to the kitchen. Roger's head was in the oven and she showed me the note on the counter." I pointed to the piece of paper. "She thought Roger was dead from gas, but the Harpers' oven has been broken for months. I pulled Roger out of the oven, determined he wasn't dead, and called an ambulance." I tightened my grip on my handbag. "Someone staged Roger's suicide. Now, if you'll excuse me, I'm going to see my daughter."

I stepped out of the nook, sidled past a gawking paramedic, and achieved the doorway without looking over my shoulder.

"Mrs. Russell, wait." Unless he arrested me, I wasn't listening to Detective Jones anymore.

I kept walking.

"Ellison." Even with my back turned I could sense Mistress K's eyebrows rise at his use of my first name.

My damn foot paused in mid-air. Fortunately, Hunter chose that moment to arrive. He wore a navy suit, a striped tie, and polished wingtips. Safe. Familiar. Just stodgy enough to limit his sexual adventures to one woman at a time. I hurried toward him. "Please. Get me out of here."

Hunter glared down the length of the hallway, closed a hand around my elbow, and led me into the morning sunshine. His steps slowed. "Are you okay? Who in the hell was that?"

He didn't mean Detective Jones. "That was Kathleen O'Malley."

"Who?"

"Mistress K. Henry and Madeline frequented her club." Roger had too. Three people, two of them were dead, and the third looked like he might join them at any moment. Had I overlooked a suspect? Was Mistress K a killer?

He shuddered. "Dreadful looking woman."

I studied his face. The corner of his lip was curled and his nose was wrinkled as if he'd smelled something distasteful. He meant it. Hunter didn't find Kathleen, her leather, her whips or her over-taxed bustier remotely attractive. I smiled at him. Not the chilly smile.

"What happened here?" Hunter asked.

"Someone tried to kill Roger Harper and make it look like a suicide."

Hunter froze for an instant. If I hadn't been walking next to him, I might not have noticed the sudden stillness and then the return to movement.

"What?" I asked. "What's wrong?"

He glanced toward the front of the Harper's colonial home. The hunter green door was closed, the shades were drawn and still he whispered. "I'll follow you home and tell you about it there."

Aggie opened the front door as soon as we pulled in the driveway. "Your mother just called, Mrs. Russell. She wanted to know what you were doing at the Harpers'."

God save me from nosy neighbors. They were everywhere. I glanced at my car. Perhaps I should invest in something less distinctive. Maybe a blue Volvo station wagon like half the mothers at the country club. Perhaps a Mercedes sedan in boring black. My British racing green Triumph was far too distinctive.

"Your sister called," Aggie continued.

Marjorie? It was official. Hell had frozen over. After Mother's less than warm welcome of Marjorie's husband, communication with my sister was as rare as an honest politician.

Hunter's hand at the small of my back propelled me inside. "I have things to tell you."

The envelopes. I wasn't sure I wanted to know what was in the envelopes. One look at the grim expression on Hunter's face told me I didn't have a choice.

Hunter settled onto one of the stools at the kitchen island. He opened a briefcase he'd carried in from his car and withdrew two stacks of documents—one of too familiar envelopes, the other of file folders.

"Iced tea?" Aggie asked.

Hunter nodded.

I shook my head. "Tab. I'll get it." I opened the refrigerator and closed my fingers around a pink can.

With drinks in front of us, there was no avoiding discussing the envelopes. I still tried. "I really ought to head up to the farm."

Hunter shook his head. No way was he letting me off the hook so easily. "Do you know Rand Hamilton?"

We belonged to different country clubs. Our children went to different schools. I'd seen his envelope in Henry's safe and wondered how their paths had crossed. "Not well. I knew Rebecca a bit from the tennis league. She was nice."

"She died."

I nodded. I hadn't known her well enough to take Rand a Bundt cake. Instead, I'd sent a note and a check in her memory to a local charity. "She'd been drinking and she went swimming alone. She drowned." Almost like Madeline. My mouth went dry and my heart beat faster.

Hunter picked up the envelope with Rand Hamilton's name on it. "What if I told you Rand killed her?"

My stomach dropped to my skinned knees. Rand had murdered Rebecca? What the hell was in that envelope? "I'd tell you my husband was a bigger idiot than I thought." I'd thought Henry had limited his blackmail to upstanding citizens eager to keep their sexual exploits quiet. Instead, he'd blackmailed a murderer. No wonder he was dead.

Hunter's lip twitched. Once. Twice. Then it curled into something resembling a sneer. "Idiot isn't the word I'd use to describe your husband."

"Maybe not," I ceded. But calling him a moron in front of Aggie seemed harsh. Almost as harsh as adding that if he wasn't already dead, I'd kill him for endangering Grace. What had he been thinking? It wasn't like we needed the money. I took a slow sip of Tab to relieve the dryness in my mouth. There was nothing I could do about the racing of my heart. Maybe it hadn't been about money. Maybe Henry had blackmailed his peers to feel powerful.

Rand Hamilton.

Respected stockbroker.

Perennial runner-up at the Worm Burner Tournament as a guest player at the club.

Murderer.

"What's Hamilton's middle name?" I asked.

Hunter opened a slim file folder. "Butler."

"What about his wife?" I asked. "What was her maiden name?"

Hunter lifted a brow. "Why do you ask?"

"The golf club," Aggie said. "The one that killed Mr. Russell. It was engraved with initials. R.A.H." She shrugged and offered me an apologetic smile. "The police were talking about it."

No flies on Aggie.

Hunter opened the file folder then pulled out a news clipping. "Rebecca Hamilton née Alling."

R.A.H. No one moved. We watched the condensation run down the sides of Hunter's glass and considered the possibility that Rand Hamilton had killed Henry with his dead wife's golf club.

I broke the silence. "It looked like a man's club."

Hunter nodded as if he agreed but said, "Plenty of women play with men's clubs."

Maybe, but I was having a hard time imagining Rand Hamilton with his paunch and his comb-over and his stick legs whacking Henry over the head with a golf club. Then again, by all accounts he had a nice backswing. I shook my head. It didn't feel right. "I'm not sure Henry's victims knew he was the blackmailer."

Hunter's eyes narrowed. I'd asked him to put in an unconscionable amount of work researching a potential murderer, he'd seen things in those envelopes he could never unsee, and now I wasn't sure the murderer was one of Henry's blackmail victims.

It was Aggie who spoke. "Why do you say that?"

I took another sip of Tab, ignored Hunter's dire expression and said, "Barb Evans."

"Barb Evans?" Hunter repeated.

Aggie went digging through the pile of envelopes. "She's the one who embezzled from the Junior League."

I choked on my soda. Barb Evans had embezzled? From the League? Was she insane? No more so than Randall Hamilton, and according to the information Henry had collected he'd killed his wife. And to think, I'd assumed all the envelopes contained pictures of sex acts.

"How much?"

Aggie pulled the papers out of the envelope and looked. "Ten thousand. She put it back, but borrowing without permission is still stealing."

Borrowing without permission versus allowing someone to spank you until your ass was the color of a brick sidewalk. All things being equal, I was more willing to accept embezzlement. Other league members might not be as forgiving. I put my elbows on the counter then dropped my face to my hands so the heels of my palms pressed into my eyes. Embezzlement. Kinky sex. Murder. What else did the envelopes hold?

I took a deep breath then raised my head to gaze at Hunter. His expression was serious and lawyerly. He looked smart and competent and utterly sure of himself.

He'd decided Rand's guilt. Rand might have access to a golf club engraved with R.A.H. If Rand knew Madeleine and Henry were the blackmailers, he had an excellent reason to kill them. Even if Rand hadn't killed Madeline and Henry or tried to kill Roger, he'd still killed his wife. How in the hell was I going to turn Rand in without revealing Henry's blackmailing?

"Why did he kill Rebecca?" I asked.

"Insurance money," said Aggie. "You always got to look at the insurance policies. Tell us about Barb Evans."

"She brought a Bundt cake to Mother's."

They both stared at me as they were still waiting for an explanation.

"I'd swear she didn't know Henry was the one who was blackmailing her."

Aggie reached across the counter and pulled the remaining stack of neatly labeled file folders toward her. She opened one and shuffled through a stack of papers. "Barbara Evans was the president of the thespian club her junior and senior year of college."

"You think she was acting?"

My ersatz housekeeper nodded.

I shook my head. "I don't think so."

Hunter frowned at me. "No one thinks Barb Evans murdered your husband."

"If Barb didn't know Henry was the blackmailer maybe Rand didn't either."

"Or maybe he did," said Aggie.

I rubbed the back of my neck. "Or maybe it was someone else."

"You offered us twenty potential killers." Hunter's frown darkened to a scowl. "Are there more?"

"I think maybe it could be Kitty Ballew or Prudence Davies."

"Who?" Aggie asked.

Hunter held up his hand to stop us from following the tangent I'd introduced any further. His right hand.

I stared at his fingers. There was an easy way to settle this. "Was Rebecca Hamilton right-handed or left-handed?"

My question required more searching of papers in the file. After a moment, Hunter gathered all the sheets in his hands then tapped them against the counter until they were in perfect alignment. "I don't know."

Neither did I, but I could figure it out. "I played tennis with her once or twice. Doubles matches. She wasn't very good. I remember Rebecca and her partner tripping over each other for balls in the center court. They both favored their forehands."

Aggie grinned at me like I was a precocious child. "The golf club they found was left-handed. Was Mrs. Hamilton?"

"I don't remember. I just remember her running into Lilly Greyson." Who'd been the left-handed player? For the life of me, I couldn't remember.

"Call her and ask." Hunter's voice brooked no dissent.

I held out my hands with fingers spread then shrugged. "I can't. Now that her kids are grown, she's summering in France. I have no idea how to get a hold of her."

Hunter's jaw, always square and firm, tightened as if he was gritting his teeth. The expression in his eyes was as hard as granite. "Aggie, would you give us a moment please?"

Aggie took one look at Hunter's jaw and hurried out of the kitchen in a swirl of purple muumuu.

"Someone has killed two people and tried to kill a third." He stood, circled the counter then stood behind me to rest his hands on my shoulders. "You have to take this seriously."

I twisted on my stool to look at him. "I am."

He shook his silver head, the expression in his eyes softened, and he squeezed my shoulders gently. "Not seriously enough. I'm worried you'll be next."

TWENTY-SIX

Hunter Tafft's hands were warm on my shoulders, his lips were parted, and his eyes, normally flinty, lawyerly chips, had heated to the approximate temperature of lava. Also, he'd just told me he cared what happened to me. For one insane moment, I was tempted to reach my fingers to the back of his neck and pull him close enough to kiss me.

He released one of my shoulders and used his free hand to brush a strand of hair away from my face, and I caught the scent of expensive ink and leather and privilege. I felt as frozen as a deer caught in headlights.

Then he sighed and drew away and my ability to move returned.

Hunter moved back to the other side of the island. "You don't think Barb Evans knew it was Henry blackmailing her?"

Really? He wanted to talk about Barb Evans? I could hardly catch my breath. I took a surreptitious gulp of air and tried to focus on blackmail. "I didn't know she was an actress."

"Your first instinct—did you think she was lying or telling the truth?"

"Telling the truth."

He offered me a tight smile. "Trust your instincts."

I blinked. *Trust your instincts?* Just a moment ago, my instincts had told me to kiss Hunter Tafft.

Hunter rested his forearms on the counter. Crisp white cotton cuffs peeked out from the arms of his navy suit. He was back to being the perfect lawyer, our moment of closeness forgotten. Maybe he hadn't felt what I had. Maybe he'd been comforting a client and missed the instant when I'd wanted to kiss him and melt into his arms.

"Your instincts tell you it's not Rand Hamilton," he said.

They did. I shrugged, unable to form more than the most basic sentences, my tongue still tied in knots by the thought of it tangling with Hunter's.

Maybe it was Rand. Maybe it wasn't. If I knew who'd killed my husband I wouldn't be sitting in the kitchen with a tempting man, I'd be with Grace.

"You said something about Prudence Davies and Kitty Ballew. Why?"

My cheeks prickled with heat. "One of them could have killed him."

"Why?"

"You know about Henry and Madeline?" It wasn't really a question and Hunter didn't really answer. He jerked his chin once then waited.

"They spent a lot of time at Club K." My voice barely rose above a whisper.

He jerked his chin again. "That woman at Roger's runs the place."

"Yes." I studied a vein in the marble island top. Shaded somewhere between Mars yellow and yellow ochre, it wove its way through at least five feet of counter. I traced a section with my finger. "Prudence and Kitty go there too."

He didn't say anything, and I was unwilling to give up my study of marble to see his reaction. We sat in silence.

He finally spoke. "They were there together? The four of them?"

I nodded without looking up.

He exhaled loud enough for me to hear it. "Why did you stay married to him?"

"I didn't know about Prudence and Kitty until after Madeline was dead."

"You knew about Madeline." His voice was kind. I *hated* kind. It too closely resembled pity.

"I stayed for Grace."

"What an asshole."

I jerked my gaze up in time to see his scowl.

"He had you and he fooled around with Madeline? He was an idiot."

Hunter thought I could inspire monogamy? I didn't know how to respond so I said, "I think both Kitty and Prudence wanted to replace Madeline."

The scowl disappeared and his face took on its usual unreadable, lawyer's mask. "That explains Madeline's death not Henry's."

"I think they were each disappointed he didn't contact them when he got back. Maybe one of them was upset enough to kill him."

Hunter chewed on that for a moment. "Where was he?"

The laugh that escaped my lips sounded bitter. "You were there when he told me. Duluth. Maybe Toledo. Failing that, he went to Provo."

"I assumed he was lying."

"That's the thing, I don't think he was." I dropped my gaze back to the marble slab. "Henry usually didn't bother to lie."

Hunter mumbled something that sounded suspiciously like *asshole*.

My husband had cheated on me with multiple women, and he hadn't cared enough about me to try to hide it. In fact, he'd taken a perverse pleasure in making sure I knew about it. He was an asshole. At least he hadn't tried to murder me.

Unlike Rand.

The marble lost its ability to fascinate. "Rebecca Hamilton drowned."

Hunter reached for the envelope with Rand's name on it. "Yes."

"Where was Rand when it happened?"

"Having dinner with her parents."

"Her parents? Without her? I assume he took the kids."

Hunter consulted his notes. "They were at summer camp."

"You've been married," I said.

Hunter's eyes rolled—just a little bit. "Three times."

"Did you ever have dinner with any of your in-laws without your wife?"

He thought for a moment. "Never."

"No man goes to dinner with his in-laws alone unless he has a damn good reason. Like creating an alibi."

He scanned the file. "Says here she came down with something but insisted he go without her."

"I don't believe it. That's a dinner you reschedule. What parent wants to think their son-in-law is out while their daughter is home sick? Rand killed Rebecca and used her parents for his alibi." Despicable man.

"How did he kill her if he was with her parents?"

"How big was the insurance policy?"

"A million dollars."

"He could have given her something to help her sleep. Only he gave her a lot of it. Then he paid someone to dump her in their pool while he was with her parents." I rubbed the bridge of my nose. "He did it. I just don't know if he killed Madeline and Henry."

"Madeline and Rebecca's deaths are very similar."

"I know but I can't see Madeline agreeing to meet a paunchy stockbroker at the club in the middle of the night. If she did, she definitely wouldn't bother with her favorite dress." I used my fingers to smooth the wrinkles in my brow. "May I see the envelope?"

Hunter slid it across the counter and I perused its contents. My guesses were spot on. Rand killed his wife but how had Henry figured it out?

I flipped through more pages and saw that Rand had withdrawn large amounts of cash from Henry's bank prior to Rebecca's death. Had Rand used it to pay the hit man? Was that how Henry found the grounds for blackmail?

Rand was a murderer. Rebecca deserved justice. Maybe I could send Henry's proof to the police anonymously. That way, no one need ever know that Grace's father was a blackmailer.

The jangle of the telephone interrupted my thoughts.

"Are you going to answer that?" Hunter asked when I made no move to pick up the receiver.

"It could be Mother. Or the police."

He grinned at me. "It could be Grace."

The ringing stopped and seconds later Aggie knocked on the kitchen door. "Mr. Tafft, it's your office. They said they were sorry to interrupt but—"

"They don't call unless it's urgent. Do you mind if I take this?"

"Go ahead. I have to pack for Grace." Aggie and I left him to his call.

She stopped me at the bottom of the front stairs. "Your daughter phoned while you were out. She gave me a list of everything she needed. I hope you don't mind but I went ahead and packed it for her."

Aggie truly was worth her weight in gold.

"I packed a bag for you too."

Maybe platinum.

"Thank you, Aggie." I looked around for something to do and lit upon the ever-growing stack of mail on the bombé chest. I scooped it up and headed to the family room to go through it.

Catalogues went directly into the trash. I wasn't in the mood to shop—not even from the comfort of home. Then I opened envelopes. I dropped the electric, phone, and gas bills into the sterling toast rack that did double duty as my filing system, wrote a quick formal regret to an afternoon tea and sent a solicitation into the waste bin with the catalogues.

Finally, only one letter remained, one addressed to Henry, the dusty one that had spent a few days under the chest.

I opened it and withdrew a single handwritten sheet. Three names with addresses. Nothing more. No signature. No explanation. No return address. I almost threw it in the trash. Almost. Then I realized the addresses were in Duluth, Toledo, and Provo and my hand shook.

It was still shaking when Hunter walked in. "What?" he said. "What's wrong? You're white as a sheet."

"Henry wasn't lying." I handed him the piece of paper.

It took him seconds to scan the addresses. "Do you know these people?"

"Never heard of them."

"I'll have Aggie check them out."

The phone chose that moment to ring again. The damn thing was possessed. It never rang this often unless Grace was at home.

I snatched the receiver from its cradle. "Hello."

"Ellison?"

"Who's calling?" I barked. I'd had it up to my eyebrows with mysterious callers.

"It's Marjorie. Daddy called me."

"Oh?" Not the most welcoming response but Marjorie only participated in our family when disaster struck. The day to day happenings that create family—remembering birthdays, sending Christmas presents, calling just to talk—Marjorie had turned her back on them all.

"I'm sorry about Henry. Is Grace okay?"

"She's up at the farm with Daddy. I'm going up there in a little while."

I could almost see my sister nod her approval. "How are you?" she asked.

"Fine."

Hunter snorted then raised a sardonic eyebrow.

I cradled the phone against my shoulder, picked up the letter opener from the desk, and tested its sharpness.

His lips twitched. I'd amused him. So happy to oblige.

"When's the funeral?" Marjorie asked.

"I don't know. The police are investigating and haven't released his body."

"Well, let me know if there's anything I can do."

A meaningless offer if I'd ever heard one. Marjorie was in Akron. She couldn't even bring me a Bundt cake. "Are Akron and Toledo close to each other?" I asked.

"Not really. Why?"

"I think Henry went to Toledo to meet with a man named—" I gestured for Hunter to hand over the paper with the addresses, "Jack Gillis."

"Jack Gillis? Really?"

"You know him?" I asked.

"I know of him. He's been throwing money around state politics." She sniffed. "New money. The man has no class."

This from a woman whose husband's top selling product was a condom called the King Cobra. Mother would have pointed that out. I refrained. "What does he do?"

"Lord, I don't know. He bribes politicians and throws parties. His wife looks like a cocktail waitress at a strip club."

How would Marjorie know what cocktail waitresses in strip clubs looked like? Besides, the King Cobra, Ten Inches of Bliss, and the Rough Rider paid her country club bill. She had no business passing judgment on cocktail waitresses.

"They're trying to buy their way into Toledo society," she said. Then she paused as if she realized she'd uttered something oxymoronic. "What I mean to say is they're supporting the symphony and the art museum and they wrote a huge check to help restore the governor's mansion. They're buying art and naming hospital wings and—"

"So they're being charitable."

"They're being social climbers."

"Any idea why Henry might have gone to see him?"

"Henry and Jack Gillis?" She laughed.

Hunter glanced at his watch.

"Marjorie knows that man in Ohio," I said by way of explanation.

"Who are you talking to?" Marjorie demanded.

"Hunter Tafft. He's representing me."

"Hunter?" Her voice turned silky. "Let me talk to him."

My fingers tightened on the phone. I forced them loose and put the receiver in Hunter's hand. "Marjorie wants to talk to you."

He took the phone. "Marjorie." One word. He said it like he was wrapping it in black velvet and tying it with a red satin bow. Bleh.

Hunter listened to whatever Marjorie was saying. Then he laughed. The sound was every bit as grating as nails on a chalkboard. It would be rude to walk out—I did it anyway. After all, the car wasn't going to load itself.

Two small suitcases waited in the front hall. I picked them up and carried them out to the car. Had Aggie packed us every volume of the encyclopedia? The damn things weighed a ton. I'd swung the first case into the trunk like I was swinging a golf club and I wanted to obliterate the ball when Hunter appeared.

"Let me do that." He effortlessly wedged the second case into the tiny trunk.

"Thank you. I have to go."

"I thought you wanted to discuss that list of addresses."

The list. The one I'd dropped on the table and forgotten in the red haze of memory. In high school, all I had to do was hint that I liked a boy for my sister to flirt with him. She was married, I was widowed, and nothing had changed. Did I like Hunter Tafft? I had in high school, then Marjorie had batted her eyelashes and they'd dated for all of their senior year.

Twenty odd years ago. I needed to get a grip.

How was it that my mother and my sister could bring out the worst in me without even trying?

I slammed the lid to the trunk. "I do have to go."

"You're angry," he said.

"I'm exhausted." It was true and it explained why I'd ended up in a ridiculous snit because my sister and my lawyer had chatted on the phone. "And, I want to see Grace."

"What about the list?"

I opened the door to the car, fingered my keys. "You said Aggie could look into it." I was eager to get away, so eager I didn't care about the list anymore. Talk about your huge mistakes.

TWENTY-SEVEN

I got one day at the farm. A respite of riding horses with Grace and sitting on the porch to watch the sun set over the hills with Daddy. A single day to hug my daughter and wipe away her tears. A brief twenty-four hours to pretend there wasn't the mother of all messes waiting for me at home. One day, thirteen phone messages from Mother, eleven from Aggie relaying messages from friends, four from Powers, three from Anarchy Jones, and none from Hunter Tafft.

Mrs. Smith, the female half of the nice old couple who took care of the farm for Mother and Daddy, noticed. "You never get calls up here." She handed me a second stack of neatly written messages.

I flipped through the notes, cream stock with Mother's monogram in navy at the top, then I handed them back to her. "You could stop answering the phone."

She tittered. She didn't realize I was serious.

Thirty plus calls to return. Fourteen if I counted Mother, Powers, and Detective Jones at one each and ignored the new stack.

"These are for Grace." A second stack was shoved into my hands.

I'd hoped the farm might be an escape for both Grace and me. Southwestern Bell was making that impossible. As if to prove my point, the phone rang.

Mrs. Smith answered it with a cheery greeting, listened to a lengthy response, then paled to the exact shade of a new golf ball. "Yes, Mrs. Walford." The poor woman mouthed *I'm sorry* then held out the receiver.

I tamped down the inclination to run away and took it from her hand. "Hello, Mother."

"Ellison Prentice Walford Russell, you have a lot of explaining to do."

All four names. I planted my feet, squared my shoulders, and braced myself for a tsunami of vitriol. Wave after wave washed over me, so dark and murky it was a struggle to breathe.

I mimed drinking a glass of water to Mrs. Smith and she had one in my hand in seconds flat then she disappeared into the laundry room. I took a sip of water, leaned against the kitchen counter, and waited for the unlikely possibility that Mother might stop for breath.

"Do you want to explain what in God's name you were doing at Roger Harper's house? Do you have any idea how it looks?" She drew out the last word.

I'd swum into a body, run over my husband's corpse and pulled a man out of an oven, and Mother cared about appearances? Wasn't she supposed to care about me? My throat swelled with unwelcome emotion. "I don't care," my voice, damn it to hell, quavered, "how it looks."

"You should care. It's a reflection on your whole family." She meant her.

I took a sip of water to wash away the quaver. "Mother, no one with half a brain would think there's anything between me and Roger Harper. Besides, the woman he took to the memorial service was there too."

I could *hear* her shudder. "Someone told me that woman runs a sex club. She's some kind of deviant who's preying on poor Roger."

"I think Roger likes it."

"*Ellison!*" She drew a ragged, scandalized breath.

"What?" I said sharply enough to be disrespectful.

Mother paused, presumably wavering between taking umbrage with my tone or my content. Content won. "That she was there while you were makes it even worse. Have you no shame?"

Me? Shame? I knew it all too well. Shame burned hot as a pool deck on a July afternoon. Hot enough for children who'd forgotten their sandals to jump like crickets in a skillet to avoid burning their little feet. I knew. When Henry and Madeline were caught in the coatroom at the Christmas party, shame had nearly charred the skin off my bones. What I felt now wasn't shame. "I guess not."

She drew another ragged breath then she made a sound somewhere between a sniff and a sniffle. "You're so lucky. Your daughter has never disappointed you."

Unlike me. My poor, put-upon mother endured disappointment after disappointment, my pulling a pajama-clad Roger Harper's head and shoulders out of a non-working oven being only the most recent.

I rolled my eyes. "I'm so very sorry if you're disappointed, Mother."

"There's no need for sarcasm."

There was *every* need for sarcasm. The alternative was to tell my mother to go to hell. No one would blame me for it either. After all, I'd been listening to a comprehensive list of my failings for—I checked my watch—twenty minutes. "You'd prefer I speak plainly?" I closed my eyes and took a large step onto a bridge I'd never thought to cross. "You're my mother and I love you, but you don't have the right to say anything you want to me." The damn bridge was made of rope and half-rotted board and it swayed beneath my weight. I took another step anyway. "What's more, my mistakes and my successes are my own. They don't reflect on you."

"Of course they do." She'd ignored my first point entirely. "You're hopelessly naïve if you think any differently."

It was as if we were speaking different languages. Either she couldn't understand what I was saying or she didn't want to. I snorted and the sound propelled me further along the bridge. It tilted from side to side.

"As for saying what I think. Well, someone has to tell you when you make a mistake. It's for your own good."

I took another step.

"Telling me I'm a disappointment is for my own good?"

"I never said that."

We were talking, but we weren't communicating. The whole conversation was pointless. Somehow, without noticing any progress, I'd passed the bridge's halfway point. "Mother, I have to go."

"I'm not done talking."

"But I am." I straightened my spine, took a breath of clean country air deep into my lungs and held it for a moment. Then I exhaled and raced toward the far end of the bridge. The damn thing swung as wildly as a five year-old with her Daddy's three-wood. My stomach lurched accordingly. "Goodbye, Mother."

"Ellison, don't you dare ha—"

I am woman, hear me roar. My roar was quiet but effective. I dropped the receiver into its cradle. Behind me, the bridge burst into flames.

The phone rang again immediately. I ignored it. Instead, I listened to the happy crackle and pop of fire eating old wood and frayed rope. Maybe I ought to roar more often.

Mrs. Smith opened the laundry room door. "You're not going to answer that?"

"No. If it's Mother, I'm not available."

Mrs. Smith, a brave soul, left the safety of bleach and starch and the smell of a hot iron and answered the phone. She listened for a moment then said, "I'll see if she's available, Detective Jones." She raised an inquiring brow.

What now? I took the receiver from her hands. "This is Ellison Russell."

There was a brief pause—just long enough for him to decide whether to call me Ellison or Mrs. Russell. Detective Anarchy Jones did neither. "Roger Harper has died."

Roger? Dead? "The oven was broken. How could he be dead?" Suddenly I didn't feel like roaring.

Detective Jones cleared his throat. "We'd like you to come back for questioning."

* * *

I took Max home with me. Daddy insisted. For some reason he thought the dog might act as protection. My assurances that Max had been less than helpful the last time an intruder made his or her way inside my house fell on deaf ears. Then again, Daddy's request that I call, apologize to Mother, and stay at their house did too. I'd sooner book a room at the Hanoi Hilton. Hell, I'd rather stay with Kitty or Prudence, and there was a real chance one of them might murder me in my sleep.

Max loved driving in my convertible. The wind caught his lips and blew them back along with his ears. He was in doggy heaven. Me, I'd just left heaven for a warmer clime.

If Detective Jones hadn't requested my presence, I might have stayed at the farm forever. No murder. No mayhem. No Mother. Instead, I pulled into my driveway.

Aggie opened the front door. She wore a black muumuu brightened with lurid Hawaiian flowers and sleeves edged with hot pink puff balls that clashed with her hair. No wonder I'd underestimated her. She looked like a lunatic with her muumuu and wild hair and false eyelashes that looked like a proliferation of long-legged spiders. Her appearance hid a sharp mind.

"Welcome home." She scratched Max behind the ears and offered me an apologetic smile. "You have a couple of messages."

Of course I did.

"Your father called. He asked that you call him when you arrive safely." Aggie tried to tuck a curl behind her ear but it sprung free the moment her fingers let it go. "Mr. Foster has called twice. When I said I expected you this afternoon, he said he'd like to take you to dinner."

"I'm meeting Hunter at the police station, and I don't know how long they'll keep me there."

"Mr. Foster said he'd be happy to play things by ear."

Powers was probably dying to hear all about how I'd found Roger's body. If I could tell the police, I could tell Powers. I glanced at my watch. It wasn't even noon and all I wanted was a nap. Burning bridges and roaring were exhausting. "Would you please call him, Aggie? Tell him to stop by for a drink around five." Surely Detective Jones would be done questioning me by then. "We can go to dinner after that. Also, would you please call Mr. Tafft and ask him to join me at the police station in about an hour?"

Aggie nodded.

I trudged upstairs to comb my hair and change. For some reason, one I didn't care to examine closely, I wanted to look my best when I sat next to Hunter Tafft and across a table from Anarchy Jones.

"Thank you for coming, Mrs. Russell." Anarchy Jones crossed his arms over his chest like I was the last person he wanted to see sitting across from him.

I wasn't exactly thrilled to see him either. We sat in a dingy interview room that reeked of stale cigarette smoke and old sweat. The dress I was wearing, a brand new Diane Von Furstenberg that wrapped then tied at the waist, would probably have to go to the dry cleaners to get rid of the smell. "You didn't leave me much choice."

Next to me Hunter glowered and looked lawyerly.

Detective Jones opened the file that rested on the battered table that separated us. "I have some questions about how you came to find Roger Harper's body."

I shifted in my chair. "Kathleen O'Malley found Roger then she called me."

"How did you come to know Ms. O'Malley?" he asked.

"Haven't we been through this before?"

Detective Jones' lips thinned ever so slightly. "Humor me."

"After Madeline died, Roger was distraught."

Detective Jones lowered his chin so that his expression looked almost disbelieving. "Distraught?"

I bet Detective Jones had never been distraught in his whole life. "Distraught," I repeated. "He passed out on my front stoop. I brought him inside and gave him coffee. He cried."

"And then?"

"Roger knew Madeline and Henry had frequented Ms. O'Malley's club and he begged me to go there with him. He wanted to see it for himself."

Detective Jones cocked his head to the side. "Did you?"

"Did I what?"

"Did you want to see Ms. O'Malley's club?"

If the detective was trying to embarrass me, he was following the wrong path. I could have lived happily ever after without seeing the interior of Club K. I pasted on my chilliest smile—one that would do Mother proud. "Not particularly."

Detective Jones glanced at his notes. "But you went anyway?"

"I did. I felt sorry for him."

"What happened at the club?"

A vision of the Berkley horse danced in my brain and I shook my head in a futile attempt to erase it. "Roger decided to stay and get to know Ms. O'Malley better."

"You let him?"

What would he have me do? Drag Roger out against his will? "He's a grown man."

"You said he was distraught."

Hunter shifted in his chair. "Where is this going?"

Detective Jones scowled and looked at the legal pad that lay in front of him on the table. "Was Mr. Harper in the habit of taking valium?"

"I don't know. Why?"

"We found a massive quantity of diazepam in his blood."

"I'm sorry." I shook my head. "I don't know. When he came to my house, the day we went to the club, he'd been drinking."

Detective Jones flipped a page in his yellow pad. "You only met Ms. O'Malley the one time?"

"Twice," I said.

"The second time?" His eyebrow rose.

"She came to see me in the hospital."

"Oh?" The damn eyebrow rose higher.

"She warned me not to talk about her club to the police."

Detective Jones didn't even pretend to consult his notes. "And you didn't."

Hunter cleared his throat. "Mrs. Russell was under no obligation to tell the police about where her husband conducted his affairs."

Detective Jones rested his forearms on the table. His lips thinned. "I would think as a concerned citizen, Mrs. Russell would have come forward."

I clasped my hands in my lap to keep them from twirling a piece of hair or picking at cuticles or doing any of the other things they did when I was nervous. "I didn't have any reason to talk about it."

Detective Jones' snort was disbelieving. "You didn't think the police would be interested in knowing that a murder victim frequented a bondage club?"

I shook my head. "Madeline was drugged and drowned, not tied and whipped."

Hunter snickered. Detective Jones scowled again.

I clasped my hands so tightly the knuckles whitened. Good thing they were hidden by the table. "There were scads of people who disliked Madeline. Any one of them could have killed her."

"Which one? Do you have any idea who did it?"

I glanced at my hands folded neatly in my lap, at the faded paint on the wall, then at Hunter. I ought to tell Detective Jones about Rand Hamilton. If I did, Grace would forever be known as the daughter of a blackmailer. I shook my head. "No idea."

Of course, he didn't believe me. The eyebrow rose like someone had pulled it with a string. "Mrs. Russell." Detective Jones ran a hand through his hair. "Ellison. There's a murderer out there. If you know something, you need to tell me. For your own safety."

"Mrs. Russell has already stated that she doesn't know who killed those people." Hunter leaned back in the uncomfortable wooden chair and narrowed his eyes. "Trying to scare her won't change her answer."

Detective Jones narrowed his eyes too.

They stared at each other like they wished looks could kill.

Maybe they were just competing to see who could look the most like Clint Eastwood. Detective Jones won. Hunter looked too civilized to pull off physical menace. "Do you have any more questions, Detective Jones?" I asked.

He tore his gaze away from Hunter. "Why did Ms. O'Malley call you?"

It was a good question. One I still didn't have an answer for. "I don't know."

"Guess," said Detective Jones.

"Don't guess, Ellison." Hunter's eyes were still narrowed. "If you want to know why Ms. O'Malley called Ellison, I suggest you ask her."

"Can you think of any reason Ms. O'Malley might have had to harm any of the victims?"

Did he suspect Mistress K? Did he think I was in cahoots with a dominatrix? I could narrow my eyes too. "I hardly know her."

"That's why I can't help wondering why she called you."

"If you have nothing further..." Hunter scraped his chair across the worn tile floor.

Detective Jones didn't move. "Three people are dead. If you know something, you need to tell me."

I shook my head. "I'm sorry, Detective. I can't help you."

"Can't or won't?"

Hunter's hand closed on my elbow. "Let's go, Ellison."

I didn't argue. I rose from my chair. I walked to the door and paused, just for a second, to look back at Detective Jones. He'd rested his forehead against the heel of his hand. Lines etched his tanned face. I'd never seen anyone look more worried.

TWENTY-EIGHT

Before I could even begin to dig my keys out of the depths of my purse, Powers opened my front door. He wore white pants, a navy blazer, and a dotted viridian green ascot. The tie brought out the green in his eyes. He probably knew that. He looked like some minor European royalty who'd decided to go slumming. "Darling," he drew out the first vowel, "you're home."

"I am." If nothing else, the past week or so had taught me I was aces at stating the obvious.

"Your new housekeeper let me in." The way Powers said *housekeeper*—twisty and sneering—let me know he disapproved of her. Had it been the muumuu that turned him off or the hair?

I didn't need his approval. "I think she's a treasure."

He sniffed. "She was good enough to take Max into the kitchen."

My lips quirked. His pants were that white, his jacket that crisp. Powers wasn't risking even one dog hair marring his perfect ensemble.

"Have you been here long?" I asked.

"No." He stepped aside and let me into my house.

I led him past the formal living room and into the family room. "I'll just go get some ice. Make yourself at home." I picked up the ice bucket.

When I returned with ice and a bottle of wine, Powers was leaning against the edge of my desk sorting through the mail.

"What's this?" He held up the paper with the addresses.

I'd forgotten all about it. "I have no idea. Someone sent it to

Henry. Gin and tonic?" I put the ice bucket down on the drinks cart.

"Do you have lime?" he asked.

"Of course."

"Then yes, please."

I mixed his drink and handed it to him. "Marjorie knows who the man in Ohio is. I've never heard of any of them."

Powers took a contemplative sip of his drink. "Odd places to live."

"I agree. Hunter is going to have his investigator look into them." That sounded so much more impressive than saying *my housekeeper is going to snoop.* "Just leave it there on the desk. I'll make sure he gets it tomorrow."

Powers put the list back. He used his now free fingers to rim the edge of his glass. "How are you holding up? How's Grace?"

"She's with Daddy. The farm is the best place for her."

He nodded. "The grapevine says you found Roger Harper's body—that he tried to commit suicide."

"Roger didn't try to kill himself."

"Oh?"

"No one tries to kill themselves by sticking their head in a broken oven."

Powers choked on his gin. More than choked. He spewed gin. On the desk. On his perfect pants. On the Tabriz that covered the hardwoods.

"Are you all right?"

He patted his chest. "Wrong pipe." Then he looked at the carpet. "Damn! Ellison, I'm terribly sorry. I don't know what happened. Do you have a towel?"

I put my wine down on the coffee table and fetched one.

"Really, I'm so sorry." Powers fell to his knees and daubed at the carpet.

"Don't worry about the carpet." I handed him a second tea towel. "Take care of your pants."

"But—"

"No buts. The great thing about Orientals is that the patterns hide stains. Not that gin is going to stain anything." I put my foot on top of the towel he'd left on the floor. "Are you all right?"

He didn't look all right. He looked pale beneath his tan— almost green.

He stared at the floor. "You're sure your rug won't be spoiled?"

"Grace has spilled everything from grape juice to Tab on this rug. Libba once dropped a glass of red wine on it. It'll be fine." I bent and picked up the damp cloth then held it up to demonstrate its unstained state.

"I am sorry."

"Stop apologizing. Let me get you another drink. You look like you could use it." It was rather sweet of him to get so upset about my carpet. He was still pale. He'd even raked his hand through his never-a-hair-out-of-place hair.

I walked over to the drinks cart, mixed another healthy Tanqueray and tonic, and brought it to him. "What were we talking about?"

"Roger." Powers' voice was muffled by its proximity to his shin. He was taking daubing his pants quite seriously.

"Right. Someone didn't know the oven was broken."

Powers' shoulders shook again. Was he laughing? "So whoever tried to kill him completely screwed up?"

I nodded.

"Are you sure? Everyone in town is talking about how Roger killed Madeline and Henry then killed himself."

"Roger knew the oven was broken."

Powers looked up from his pants long enough to take a gigantic gulp of his new drink. "The neighbors saw him wheeled out."

"He was taken to the hospital not the morgue."

Powers daubed more vigorously. "Which hospital? I should send flowers."

"You can't. He died."

"I thought you said the oven was broken."

"It was. He died of a drug overdose." I took a sip of my wine.

"Roger once told me that Madeline was the best thing that ever happened to him." I wiped unexpected wetness from my eyes. "Can you imagine?"

Powers raised his glass in memory. "Poor Roger." Then he squared his shoulders. "I'm supposed to be cheering you up."

"I'm not sure that's possible."

"Of course it is. You have a show coming up. How's the painting coming?"

I'd forgotten all about the show. There was no way the light-hearted, happy canvases in my studio would gel with anything I'd paint now. "About that..."

Power's spring green gaze searched my face. His brow wrinkled. "You're postponing."

I shook my head. "I'm cancelling. I'll bring you what I have and you can sell it without an opening."

He opened his mouth, presumably to argue, then snapped it shut. We both knew I'd make less money without an opening. He didn't have to point it out.

"You've had a rough time." Powers Foster, master of understatement. "I know just the thing to take your mind off your troubles."

Powers proceeded to share with me every scandalous tidbit he could think of. Some of them were even funny. Then we went to the crêperie and ate crêpes filled with cheese and ham and bits of mushroom. Frankly, I couldn't see why Powers was so wild about the place. I begged off going out for more drinks. He had me home in time for me to put on my nightgown and crawl into bed for the ten o'clock news.

At ten-thirty, I called Grace. "Honey, how are you?"

"Okay." Her voice still sounded flat, like champagne without its sparkle. "Have the police found out anything yet?"

"If so, they're not telling me."

"Mom..."

"Yes, honey?"

"Be careful. Do you have Max with you?"

"He's curled up at the foot of the bed."

Max raised his head and looked at me. I swear the dog knew we were talking about him.

"I love you, Mom."

"I love you too."

We hung up. I punched the pillows a time or two. Max grumbled. I closed my eyes, sure I wouldn't sleep. I did.

I know because Max's growl jarred me out of a dream. The sound was deep, low, and menacing. He jumped off the bed and went to stand by the door.

I stayed in bed and strained to hear whatever it was that had disturbed the dog.

Nothing. Well, nothing but the dog's growl. He looked over his shoulder, a clear why-aren't-you-getting-up look on his doggy face and then I heard it. A thump as if someone had walked into a piece of furniture in the dark.

My heart, which had been stuttering along, switched into overdrive. It raced. It careened. It slammed into my chest.

I picked up the phone and got a busy signal.

Max growled again.

Someone was in my house. They'd taken the phone off the hook so I couldn't call for help. I was in my bedroom with nothing but a dog and a .22 for protection.

I opened the drawer to my bedside table, closed my fingers around the gun, and released the safety. Then I eased out of bed and tiptoed to the door.

Max watched as my fingers closed around the knob and turned. I'd opened the door no more than an inch or two when he nosed past me and ran down the stairs at full speed. Someone once told me that a barking dog is offering a warning. Max didn't bark. Whoever was in the house would meet Max with no more than the sound of his claws on the hardwood as warning.

Downstairs something crashed. Then something else. Then came a muffled voice uttering profanities. A cry of pain. Max barked. Then the back door slammed.

I stood frozen at the top of the stairs, my heart still trying to escape my chest, my fingers sweaty against the gun's handle.

I didn't move until Max appeared at the bottom of the stairs and looked up at me.

Then I sat, my legs suddenly too weak to hold me.

I don't know how long I sat there—long enough for my heart rate to return to a human pace, for my hands to stop shaking, and for the dog to take a position at the bottom of the steps that assured me no one would make it past him.

Finally, I found the courage to creep down the stairs.

The shadows seemed darker, the white noise filled with menace. Despite Max's obvious swagger, I worried the intruder might still be in the house. The front door was closed. I tiptoed toward it and felt for the security chain. It was still in place. Whoever had entered my house hadn't done it through the front door.

I inched toward the kitchen. Next to me, Max's nails clicked on the floor. My fingers grazed the top of his head. The dog had earned his very own t-bone steak.

The kitchen was pitch dark. I should have left lights on. Too late now. I steadied my shaking hand and flipped the light switch. Everything was as it should be except the back door hung open and the phone was off the hook. I put the receiver back in its cradle, counted to three, then picked it up again and wedged it between my ear and my shoulder. One hand clutched the gun, the other dialed the operator.

"I need the police," I said. "Someone has broken into my house."

A slightly bored voice asked, "Address?"

I gave it to her then I glanced at the oven clock. Two o'clock. The neighbors weren't going to like yet another night of having their rest disturbed by flashing lights and sirens. One of them would call Mother. I shuddered. Then I remembered Mother wasn't speaking to me. I doubted a little thing like an intruder in my house would change that.

I heard the first siren followed almost immediately by the doorbell.

With Max at my side, I peeked through a window before I opened the door to two police officers.

They stared at me, their mouths open, their eyes wide, and I realized I was wearing nothing more than a sheer nightgown accessorized with a gun.

"Are you all right, ma'am?"

How many times over the past week or so had I been asked that very question? How many times had I lied and said I was fine? I was tired of lying. "No."

Before they could respond, another car, this one without flashing lights or a siren, pulled into the driveway. I knew before I saw so much as a loafer touch my driveway that Anarchy Jones was behind the wheel.

He strode up to the house with a scowl affixed to his lean face. The scowl deepened when he saw me standing in the doorway. "Are you all right?"

"She says 'no,'" said one of the uniformed officers.

Anarchy looked at me closely and despite the warm night air, goose pimples raised on my arms.

"Are you hurt?" he asked.

I shook my head. My traitorous throat felt tight and quivery and not up to the task of speaking.

Again, I felt his gaze on me. It searched my face then moved lower. The damn nightgown didn't hide a thing. In fact, it was designed to show off everything. I crossed the arm without the gun over my chest and felt heat rise to my cheeks.

A slow grin spread across his face and the chilly expression in his eyes thawed. Hell, it grew warm. He reached out and gently took the gun from my fingers. "Let's get you something more to put on."

I let him take the gun. No way was I letting him take me upstairs to find something more appropriate to wear to a burglary. Instead, I yanked open the front hall closet, grabbed a khaki raincoat and shoved my arms into the sleeves. I might look like a flasher but I wouldn't be in my bedroom while the police poked around my house.

"You want to tell me what happened?" he asked.

"Max heard something. Then I heard something." I bent and scratched behind my hero's floppy gray ear. "When I let him out of my bedroom, he raced downstairs and I heard a crash or two. Then I called the police."

"Where were the crashes?"

"The family room, I think."

He raised a brow. "You're not sure? Haven't you been in there?"

"No."

"Why not?"

I wrapped the raincoat around me and tied the belt. "If Max killed the burglar, I didn't want to be the one who found the body." I was only half-kidding.

Detective Jones pressed his lips together. Tightly. Like he was trying to hide a smile.

We stared at each other a moment. He'd probably prefer it if I quietly disappeared, went to Mother's, let him investigate without me around. Wasn't going to happen.

Finally, he sighed. "Let's go."

I turned on my bare heel and led him and the two uniformed officers down the front hall to the kitchen. We all stopped to consider the gaping back door.

"I assume you locked it before you went to bed," said Detective Jones.

I rolled my eyes.

Such a childish response was beneath his notice. He ignored me to inspect the door and then the lock. "It hasn't been forced. Who has a key?"

"Me, Grace, the housekeeper, Mrs. Landingham, our next door neighbor to the west—" As opposed to our neighbor to the east, who I was fairly certain donned black and rode a broom. She was probably outside casting an evil spell because I'd disturbed her rest. "My parents each have one."

"That's it?" Who knew Detective Jones had a sarcastic streak?

"If I think of anyone else, I'll let you know."

Watching Detective Jones examine the door wasn't exactly scintillating. I moved toward the family room.

He caught my arm and stopped me. "No telling what's in there. I'll go first."

I shrugged and followed him into an unholy mess.

TWENTY-NINE

Why any burglar would bother with our family room was beyond me. My grandmother's sterling tea service was displayed on the buffet in the dining room. Henry's grandfather's collection of Fabergé eggs glittered behind the glass of a curio cabinet in the living room. A framed Babe Ruth baseball card, which in better times Henry told me could fund our retirement, hung in the study. Those damned Toby mugs were there too. Some of them were quite valuable.

The family room held nothing but a bunch of comfortable, approaching shabby, furniture, and a television.

An undisturbed television.

By contrast, the area around my desk was destroyed. Drawers were emptied, papers were swept to the floor, and a Lalique paperweight that might have been worth stealing lay shattered near the window.

"Any idea what they were looking for?" Detective Jones asked.

I shook my head. "None." It made no sense. Why would one of Henry's blackmail victims think they could find something incriminating in my desk?

"You're sure?" he asked.

"No idea."

"There's some blood over here," one of the uniformed officers said. "Looks like maybe the dog bit someone." He pointed to a bit of torn dark fabric on the floor.

Max, who'd settled next to me, grinned his best doggy grin and looked proud. I scratched behind his ear. "You get a steak tomorrow."

"We'll have to dust for fingerprints," said the other officer.

Poor Aggie. She'd finally gotten the study put to rights.

"Tell me again who has a key," said Detective Jones.

I counted everyone off on my fingers.

Detective Jones put the thumb of his right hand on one temple and his ring finger on the other then he squeezed. Almost like he was fighting a headache...or controlling the need to scold me. "You ought to get your locks changed. That door wasn't forced."

Did he actually believe one of the people who had a key to the house had turned to burglary? "I guess I should check under the flower pot."

"The flower pot?" His voice held a certain soupcon of incredulity.

"The one by the back door."

Detective Jones left off squeezing his temples in favor of rubbing his brow with the heel of his hand. The man had a headache. That or he despaired of my intelligence. He jerked his chin toward one of the uniformed officers who promptly disappeared down the short hallway to the kitchen.

He returned a moment later. "No key."

Detective Jones' eye twitched. "Three murders and you left a key outside your door?"

When he put it that way, it made me sound reckless. Or stupid. I was neither. I just hadn't thought about the key being there. "Grace sometimes forgets her key. Besides, we've kept a key under that pot for years and never had a problem."

He snorted. "I think it's safe to say circumstances have changed."

I couldn't argue with that. I could argue with his tone. "No one likes a smart ass, Detective Jones."

The uniformed policemen, one furiously scribbling notes on a pad, the other poking behind the drapes, froze. Detective Jones glared at me through narrowed eyes. "Kitchen."

When I didn't move, he stepped forward, grabbed my elbow, and dragged me out of the family room.

Max growled. The same low, deep-in-his-throat sound he'd used to alert me someone was in the house. It promised blood and violence.

Detective Jones left off glaring at me and glared at the dog. The growl in Max's throat faded to silence. Unfortunately that meant the detective was free to return his scowl to me. "Two couples. Four people. Three are dead. You do understand you could be next, don't you?"

I understood it but I didn't believe it. I shook my head. "I don't think so."

He hadn't released my arm. His grip tightened. "Why? You know something. I know you do. You've got to tell me."

That my husband was a blackmailer? Not likely. If my arm had been free, I would have crossed it over my chest, a not so subtle sign I had no intention of telling him anything. But it wasn't free. When he used his other hand to catch my chin and force me to look into his brown eyes, my determination slipped.

"You have to tell me," he insisted. "I can't keep you safe unless I know what I'm up against." His eyes were flecked with gold. Honest eyes. Sincere eyes. Keep me safe eyes.

I had so many suspects. Rand Hamilton. The other names on the envelopes. Kitty Ballew. Prudence Davies. I had to tell him something.

"You know Henry went to that sex club..." My voice was barely above a whisper and Detective Jones leaned closer. He smelled faintly of Yardley cologne and strongly of man. Heat rose to my cheeks. With any luck, he'd think it was because I was embarrassed to be talking about a sex club. There was something wrong with me. Had to be. My husband wasn't even buried and Detective Jones made my heart flutter.

"And?"

"He went with Madeline Harper. When they were there—" I shifted my gaze from his eyes to his shoulder.

"Tell me, Ellison." Somehow, he managed to be gentle and demanding in the same breath.

I focused on his shoulder. No plaid pants tonight. Instead, a plaid shirt. I followed a blue thread that got lost when it met tan and green stripes. "When they were there, they were also with Kitty Ballew and Prudence Davies. Kathleen O'Malley said Henry played Kitty and Prudence against each other to supplant Madeline."

"You think one of them killed Madeline?"

I nodded. "It's possible."

"Why kill Henry?"

I shrugged. "Maybe she was angry he ignored her at the country club the night he got home. They were both there and he didn't bother to acknowledge either one of them."

"What about Roger Harper?"

"The fall guy."

He released my arm. Not my chin, that he still held between strong fingers. I left off my study of his plaid shoulder and risked a glance at his eyes. His pupils were so large it was hard to see the irises were brown. His expression was intent, as if he was weighing pros and cons and repercussions. My heartbeat skipped.

With his free hand, he pushed a strand of hair away from my face.

My breath, already shallow, caught in my lungs.

He bent his head, drew closer.

My lips parted.

Time stopped.

Then Detective Anarchy Jones took a giant, abrupt step backward and released my chin. He turned his back to me and rested his hands against the kitchen island as if it was holding him up. "We'll bring them in for questioning." His voice was as sharp as the broken shards of my Lalique paperweight.

His rejection felt like diving into icy pool water. It stole my breath. It chilled me. It made me wonder what the hell I was doing.

Before I had a chance to figure it out, Hunter Tafft appeared in the doorway from the front hall. "Your mother telephoned. One of your neighbors called to complain that the police were at your house again." His sharp gaze took in Detective Jones' stance and me with my back pressed against the kitchen counter. He raised a brow.

"I was just telling Detective Jones who Henry spent his time with at Club K." Hopefully talking about a sex club would explain away the embarrassed flush warming my cheeks.

Detective Jones straightened his shoulders, gave up the island's support and turned to face Hunter. I checked to make sure my raincoat was securely fastened.

Hunter looked mildly amused. He also looked like he'd just stepped out of an ad for expensive cologne or champagne—sure of himself, sophisticated, perfectly dressed.

No one spoke for a full minute. I know. I watched the seconds tick by on the oven clock.

Finally, I broke the silence. "I'm going to go change." Looking like a flasher wasn't doing me any favors. "Maybe one of you could make coffee?" I brushed past Hunter and marched up the stairs with Max at my heels, the only male I could count on.

When I came back downstairs with brushed hair, brushed teeth, and khaki shorts instead of a khaki raincoat, the smell of coffee met me in the hallway.

One of them had figured out Mr. Coffee. There were grounds all over the counter to prove it.

At least he'd pushed the button then left. I had the kitchen to myself.

I poured myself a cup, brought the cup to my lips, sipped and spit. Whoever had violated Mr. Coffee had made tar laced with tiny bits of coal. The foul concoction now decorated the countertops, part of the wall and my white tee shirt.

"Too strong?" Hunter asked.

I nodded, unable to speak, the coffee having melted my throat. I filled a glass with water then drank. Deeply.

"I wasn't sure how much to put in."

So he went with half a can? I emptied the pot into the sink, rinsed it twice, then dared pull the handle to the filter. It was filled to the brim with grounds. Wet globs of them dripped onto the warming burner. There were probably even grounds in the water reservoir.

Grace was the proud owner of a fabulous I-can't-believe-you'd-do-something-so-stupid look. It involved dropping her chin slightly toward the left collarbone, wrinkling her brow, and looking up through her eyelashes. She used it if I sang with the radio when we drove. It was also employed when I asked her vegetarian friend, Pamela, if she wanted bacon with her pancakes. On one memorable occasion, when I was late picking her up, Grace managed to hold the expression for the length of an entire car ride. I used it now.

"What?" he asked.

I grabbed a paper towel, held it beneath the hole at the bottom of the filter basket until it was over the trash basket, then upended it. Wet grounds plopped into the trash. I shook again, waiting for the filter. Nothing but sodden coffee grounds. The man hadn't used a filter. Unbelievable.

Then again, my life had become unbelievable. Murders and break-ins and fights with Mother that wouldn't be easily resolved.

I tossed the coffee grimed filter basket into the sink and turned on hot water, poured some dish soap onto a sponge and began to scrub. I scrubbed the pot too. Hard.

"Out, damned spot."

I glanced over my shoulder at Hunter. He wasn't leaning against the coffee spattered counter, he was lounging. His hands were in the pockets of his pressed khakis. His navy blazer was unbuttoned. He needed just a breath of wind in his hair and he'd be on the deck of a yacht. His eyes ruined the illusion, they were serious. Also, a few lines puckered his forehead. And he was quoting Macbeth.

"Pardon me?" I snapped.

"'Out, damned spot.' It's what Lady Macbeth says when she feels guilty over Duncan's death."

"If anyone should feel guilty, it's you. You may have killed Mr.

Coffee." I returned to my scrubbing, this time with a bristled pot scrubber.

"Liar." He stepped closer. I could sense him right behind me. "You're wondering if you'd turned over the files if Roger Harper would still be alive." His voice was so low I could hardly hear him. "You're wondering if this would all be over."

I hadn't been thinking that at all. I'd been debating between Kitty and Prudence as the most likely murderess. Hunter must have been thinking the files held the key. Hunter felt guilty. The lawyer had a conscience. Who knew? I held up my brush and turned to face him. He was inches away. "Would you like to scrub for a while?"

"You seem to be doing an able job."

"Then maybe you'd like to wipe off the counters." I jerked my chin toward a roll of paper towels.

He didn't move. He was close enough for me to feel his warmth, to smell fine fabric and a trace of expensive cologne, to see the flecks of ice melting in his eyes. Oh dear Lord. I'd already had one near encounter in the kitchen. I wasn't up for a second.

I thrust the dripping brush like a sword, stopping it just short of his immaculate jacket. "Scrub or wipe."

He retreated and I took a deep breath of air untinged by his scent.

"I'll wipe." He tore a paper towel off the roll.

"Thank you." I nodded toward the hallway that led to the family room where the police poked and prodded and covered my belongings in dust. "We can discuss Macbeth another time."

"In the morning."

"It is morning."

"In the morning when we get up."

I froze. My heart, my muscles, my lungs, all cast in ice. Just for a moment. Then I waved the scrubber in Hunter's direction. Who cared if I covered the freshly wiped counters with soapy water? Not me. "*We* are not getting up. I am getting up. You are getting up. There is no *we*."

THE DEEP END 233

"I'm spending the night." He crossed his arms over his chest.

I should have stabbed him with the scrubber when I had the chance. Too late now. "You're not."

Hunter snorted. "Ellison, someone—maybe the murderer—has a key to your house. I'm spending the night here. Or, if you'd prefer, you can come back to my place."

I didn't want him here and I sure as hell didn't want to go home with him. "Max will protect me."

Hunter tried out Grace's I-can't-believe-you'd-do-something-so-stupid expression. He looked like Atticus Finch staring down one of Tom Ewell's lies. "We both know that dog can be bought off with a bone."

He wasn't wrong. I tried a different tack. "You can't spend the night with a client. Isn't there a lawyer rule against that?"

"You're not my client. Your mother is. She's the one who sent me over here tonight. Remember?"

I ought to have written him a retainer check days ago. Where was my checkbook? The blasted thing had been in my desk, in the family room, with the police. Damn.

Before I could stop, consider or talk myself out of it, I marched into the wreck of the family room, located my checkbook and picked it up off the floor.

Detective Jones and the two uniformed officers stopped wreaking havoc and gawked at me.

I waved it at them. "I need this." Then I narrowed my focus to Anarchy Jones. "And I want my gun."

THIRTY

I didn't sleep.

When the police left after two hours of investigating my rifled desk, I marched up the stairs, wordlessly pointed Hunter, who refused to accept a check, toward a guest room.

I took refuge in my bedroom. It had taken seven attempts to get the color of the robin's egg blue walls exactly right. The hassle was worth it. My walls were cool and serene and calm. The exact opposite of me.

Max curled up at the end of the bed. I didn't have the energy to shoo him off.

Instead, I curled up on the window seat and watched the night.

My husband was dead and I felt no grief. Surely I ought to feel something. Well, something besides guilt for not feeling.

My daughter was grieving and my heart bled for her. Thank God I'd left her with Daddy. Distance from the chaos swirling around my life was the best thing for her. If I repeated that often enough, I might even believe it.

Mother was...well, Mother was Mother. Furious with me for failing to fall in line with her plans and for scraping together the courage to hang up on her. Yet, she'd cared enough to send Hunter.

My lawyer. Suave, demanding, more handsome than was good for me. He bent rules as easily as twisty straws and he seemed to think he could take up residence in my life without permission. I could let him. I could unlock my door and walk down the hallway, tap on the door to his room and change everything. Making such a momentous decision in the midst of a murder investigation seemed as foolish as trying to chip out of a sand trap with a driver.

Then there was Anarchy Jones, the policeman who colored inside the lines, the man who even yet might arrest me. I'd wanted to kiss him. He'd wanted to kiss me. I'd sensed it. A connection had arced between us, alive with possibility, energizing and terrifying at the same time. Later, in the family room, I'd wanted to take my gun and hit him over the head with it. *Are you sure you know how to use it?*

As soon as I was old enough to beg to go hunting with Daddy, he'd made sure I knew how to shoot a gun. Killing animals hadn't appealed to me. The art of putting a hole in the center of a target had. That and my winning marksmanship competitions had made Daddy happy.

When had I stopped shooting because I liked it and kept at it because it made my father happy? Who knew?

I knocked my forehead against the window.

I'd spent so much of my life, so much time and energy, making other people happy—Mother, Daddy, Henry, even Grace—that I'd overlooked my own unhappiness. I'd ignored their resentment when I disappeared behind a locked door to paint. It had been waiting for me when I came out, caustic and real enough to make me feel guilty about the one thing that was mine.

None of this was part of the plan all the girls I'd grown up with had been given. Not a written plan, unless the book about Cinderella counted. The plan was in the water we drank, the air we breathed. It was poured into the pavement on the streets we called home. Marry a nice man, one who was a good provider, and live happily, or at least comfortably, ever after.

Safe to say I'd followed the plan. I'd married a banker. Had a baby. But the plan had failed me. It left me alone huddled in a window seat with every emotion I'd refused to let myself feel seeping through my pores until the air in my bedroom was heavy with sadness and angst and confusion.

I sat there until the sky began to lighten with soft shades of lavender and gold and pink dotted with bits of fluffy clouds. It reminded me of the sunrise the morning I found Madeline. I missed my morning swim. With that thought, I abandoned my perch, took a shower, and pulled on some clothes. Max raised a sleepy brow then snuggled more deeply into my covers. He was welcome to the bed. I grabbed my purse, pausing just long enough to drop the gun into its depths, then tiptoed down the back stairs, holding my breath with each creak. No way was I waking up Hunter.

I drove with no destination in mind, until manicured lawns and neat storefronts gave way to smaller houses with crumbling front walks, until warehouses gave way to wheat fields. I drove past neat farms and farms with rusted cars dotting their yards to a little town I'd never heard of. I stopped in front of a diner with a herd of pick-up trucks parked in front.

Inside men wore overalls and John Deere hats and talked about rain and tornadoes and taxes. I ordered a cup of coffee, eggs, toast, and fried potatoes and listened to them. I was used to men who wore Brooks Brothers suits and talked about the stock market and their golf games and, yes, taxes.

I pretended I didn't notice that everyone was staring at me. The stranger. As out of place in their world as they would be in mine.

I ate my food, stared out the window at the row of dusty Ford trucks, and wondered what the hell I was doing. The waitress poured me more coffee, brought me more cream. The men in overalls filtered out to the trucks like sunlight through a gauzy curtain. One instant they were inside, the next in their trucks and the next the trucks were gone.

It was just me and the waitress. Her nametag said Flo.

"You want more coffee?" Flo asked.

I pushed my cup toward her.

She filled the cup to the brim.

What in the world was I doing? Running?

If I was running, where was I going? Nowhere without Grace.

I couldn't run. Not really. Maybe I could hide.

Grace and I would spend the rest of the summer in Europe, far away from vicious chatter. We might even stay there. I could find a tutor or enroll Grace in school in London. I could paint. We could go to museums and the theatre and the opera. We'd be so cultured, we'd quote Shakespeare in our sleep. When Grace was ready for college, I'd travel the whole world. All the places I'd wanted to go that Henry had refused. A safari in Kenya. Trips to see the Great Wall and the pyramids at Giza. I'd kiss the Blarney Stone, ride a camel in the desert, and snorkel in the Great Barrier Reef. Alone.

The murders, my battle with Mother, Hunter Tafft, and Anarchy Jones would fade into distant memory.

Maybe.

Maybe they'd haunt me. Riddles left unanswered. Problems left unsolved.

Something deep inside me twisted. No way could I hide from my life.

I laid a twenty on top of the three dollar check and headed home.

A police car and Hunter's Mercedes were parked in my drive. I drove right past them. I needed a different destination, one that didn't involve where-have-you-been questions or the shadows of death. I might not want to hide, but I wasn't quite ready to go toe to toe with my issues either.

Driving to Power's gallery to pick up my check seemed an attractive alternative. Besides, after seeing the cars in the driveway, Europe was looking more attractive and Powers was sure to tell me my travel plans were genius.

The bell on the door to Powers' gallery jingled when I opened it. I took a moment to look at the canvases he had hanging. A Frank Stella, a couple of Jasper Johns prints, several of Philomene Bennett's paintings, a handful of other regional artists, and me. My paintings were keeping excellent company.

"Hello," I called.

"Sorry, sorry." A young man emerged from the office. "I didn't hear you come in."

The young man had dark hair, dark wings for eyebrows, and cheekbones that could cut metal. He also had full lips and eyes as brown as Anarchy Jones'. He wore a tight lavender shirt and white pants, and he simpered when he walked. Where had Powers found him? Would it be rude to ask? "You're new."

He smiled, displaying dazzling white teeth. "I am."

"I'm Ellison Russell."

He blinked.

I waited.

Nothing. No sign of recognition. How does one work in an art gallery and not know the names of the artists hanging on the walls? Apparently, Powers hadn't hired him for his intellect.

"I'd like to see Powers."

"Mr. Foster is coming in late today. May I help you with something?"

I pointed to a canvas. "I painted that. Powers said I could stop by and pick up a check."

The smile grew brighter. "He's not here."

"You already said that."

His smile began to look a bit forced. "It's still true."

"I don't need him to be here to pick up a check."

The young man's hands fluttered like butterflies. "I could call him."

Powers might find Madeline's replacement charming or funny or handsome. I found him distinctly annoying. "I don't believe I caught your name."

"Freddy. Freddy Merlot. Like the wine."

"Well, Freddy, where exactly is Powers?"

"He called and said he'd had a rough night. He's not coming in until this afternoon."

"There's no need to disturb him." Where had Powers gone after he left my house? "In the office, there's a file cabinet. All of Powers' clients and artists have files. My check will be in the file. Why don't you go get it?"

"I couldn't."

A deep breath was in order. "Why not?"

"I'm not supposed to get into the files."

I swallowed my impatience. "Then I'll get it."

"Oh, no."

"Oh, yes."

I brushed past him and opened the door to Powers' office. A Calder hung from the ceiling. A Picasso graced one wall. Beneath it sat a huge credenza. I tried to open it. It was locked. Like that could stop me. I picked up a small Henry Moore sculpture off the desk and grabbed the key.

Freddy Merlot stood in the doorway. His hands were still fluttering, and he'd caught the corner of his bottom lip in his very white teeth. "I don't think this is a good idea."

"That's because it's an excellent idea."

The jingle of the front door opening underscored my point.

Freddy didn't move.

"Aren't you going to see who that is?" I asked. "It could be a customer."

Still he lingered, clearly unwilling to leave me alone in Powers' office.

"Freddy, Powers is a dear friend. He won't care if I grab my check. I promise. He will care if someone steals something because you weren't out front."

With a telling sniff, Freddy spun on his heel and sashayed off.

I hadn't made a friend. I didn't care.

I opened the file drawer and flipped through the Rs. Rice. Roper. Runyon. Russell.

Wait. Runyon? I recognized the name.

I pulled the Runyon file out of the drawer and opened it. George Runyon lived in Duluth, Minnesota. Powers had sold him a Picasso for an impressive amount of money.

It had to be a coincidence. Why hadn't Powers said anything when he was looking at the list?

I flipped through the files. Jack Gillis, the man in Toledo. He too had purchased a Picasso.

I knew the next one would be there. Albert Smithers of Provo, Utah. I looked anyway. Sure enough, Smithers was the proud owner of a Picasso.

Why did Powers have files for the men on Henry's list? I opened the Smithers' file with numb fingers.

The copy of the provenance, a piece of art's history of ownership, wasn't there. What the hell?

Had Powers been selling fakes? Had Henry and Madeline found out?

I stared at the Picasso over the credenza. Filled with hard edges and stark color it mirrored my thoughts. What if Powers had sold forgeries? What if Henry and Madeline had blackmailed him? What if Powers had killed them?

I had to be wrong. There had to be some other explanation. There was no way my flamboyant, loving friend was a murderer. Not Powers.

The door jingled. Freddy Merlot had succeeded in scaring away a customer. I shoved the files back into their places. Slipped my check out of my file and closed the drawer.

Just in time, too. Especially since it wasn't Freddy Merlot who appeared in the office doorway, it was Powers.

For once in his life, Powers didn't look ready for a photo shoot. There were purple shadows underneath his green eyes. "What are you doing?"

I held up my check as explanation. "Are you all right? You don't look yourself."

He limped into the room.

I stood, grabbed his elbow and helped him settle into his chair. "What happened?"

"A little car accident. Nothing too serious, but I'm sore as hell." He leaned back in his chair and sighed.

If I could overlook the fatigue on his face, Powers looked almost like Powers. Mint green shirt, tan blazer, white pants, Italian loafers, no socks. Then he crossed his leg and I saw a bandage that covered most of his calf.

How did he hurt his calf in a car accident?

In that second, my doubts disappeared. His injuries weren't sustained in a car accident. They were the result of a run-in with one very protective Weimaraner.

He'd killed Madeline and Henry. He'd hit me over the head with a fireplace poker. He'd killed Roger. Last night he'd broken into my house.

My friend killed people, apparently without remorse.

"Ellison, you look pale. Are you going to faint?"

"No. Of course not. I'm just tired." I attempted an insouciant shrug of my shoulders and forced myself to look at his face, not his leg. Powers had killed three times. I couldn't let him know I suspected as much. "Someone broke into the house last night. I didn't get much sleep."

"You poor darling. What was taken?"

"I'm not sure. Whoever it was started in the family room and there's not much of value in there." Except I was sure. One piece of paper had been stolen, a list with three names, proud owners of Picassos without provenances.

"How dreadful." His voice was filled with ersatz sympathy.

"Yes."

Powers rubbed his chin. "Any idea who did it?"

"None." Did I sound too definitive? Like I was protesting too much? "The police are still at the house dusting for fingerprints and making a mess."

"Well, maybe the burglar didn't wear gloves."

"Maybe not." The burglar hadn't worn gloves. His prints were all over the room anyway. "I suppose I ought to be on my way."

"Stay. Have a cup of coffee with me."

Powers had drugged Madeline and Roger. There was no way anything he offered was passing my lips. My heart thudded against my chest and my hands slicked with sweat.

"I can't," I squeaked then I lowered my voice, "I mean, I have errands and I have to check on the plans for Henry's funeral and..." My voice trailed off because Powers' eyes had narrowed.

I picked up my purse off the desk, stuffed the check inside, and backed toward the door. "I do have to go. I'll call you later."

Powers struggled out of his chair.

I took a giant step backward, opened the door, and walked into the lavender clad chest of Freddy Merlot. His hands closed around my upper arms.

I struggled to get free. "Let me go."

His grip tightened.

I lifted my knee and brought my foot down hard on his instep. He gasped and released me. I swung my purse, heavy with the weight of my gun, at his head. The sound it made when it connected was hollow, as if there was nothing inside his skull but air. Freddy fell to the floor.

I ran, wresting open the door to the gallery. Then I threw myself into my car. It took three tries to jam the key into the ignition with shaking fingers.

I turned the ignition just in time to see Freddy help Powers into his car. He planned to follow me.

THIRTY-ONE

My Triumph roared to life and with one eye fixed on my rearview mirror, I put the car in gear. I released the clutch too quickly and the engine died. My heart died with it.

Powers tried to maneuver Bitty Sue's tank of an Eldorado out of its spot. After about five seconds, he gave up on careful and collapsed the bumper of the car in front of him.

Almost screaming with frustration, I started my car again and zipped into oncoming traffic. Someone honked and I saw the shadow of a rude gesture as I sped by.

The closest policemen I knew of were at my home. I pointed the car in that direction.

They say misfortune comes in threes. They're right. First, Powers, my dear friend who was also a murderer, followed me. Second, the engine in his car was twice the size of mine. Third, the puffy clouds I'd admired at dawn had coalesced into a grey ceiling that began to spit raindrops, and me with the top down.

I drove. Fast. Every few seconds I wiped water from my eyes without knowing if it was rain or tears.

A quick glance in the rearview revealed that Powers had closed the gap between our cars.

I was already in fifth gear, driving so far over the speed limit as to boggle the mind. Half-blinded by the rain, I could see just enough to know the pavement was dangerously slick. I drove faster. So did Powers.

The road wound around the edge of the golf course. A spilt rail fence was all that separated me from a deep creek bed and the seventh fairway.

My hands gripped the wheel.

My right foot pushed so hard on the accelerator it was a wonder it didn't break through to the pavement.

I heard a sob in the rush of wind and speed and realized I was crying. Hard.

I gulped a damp, ragged breath. No way was I going to lose control. No way was Powers going to kill me the way he had Madeline and Henry and Roger. I took another curve going eighty and felt the wheels leave the pavement. My heart stopped as I fought to control the little car.

How ironic would it be if I killed myself in an automobile accident while fleeing a murderer?

The wheels grabbed traction in the strip of grass next to the road and I sped on.

I risked a second glance in the rearview. Powers was inches from my bumper. The Triumph couldn't go any faster. Powers' Eldorado could.

He rammed me.

Somehow I kept the car on the road. The obscenities I screamed were lost to the wind and rain and speed.

The Eldorado's grill met the trunk of my car a second time.

I spun a dizzying, tilt-a-whirl circle then slammed through the fence, losing a side mirror. The car jolted down the embankment, scraping against rocks and trees before coming to a rest with its nose in the rising creek.

Thunder clapped as if I'd just provided an amusing show.

I couldn't breathe. Couldn't think. Couldn't move.

I had to.

Powers wouldn't be satisfied with knocking me off the road. He had to make sure I was dead. He'd be coming.

My purse had fallen to the passenger-side floorboards, and I reached for it. Even the slightest movement sent waves of sharp pain careening through my chest. My fingers stretched, strained to grab hold of the handle that was just out of my reach.

I shifted then whimpered as new pain knifed through me. But I had it. I pulled the purse toward me and dug for my gun. A checkbook, a billfold, the bag that held make-up, house keys, tissue, random bits of paper, a hairbrush—my questing fingers touched it all. Finally, they found the comforting coolness of metal. My hand closed around the gun.

"Ellison!" Powers' voice was full of concern and for one hopeful, insane, delusional moment, I let myself believe it was all a mistake. Powers, the man who'd appeared at my door with a bottle of bourbon and a box of donuts the morning after the coatroom incident, wouldn't hurt me. Powers, with his snippy gossip and wickedly funny one-liners, wasn't a killer. Except my destroyed car was half-submerged in a creek, each breath I took was a new agony and, when I peered through the falling rain, I could see him using a golf club as a cane to help him down the slope of the hill.

A silly, petty part of me was glad he was ruining his Gucci loafers in the mud.

A more sensible part, a part that wanted to stay alive, struggled to get out of the car. I pulled on the door handle and nothing happened. Nothing. I tried again. Still nothing.

Powers yelped. I looked up in time to see him slide several feet down the hill in his white pants.

The slide ruined a nice pair of linen trousers and brought him that much closer to me.

I gave up on the door and climbed over it. My left hand clutched my right side as if mere fingers could somehow hold ribs in place. My right hand clutched the gun.

I freed myself from the car only to have my feet sink in mud. A bubble of hysterical laughter escaped me. It was a bad day for Italian leather. I abandoned my Ferragamos.

Down the hill a rain-swollen creek looked ready to sweep me away. To my left was Powers. To my right, the embankment grew steeper. It wasn't like I had much choice where to go. I scrabbled around the car then ran—barefoot—on rocky ground.

Rain, mud, the screaming pain in my side and the damn rocks underfoot. Did every single one have a jagged edge? I wiped pink water from my face and added blood to my list of complaints. I tripped, caught a sob in my throat, then pushed myself to standing with my free hand. A sharp clap of thunder was followed by the explosion of bark from a tree a foot to my left. Not thunder. A shot.

Thank God, Powers couldn't hit the wide side of a barn under the best of circumstances. I clutched my gun more tightly and clambered over a large rock.

"Ellison, stop! We'll work this out."

I dared a peek over my shoulder.

He was twenty-five feet away. How had he gotten so close? Powers might actually be able to hit a barn if he got close enough to it.

I gave up on scrabbling through mud and rocks and starter oaks. Instead, I turned and raised my gun. "I'm listening."

Powers' white pants weren't white anymore, his mint green shirt was torn and his blond hair was plastered to his skull. He held a .45. It was pointed at me.

"Tell me why." My voice sounded strangled, as if I was fighting terror or tears. I wasn't. Of course I wasn't. The hand that held the gun shook and I loosed my hold on my ribs to steady it.

"It was Madeline's fault."

If I could keep him talking, someone might drive by and notice the hole in the fence, might peer over the edge and see my car in the creek, might send help. "Madeline?" I blinked away pink-tinged rain.

He nodded. "She snooped in my files."

"So you killed her?"

"She figured out I'd been selling forged Picassos. She wanted a cut."

Of course she did. She'd also told Henry and put us all on a road to misery. "Why sell forgeries?"

"The money."

He didn't say *duh* but the sentiment hung in the air like mist.

"You have plenty of money."

"Not enough to open a gallery in New York."

The pink-tinged rain that clouded my sight seemed redder, as if the mix of blood to water had increased. "New York?"

"I need to get away from here."

"Bitty Sue won't give you the money?"

The sound that escaped his lips was harsh, explosive, caustic.

I flinched.

"If I move to New York, Bitty Sue will cut me off." Powers' voice trembled. His hand trembled. A .45 is a heavy gun. Especially for a man whose heavy lifting usually consisted of martinis with four olives.

"So you sold fakes."

"I was careful. There was no way men in Duluth and Provo and Akron would ever meet or compare collections. It was the perfect plan."

I allowed myself a quick glance up the hill. The damned road was still deserted. "Until Madeline discovered it."

"She wanted to expand. To sell more. She didn't understand the more I sold the more likely I was to get caught."

I swallowed. "So you killed her."

"I told her to meet me at the gallery and we'd discuss it. I had a pitcher of martinis waiting." His left hand covered his mouth, squeezed his cheeks, his gaze turned inward.

I took a tiny step backward. A shade more distance between Powers' gun and me.

Then he laughed, cackled really. "She downed the first one and poured herself a second before I had time to find out if she'd told anyone."

She'd told Henry, my grasping, rapacious husband, who'd enjoyed having power over others.

"She slurred out something about mailing insurance to Henry. Why do you think I kept going through your mail?"

Because he was a snoop. "Why dump her in the swimming pool?" I asked.

"I didn't know she was dead. I thought if she drowned it would look like an accident."

"And Henry?"

"I came back to your house to search for whatever Madeline sent Henry. He came home."

"You killed him."

"He wanted money to keep quiet about the paintings...and Madeline."

My stomach turned. I already knew Henry was willing to blackmail a murderer, but Madeline had been his...Apparently she really had meant nothing to him.

"It was a stroke of luck that Roger and I confused our golf clubs the last time we played. After that, he looked so guilty. The cuckolded husband kills his wife and the man she's been sleeping with. He's overcome by guilt and kills himself." He wiped the rain from his face. "God damn Madeline. Who doesn't get their oven fixed? It would have been perfect if Roger had just died the way he was supposed to."

"What now?"

For an instant, the man with the gun looked like the Powers I knew. "That depends on you."

"On me?"

"They were bad people, Ellison. They deserved to die." His spring green eyes blazed with certainty. "You stay quiet, and I get out of here. I go to New York and get out from under Bitty Sue's thumb."

He wanted my silence. Bad enough that he'd forged paintings. He'd murdered three people. I shook my head. "I don't think we get to decide who lives and dies. Besides, Roger wasn't a bad person."

Powers shrugged. "He was a weak one. No one will miss him. So, you promise me you keep your mouth closed and we both walk away from this."

He didn't mean it. I saw the lie in his eyes, I saw it in the way his nose twitched, and in the set of his mouth. If I lowered my gun, I was dead.

"I can't do that, Powers."

"I was afraid you'd say that."

"Oh?"

"I never wanted to hurt you, Ellison."

I blinked my disbelief. He'd left a body in a pool where he knew I swam every morning. He'd hit me over the head with a fireplace poker. He'd murdered my husband then left the body in the driveway for me to run over. Now, he pointed a gun at me.

"Powers, if you shoot that thing at me, chances are you'll miss. We both know it." I lifted my gun slightly. "I won't miss."

He actually laughed. "You won't shoot me, Ellison."

"How do you know?"

"I just know. You've never stood up for anything but your art and Grace. You're not going to start now."

He took a step closer and raised the .45.

"You're wrong." I tried to sound menacing, as if I meant to shoot him, as if my insides hadn't turned to gelatin, as if I could kill a man.

He shook his head in disbelief. "I know you can't do it." He lifted the gun a bit higher. "I'm very sorry about this."

"I am too," I murmured. Powers had been so busy killing people he hadn't noticed the change in me. I pulled the trigger.

Daddy once told me that if I pointed a gun at someone, I should shoot to kill. I watched red bloom bright on Powers' green shirt. I watched as he looked down, surprise writ clearly on his face as he collapsed into the mud.

For a moment, I didn't move. I stared in horror at the man lying on the ground. When my legs wouldn't hold me any longer, I sank onto the large rock that extended from the embankment. Someone was screaming. I wished she'd stop. It was too loud. It threatened to disturb the stillness in my head.

The first policeman to arrive slipped in the mud at the top of the hill and slid halfway down on his ass. The second one did the same. The third one to arrive held onto trees as he descended. He didn't spoil his plaid pants.

That one approached me slowly with his hands held in front of his body and a furrow between his brows. "Ellison." His voice was so soft it sounded as if he was singing. "Ellison," he crooned. "Put down the gun."

I looked at my hand and was surprised to see the .22 still clasped in my fingers. I couldn't let it go. "Is he dead?" I asked.

One of the policemen who'd slid down the hill looked up from Powers' body. "He's dead."

Slowly, with great care, I put the gun down on the rock then I closed my eyes on the mud, and the blood and the rain.

An arm circled my shoulders and for an instant I allowed myself to relax into its comforting warmth. I hid my eyes against wet cotton and a muscled chest, and pretended the man who was stroking my wet hair was more than a policeman. When I looked up, Anarchy's brown eyes searched my face. "Are you all right?" he asked.

"I killed Powers."

His arm tightened around me. "What happened?"

"He killed them then he ran me off the road."

"Mr. Foster killed Mr. and Mrs. Harper and your husband?"

I nodded, suddenly too exhausted to speak. I rested my head against Anarchy's shoulder.

He held me there for a moment. Then his fingers explored my hair. He pulled them away. Blood covered them. I felt his swallow. "Ellison, you've hurt your head. We need to get you out of here."

The arm that circled my shoulders dropped to my waist. Before I could object, Anarchy lifted me off the rock. The pain in my ribs turned my sight as crimson as the blood on his fingers. I gasped for air, teetering on the edge of agony. Then I dove head first into blackness.

THIRTY-TWO

Everyone said the service for Henry was lovely. Unless a pallbearer trips and drops the casket, that's what people always say. One of those polite lies that gets us through our lives. *All brides are beautiful. No, darling, you can't tell at all—you just look younger. Lovely service.*

Except, since Mother made all the plans, the service really was lovely. Lovely despite Kitty and Prudence's sobbing near the back of the church.

I sat numb in the first pew. Grace clutched my hand. The minister, faced with eulogizing a philandering blackmailer who flogged women in his spare time, made Henry sound like a pillar of the community.

After the service, it seemed like the whole congregation came over to the house. There were pitchers of martinis and Tom Collinses. Endless bottles of wine. Canapés. Crudités with fresh dill dip. Tiny little ham sandwiches. Not made with the ham Bitty Sue gave me. Somehow, I couldn't bear to serve that after killing her son.

Not that she would have known.

She didn't come.

I didn't blame her.

Daddy hovered.

Grace withdrew to the comfort of her girl friends. They curled up in the corner of the family room to drink Tab, dip bits of French bread in cheese fondue, and talk.

Mother, looking very much as if she was sucking lemons,

offered me an olive branch. "Your new housekeeper is doing a nice job."

If she could extend the branch, the least I could do was reach out and take it. "Thank you. The service was lovely. I appreciate your planning it."

We stood, caught in an awkward pause, neither willing to reach any further. Mother opened her mouth as if she meant to say something then snapped it shut, a sure sign she was trying to find some way to criticize without sounding critical.

Hunter's approach saved us. His smile was enough to make her forget any unsolicited advice she might have thought to share about my attire, my hair, or the strength of the martinis. She beamed up at him. "Hunter, I don't know what we would have done without you. Isn't that right, Ellison?" Only the lack of a foot-covering table kept her from kicking me to make sure I came up with the right response.

"Absolutely." It was nothing less than the truth. Hunter and Aggie had opened all Henry's envelopes—except one. He'd advised me as to what I should say to the police. He'd even put up with Mother's transparent attempts at matchmaking. I smiled at him.

He smiled back. "May I have a word?"

"Look!" Mother pointed at someone across the room. "There's Lorna. I must speak with her. Hunter, why don't you keep Ellison company?" She was about as subtle as a fireplace poker to the skull. Undoubtedly she was rubbing her hands together with glee, under the mistaken impression that something was developing between Hunter and me.

Hunter had enough sensitivity not to comment on Mother's machinations. "What do you want to do about the files?"

"I don't know. Well, I don't know except for Rand Hamilton. Can we send that one to the police? Anonymously?"

"If that's what you want."

"We can't let a killer go free."

"Of course not." Hunter cleared his throat. He stared across the room to where Mother was deep in conversation with Lorna.

His tanned cheeks looked almost flushed. "Ellison, now that this is over..." He straightened his tie, a nice, conservative yellow and blue stripe. "Would you have dinner with me?"

"A date?"

My voice might have squeaked. A date? With Hunter? Mother would be giddy. Me? I wasn't so sure. Not that Hunter wasn't handsome. He was. He was also charming and sophisticated and a fabulous lawyer. I just wasn't sure I wanted to get involved again. Ever.

He shifted his weight from foot to foot and jammed his hands in his pockets. "A date."

"I...um...I...That is to say..." I brushed a strand of hair away from my cheek. "I don't think I'm ready to date."

"When you are?"

I nodded. No need to tell him I'd never be ready. Men couldn't be trusted. I had all the proof I needed. My husband had cheated and blackmailed and lied. My father did something bad enough to end up with his name on one of Henry's damned envelopes. Powers murdered three people before trying to kill me. I was done with men. End of story.

"I won't rush you, Ellison. But I do want to know you better."

My skin tingled with the thought of knowing Hunter Tafft better.

Barb Evans chose that moment to approach us, and Hunter, with a look that said quite clearly that we weren't done talking, excused himself and melted into the crowd.

"Are you holding up?" she asked.

"When this is all over..." I waved a hand at the crowd of people. "I'm putting Grace on a plane and we're going to Europe until school starts."

"Can't say I blame—" Her hand closed on my arm. "Who is that?"

I followed her gaze.

"That's the police officer who investigated the murders."

Anarchy was wearing a navy suit—wearing it well—and he was

attracting attention. More than one woman watched him weave his way through the crowd.

He stopped in front of me. "Mrs. Russell."

"The investigation is over, please call me Ellison." Barb seemed to have grown roots. She wasn't moving nor was she releasing my arm. "This is my friend, Barb Evans. Barb, this is Detective Jones."

He glanced at her for half a second. "Pleased to meet you." His gaze returned to me. "I have a question for you, Ellison."

What questions could he have now? With Hunter's help, I'd explained that Powers had sold fake Picassos and that Madeline had discovered his crime. Of course she'd told Henry. We'd posited that Powers killed them both to keep them quiet. He'd killed Roger in a botched frame up. There was no mention of blackmail. Grace's father's reputation was safe. Had Detective Jones discovered all that we'd omitted? My heart stuttered. "Of course, although I don't know where we'll find any privacy."

He nodded to Barb, grabbed my free arm, and led me through the crowd to the kitchen, past the caterers and onto the back patio.

The late afternoon heat prickled on my skin. The air was almost too humid to breathe. It settled into my lungs like a soggy lump of dread. "What's your question, Detective?"

"Anarchy," he corrected.

"What's your question, Anarchy?"

He leaned forward as if he meant to whisper a secret in my ear. Except, he didn't. Instead, his lips brushed against mine. My heart, which had been stuttering along, raced faster than the winner of the Kentucky Derby.

"Will you have dinner with me tomorrow night?" He traced the edge of my jaw with the tip of his finger.

I blinked, suddenly unable to remember the pathway by which words traveled from my brain to my mouth.

"Will you?" he asked.

It had to be some kind of record. How many women were asked out at the reception following their husband's funeral?

How many women were asked out twice?

"I don't think I'm ready to date."

His lips curled into a slow smile. "I'll wait."

I used my hand to fan the heat. Who knew if all that warmth was a result of the sun beating on my shoulders or the flush of my cheeks?

Anarchy Jones would be waiting a long, long time.

It was hours before everyone was gone, then the caterer had to pack up and Aggie had to clean up.

Grace, who looked positively gray with fatigue, trudged up the stairs.

My daughter had the right idea. I went upstairs, kicked off my shoes, shucked off my dress, and unclasped the heavy rope of pearls at my neck. I tossed them on the bed and opened the safe.

It was waiting for me. Poison in a manila wrapper.

I stood there in my underwear and stared at it.

Quite of their own volition, my fingers closed on the envelope. My nail slipped under the flap.

I had to know.

I couldn't go through the rest of my life not knowing. What if it was something inconsequential—a deliberate miscounting on a golf scorecard, a careless mistake on his taxes? I'd have put myself through hell for nothing.

I opened the envelope. Reached inside. Pulled out a picture of a blonde woman. She wore a blindfold, handcuffs, stockings, stilettos, and not much else.

Oh. Dear. Lord.

My stomach turned. Twice.

It was a good thing Henry was dead because if he still breathed I would have had to kill him. How could he? One time, to please him, I'd donned the ridiculous outfit and let him tie me and blindfold me. One time and he'd taken pictures and extorted money from Daddy.

Embarrassment swamped me. It left me drowning in a bottomless pool of shame. My father had seen those pictures. What he must think of me. I was so appalled I could hardly breathe. I sat on the edge of the bed, clutched my stomach and rocked.

I don't know how long I sat there. Long enough to plan an escape wherein I never had to look him in the eye again. I mapped out an itinerary of Europe and Asia and Australia. I sat long enough to have two tiny thoughts that made the whole thing bearable.

Daddy loved me enough to pretend he hadn't seen the pictures. Maybe we could keep pretending. We could pretend for the rest of our lives.

More importantly, Daddy hadn't done anything worthy of blackmail.

Henry really was a worm. I'd been right about that. And I'd been wrong. A girl *could* count on her father after all.

Maybe she could count on another man as well. When I got back from Europe, I'd call him and find out.

JULIE MULHERN

Julie Mulhern is a Kansas City native who grew up on a steady diet of Agatha Christie. She spends her spare time whipping up gourmet meals for her family, working out at the gym and finding new ways to keep her house spotlessly clean—and she's got an active imagination. Truth is—she's an expert at calling for take-out, she grumbles about walking the dog and the dust bunnies under the bed have grown into dust lions. She is a 2014 Golden Heart® Finalist. *The Deep End* is her first mystery and is the winner of The Sheila Award.

Henery Press Mystery Books

And finally, before you go...
Here are a few other mysteries
you might enjoy:

PILLOW STALK

Diane Vallere

A Mad for Mod Mystery (#1)

Interior Decorator Madison Night has modeled her life after a character in a Doris Day movie, but when a killer targets women dressed like the bubbly actress, Madison's signature sixties style places her in the middle of a homicide investigation.

The local detective connects the new crimes to a twenty-year-old cold case, and Madison's long-trusted contractor emerges as the leading suspect. As the body count piles up like a stack of plush pillows, Madison uncovers a Soviet spy, a campaign to destroy all Doris Day movies, and six minutes of film that will change her life forever.

Available at booksellers nationwide and online

Visit www.henerypress.com for details

FINDING SKY

Susan O'Brien

A Nicki Valentine Mystery

Suburban widow and P.I. in training Nicki Valentine can barely keep track of her two kids, never mind anyone else. But when her best friend's adoption plan is jeopardized by the young birth mother's disappearance, Nicki is persuaded to help. Nearly everyone else believes the teenager ran away, but Nicki trusts her BFF's judgment, and the feeling is mutual.

The case leads where few moms go (teen parties, gang shootings) and places they can't avoid (preschool parties, OB-GYNs' offices). Nicki has everything to lose and much to gain — including the attention of her unnervingly hot P.I. instructor. Thankfully, Nicki is armed with her pesky conscience, occasional babysitters, a fully stocked minivan, and nature's best defense system: women's intuition.

Available at booksellers nationwide and online

Visit www.henerypress.com for details

DINERS, DIVES & DEAD ENDS

Terri L. Austin

A Rose Strickland Mystery (#1)

As a struggling waitress and part-time college student, Rose Strickland's life is stalled in the slow lane. But when her close friend, Axton, disappears, Rose suddenly finds herself serving up more than hot coffee and flapjacks. Now she's hashing it out with sexy bad guys and scrambling to find clues in a race to save Axton before his time runs out.

With her anime-loving bestie, her septuagenarian boss, and a pair of IT wise men along for the ride, Rose discovers political corruption, illegal gambling, and shady corporations. She's gone from zero to sixty and quickly learns when you're speeding down the fast lane, it's easy to crash and burn.

Available at booksellers nationwide and online

Visit www.henerypress.com for details

FRONT PAGE FATALITY

LynDee Walker

A Headlines in High Heels Mystery (#1)

Crime reporter Nichelle Clarke's days can flip from macabre to comical with a beep of her police scanner. Then an ordinary accident story turns extraordinary when evidence goes missing, a prosecutor vanishes, and a sexy Mafia boss shows up with the headline tip of a lifetime.

As Nichelle gets closer to the truth, her story gets more dangerous. Armed with a notebook, a hunch, and her favorite stilettos, Nichelle races to splash these shady dealings across the front page before this deadline becomes her last.

Available at booksellers nationwide and online

Visit www.henerypress.com for details

THE AMBITIOUS CARD

John Gaspard

An Eli Marks Mystery (#1)

The life of a magician isn't all kiddie shows and card tricks. Sometimes it's murder. Especially when magician Eli Marks very publicly debunks a famed psychic, and said psychic ends up dead. The evidence, including a bloody King of Diamonds playing card (one from Eli's own Ambitious Card routine), directs the police right to Eli.

As more psychics are slain, and more King cards rise to the top, Eli can't escape suspicion. Things get really complicated when romance blooms with a beautiful psychic, and Eli discovers she's the next target for murder, and he's scheduled to die with her. Now Eli must use every trick he knows to keep them both alive and reveal the true killer.

Available at booksellers nationwide and online

Visit www.henerypress.com for details

LOWCOUNTRY BOIL

Susan M. Boyer

A Liz Talbot Mystery (#1)

Private Investigator Liz Talbot is a modern Southern belle: she blesses hearts and takes names. She carries her Sig 9 in her Kate Spade handbag, and her golden retriever, Rhett, rides shotgun in her hybrid Escape. When her grandmother is murdered, Liz high-tails it back to her South Carolina island home to find the killer.

She's fit to be tied when her police-chief brother shuts her out of the investigation, so she opens her own. Then her long-dead best friend pops in and things really get complicated. When more folks start turning up dead in this small seaside town, Liz must use more than just her wits and charm to keep her family safe, chase down clues from the hereafter, and catch a psychopath before he catches her.

Available at booksellers nationwide and online

Visit www.henerypress.com for details

CPSIA information can be obtained
at www.ICGtesting.com
Printed in the USA
LVOW07s0752011017
550624LV00001B/3/P